CRITICA
JAMES (

'Brilliant and uncompro
is one of the best writers working today' – Ace Atkins

'full of wry humor and thoughtful writing'
– ***Kirkus Reviews***

'engrossing and wonderfully realized' – ***Publishers Weekly***

'[I]mbued with the magical realism of García Márquez… [and] the frontier brutality of Cormac McCarthy… Blake's story will entertain fans of historical and adventure novels alike' – ***Shelf Awareness***

'A literary page-turner … a romantic, violent, panoramic historical saga (written) with a journalist's eye for detail and a poet's love of words… a fascinating read'
– ***San Antonio Express***

'[A] worthy book… *Country of the Bad Wolfes* is a poetic... offspring of Gabriel Garcia Márquez and Cormac McCarthy…' – ***Tucson Weekly***

'A great read from start to finish, full of grit, local color, and a large cast of vibrant characters … this brawling, high-spirited, and superbly realized family saga… offers many pleasures, including endearing characters, unlikely love stories, and all manner of mayhem. Highly recommended for fans of literary fiction'
– ***Library Journal***

'Full of fascinating history, the Wolfe family saga is ribald, raunchy and essential reading… don't miss it'
– ***Poisoned Pen***

'This is historical fiction in the manner of Umberto Eco… many-faceted, slow, and savory' – ***Booklist***

'Blake's literary badlands are uniquely his own' – ***GQ***

'For anyone who has never experienced the exceptional talent of the idiosyncratic Blake, this is a wonderful novel to start with... Passionate, bloody and yet incredibly romantic, it is a tribute to the genius of its author' – **Geoffrey Wansell, *Daily Mail***

'Nobody writes about blood and guts better than James Carlos Blake' – ***Washington Post***

James Carlos Blake writes with the muscularity of great pulp novels and the grace of a dancer - from the edge of an America that is forever frontier – **James Sallis**

'Blake's prose is muscular, his dialogue and details are keenly observed… one hell of a ride' – ***Booklist***

'Blake writes with a fearless precision and a ruthless sensibility, his prose is spare and tough, and his descriptions detailed and cinematic' – ***Publishers Weekly***

'One of the greatest chroniclers of the mythical American outlaw life' – ***Entertainment Weekly***

'James Carlos Blake is a formidable writer [and] a deft stylist, welding the language with power and authority'
– ***Tucson Weekly***

'James Carlos Blake is of the Cormac McCarthy/Sam Peckinpah school of storytelling: Make it bloody as hell, but make it beautiful' – ***Dallas Morning News***

'One of the most original writers in America today'
– ***Chicago Sun-Times***

'An epic chase' – ***Men's Journal***

'Riveting' – ***Latinidad***

Other Works by James Carlos Blake

Novels

The Pistoleer
The Friends of Pancho Villa
In the Rogue Blood
Red Grass River
Wildwood Boys
A World of Thieves
Under the Skin
Handsome Harry
The Killings of Stanley Ketchel
The Rules of Wolfe
Country of the Bad Wolfes
The House of Wolfe
The Ways of Wolfe

Collection

Borderlands

THE BONES OF WOLFE

JAMES CARLOS BLAKE

NO EXIT PRESS

First published in 2021 by No Exit Press,
an imprint of Oldcastle Books Ltd,
Harpenden, Herts, UK
noexit.co.uk
@noexitpress

 A CIP catalogue record for this book is available from the British Library.

ISBN
978-0-85730-451-3 (Print)
978-0-85730-452-0 (Epub)

2 4 6 8 10 9 7 5 3 1

Typeset in 11.1 on 13.3pt Janson Text with Charlemagne Std display
by Avocet Typeset, Bideford, Devon, EX39 2BP
Printed and bound in Great Britain by Clays Ltd, Elcograf S.p.A.

To

The Distler IV

Joseph

Nancy

Emma

Morgan

Bone of my bone thou art, and from thy state
Mine never shall be parted, weal or woe.

–John Milton, *Paradise Lost*

Do what thy manhood bids thee do
From none but self expect applause;
He noblest lives and noblest dies
Who makes and keeps his self-made laws.

– Sir Richard Francis Burton

Yes, I am proud; I must be proud to see
Men not afraid of God, afraid of me.

–Alexander Pope, 'Epistle to Dr. Arbuthnot'

Life is contemptuous of knowledge; it forces it to sit in the anterooms, to wait outside. Passion, energy, lies: these are what life admires.

–James Salter, *Light Years*

CONTENTS

I

THE SHIPMENT

EDDIE AND ALBERTO

The Gulf of Mexico on a moonless midsummer night. Star-clustered sky over placid black water. A frail and tepid offshore breeze. Eddie Gato Wolfe throttles back the engines as the boat closes in on a barrier island partitioning the Gulf from the southernmost reach of the Mexican Laguna Madre and the long stretch of uninhabited marshland beyond it. The vessel is an artfully customized trawler model fitted with a reinforced shallow draft hull and powered by supercharged twin Hemis. Even with a full load it can fly, and empty of cargo it can outrun almost anything short of a speedboat. Its hull registration number belongs to a commercial fishing boat whose sinking eight years ago was never reported, and its registered owner is a man who perished in a Veracruz nightclub fire six years ago with fifty-two other victims, his remains never identified. The name *Bruja* and home port of La Pesca displayed on the transom are also falsehoods.

Eddie's crew consists of Romo at the bow with a pair of night-vision binoculars, scanning for signs of other boats; Tomás at the stern and doing the same; and Gustavo in the wheelhouse, attending the navigation screen and keeping Eddie advised of the heading for the lagoon inlet. They have all slathered themselves with repellent in readiness against the mass of mosquitoes. Each man carries a Beretta nine-millimeter pistol, and the wheelhouse locker holds three fully loaded M4 carbines and three extra thirty-round magazines per man.

The island is profuse with mangroves. Its width ranges from sixty to eighty yards, and the breadth of lagoon between it and the mainland is less than a quarter mile. Both the island and a sizable expanse of the marshy coast are owned by Eddie's Mexican kin. The inlet he approaches was excavated by them decades ago and is not to be found on any nautical charts but their own and those of their Texas relatives. It is hidden from aerial view by a canopy of dense tree growth, and the design of its channel – like a horizontally elongated *N* that on the chart looks like a wide, wry smile and inspired its name of Boca Larga – obscures offshore detection of its entrance. The inlet is never used in daylight lest the boat be seen entering or exiting, and to navigate it at night, even with GPS assistance, requires an expert hand at the wheel. The spotlight at the fore of the wheelhouse roof is strictly for emergencies. Eddie knows this night passage well. He has steered through it many times before.

The inlet's mouth is barely twice the width of the boat, and not until they're within forty feet of it can they distinguish the deeper blackness of its gap against the extensive wall of mangroves. Eddie slows the *Bruja* to a brisk walking pace and they pass into the channel with the engines growling low. The darkness in here is nearly absolute, the air danker. GPS emitters implanted at intervals along both banks enable Gustavo to keep Eddie on a course exactly in the center of the channel. They make the starboard turn into the long middle portion of the passage, which is also its widest and allows the boat almost six feet of leeway to either side, and at the end of this stretch Eddie wheels left into the channel's other short arm and they pass through it into the lagoon. Though the depth here does not at any point exceed four feet and in places is around three, the *Bruja*'s shallow draft easily clears the bottom. From somewhere in the darkness comes the loud splattering of a school of fish in flight from a predator. Eddie's watch shows 9:45.

They're moving even more slowly now, holding to the centerline of the lagoon, and Eddie brings the boat to an idling halt. Romo turns on a large flashlight, pointing it directly ahead, slowly raises its beam straight overhead, and as slowly sweeps it to the left and right three times and turns it off. Several seconds elapse and then a row of low-watt yellow lights appears along a short stretch of cleared bank. Eddie heads toward it. As they advance on the landing, they make out the figures of four men standing in the ground lights' hazy glow.

Shortly the *Bruja* ties up at mooring posts alongside the clearing and a Mexican cousin of Eddie's named Alberto Delmonte hops aboard. They greet each other with laughter and backslapping hugs.

Been waiting long? Eddie asks in Spanish. Like all their family on both sides of the border, he and Alberto are fluently bilingual.

About half an hour, Alberto says. Left the capital early this morning and made good time. Gonna be a long night for me and my guys, though. We gotta deliver this load to Irapuato by tomorrow afternoon, two o'clock. Thirteen-fourteen-hour drive and the first hour is on this slow-ass turtle trail back to the graded road.

Eddie takes a flashlight off his belt. Well, hell, let's get to it.

They go belowdecks and into the dimly lighted hold. Because of the reconfiguration of the hull, the hold's headspace was much reduced and they can stand no higher than a half crouch. The load comprises two crates of M4A1 carbines and two of M240 machine guns, plus a crate of 5.56 ammunition and one of 7.62. Each crate is stenciled with U. S. ARMY and abbreviated military descriptions of its contents.

Eddie opens a carbine crate and shines the light into it, and Alberto takes a look. Every load Eddie has ever delivered to Boca Larga has been collected by Alberto, and their examination of the cargo before its transfer between them is simply a rite of formality by which they assure themselves they are not becoming lax in their professional roles.

'I said it before and say it again,' Alberto says in English as he pats one of the M4s. 'This baby's the best there is for both open-field and street fighting, and I mean the AK, too. I know some say these jam too easy in sandy conditions, but I don't know anybody it's happened to.'

'Neither do I. M4's our steady bestseller.' Eddie closes the crate and opens one that contains machine guns.

Alberto grunts as he raises one of the guns partway out of the crate with both hands. He works its action and dry-fires it with a loud snap. 'I shot one of these at a ranch in Puebla last year. Felt like God.' He puts it back in place. 'Gotta have some muscle to tote the son of a bitch, though. Weighs, what, twenty-five pounds?'

'Twenty-seven,' Eddie says. 'Add a tripod and that's another eleven. So yeah, takes an ox to haul it around.' He resets the crate cover. 'Wasn't easy for Charlie to get them on short notice, let me tell you.'

'It's a special fast-lane order, but Rigo knew Charlie could fill it. I've always wondered how the hell he does it. Got inside men at a thousand armories or what?'

'Got his ways is what he's got. Who's the buyer?'

'Zetas.'

'Woo. *Serious* people.'

'Fucking A,' Alberto says. 'Pay top dollar for what they want, though. The word is, they're getting it for one of their enforcement crews along the lower border, but you know how it is with the word. About as reliable as Tina Maria.'

'Tina? Didn't you break up with her three, four months back?'

'Yeah. Gotta tell you, though, I kinda miss her. I mean, she really knew how to deal with a dick. I ain't kidding, Ed, soon as I'd ring her doorbell I'd get a boner. I told her that once and she said, "Pavlov's dong." Another thing about her, she was good for a chuckle.'

'Always tough to lose a sex artist,' Eddie says, 'but one with a sense of humor is a major loss.'

They go topside and tell the crews to get busy, then help them to unload the cargo and transfer it to a large pickup truck about fifty feet away – a dark Dodge Ram with a buttressed chassis, a quad cab, and a bed topper. Despite its big backcountry tires, Alberto did not park the truck any closer to the bank for fear of miring in the soft ground under the additional weight of the cargo. The vehicle stands on a narrow crushed-shell trail that was also constructed by his family and also is not on any official map. It snakes through sixteen miles of palms and marshy terrain before connecting to a dirt road that runs north to a gravel works and a junction with a main highway.

Each crate is borne by two men at either end of it. Mosquitoes keen at their ears, and the men curse the unsure footing that makes the work all the more laborious. Huffing as they lug the crates to the truck, they hoist them up to the bed and muscle them into place. When the last one is worked in among the others, Alberto swings up the tailgate and snaps it shut and then fastens the windowless topper gate to it with a large padlock. The lock is meant to thwart street kids skillful enough to hop onto the back bumper of a slow-moving truck in city traffic and peek under the topper to see if it's carrying anything that might interest their robber employers.

Eddie checks his watch and says, Seventeen minutes. Not bad. A couple of Alberto's guys retrieve the landing lights from along the bank and put them in the Ram, while Romo and Gustavo hop aboard the *Bruja*, dig out icy bottles of

Bohemia from a large cooler, and hand them out. The men raise their beers, say, 'Salud,' take deep swallows, burp, and sigh with pleasure.

Alberto takes a satellite phone off his belt and presses a few buttons. The order is complete, he says into the phone, then pokes a button on it and returns it to his belt. He chugs the rest of his beer and pitches the bottle into the water and his men do the same. 'Gotta boogie,' he says. He and Eddie once more exchange hugs and back slaps, and Eddie tells him to give his regards to the rest of the Mexico City family. Alberto says for him to do the same with his Texas cousins.

A minute later the big Ram has slowly rumbled away into the darkness and the *Bruja* is making its way back across the lagoon. Eddie activates his phone and says into it, 'I'm an old cowhand,' a code phrase apprising the listener that the transfer has been completed without incident.

He nimbly steers back through Boca Larga and out into the Gulf, then opens the throttles, rousing the Hemis to a roar as the boat accelerates with its prow rising, the men laughing as they hold tight against the rearward lean.

They don't switch on the running lights or cut back to cruising speed until they're a mile out and turn north for home.

THE CREWS

The Ram lumbers through the underbrush along the twisting shell track glowing pale bright in the headlights and holding the truck to a speed of around fifteen. The driver, Jorge, turns the air conditioner up another notch, grousing that he can walk faster than he can drive on this so-called road. Alberto's riding shotgun. Neto and Felipe are in the rear seat.

They are discussing whorehouses, a subject initiated by Neto's enthusiastic account of a recent visit to a new brothel in Mexico City called El Palacio de Los Ángeles. He claims it has the prettiest girls of any house he's ever been to and it fully guarantees that they're free of disease.

He and Jorge both favor the simplicity of brothels. You pick out a girl, you pay a fixed price for exactly what you want, you get it, and when you're done you say, So long, darling, maybe I'll see you again. Lots of variety and none of the problems of a regular girlfriend.

Alberto admits to the practicalities of clean whorehouses, but he much prefers sex that includes some affection.

Affection? Jorge says. You talking about *love*? Hey, man, every time I go in a whorehouse I fall in love. Then it's over and I leave and I'm not in love no more. Works out great.

Not for me, Alberto says. It's not as satisfying when you pay for it. If you want variety, do what I do and get a lot of girlfriends.

Any way you get it you pay for it, Neto says. You don't spend money on your girlfriends? And every girlfriend sooner or later becomes as much of a nag as a wife. Who wants a lot of *that*?

He's convinced me, Felipe says. Soon as I get home I'm kicking my girl's ass out the door.

What girl? Alberto says. You haven't had a girlfriend since Bettina kicked *you* out.

Yeah, well… if I *did* have a one, out she'd go.

Let's have some music, Jorge says.

He switches on the CD player and ranchero music resounds from the speakers. The others all groan and Felipe says, No more of that hick shit, man. We had to listen to it all the way up here.

The driver picks the music, Jorge says, that's the rule. Chief said so.

Well, I'm making a new rule, Alberto says. We take turns picking the music and it's my turn.

He fingers through a row of CDs in the console and picks one. He ejects the ranchero disc from the player and inserts the selected CD, and the speakers begin booming the heavy-metal tempo of a band called Asesino.

Oh, yes! says Felipe. That's more like it!

As Jorge grumbles about the unfairness of changing the music rule in the middle of a run, they enter a hairpin turn that forces him to cut their speed even more, the headlights dragging across palm trunks and high brush as the truck crawls through the bend. Then they're out of the turn and facing a straight stretch, and the headlights expose a ponderous dark vehicle standing ten yards ahead and blocking the trail. It faces in the other direction, its lights off, its interior hidden within black glass.

Jorge stomps on the brakes and the truck crunches to a halt. 'What the hell?' Alberto says, and starts to reach for the volume knob on the player just as the dark brush on both sides of the mysterious vehicle detonates into a crackling, flaring barrage of automatic gunfire.

The men shriek and convulse as bullets punch through the Ram's windshield and transform it into a thickening web of starbursts. The windows come apart in shards. The tires blow and the truck lurches and slumps and the engine quits. The music cuts off. The headlights go last – the ambushers having no further need of them to delineate their target.

Fifteen seconds after it commenced, the shooting stops. All screaming has ceased. The only light is the cab's dashboard glow. The only sounds are a harsh hissing under the hood, the clacking of weapons being reloaded with full magazines, the snapping of cocking handles.

The vague form of a man holding a firearm at waist level with both hands appears from the gloom on the forward right side of the truck and cautiously approaches it. When he's abreast of the cab he can see the men inside in the dim dash light, motionless, slumped in unnatural attitudes. A faint scent of blood exudes from the shattered windows and threads into the mix of gunfire fumes and marsh odors. He fires a luminous burst through the front window, jarring the two bodies, the near one folding atop the console, the driver crumpling lower against the door. He then sidles over and looses a burst into the men in the back seat. Then lowers the weapon and says, 'Luz.'

Lights come aglow on both sides of the trail and three men emerge from the scrub, two from the left, one from the right, each of them wearing a utility light strapped to his forehead like a miner and each man armed with an M4A1 carbine. They curse the mosquitoes that in this part of the marsh are so fierce even the strongest repellent is of small effect.

In the light of the head lanterns, the man at the truck is revealed as young and clean-shaven, with a pale wormlike scar that angles vertically down the right side of his mouth.

He presses a button on his wristwatch to illuminate its face and show the time. Chico, he says, the vehicle, *move*.

Got it, chief, Chico says, and jogs up the trail to the huge black Suburban. The chief calls another crewman to the rear of the Ram and has him shine his light on the padlock securing the topper gate to the tailgate. He stands to the side of the lock to avoid possible damage to the cargo, puts the muzzle of his carbine to the juncture of lock case and shackle, and blasts the lock apart. He raises the topper gate and the crewman shines his light on the crates inside. Because of the attack's diagonal lines of fire into the cab, the shipment shows no sign of having been struck.

Good, says the chief.

Driving in reverse, Chico brings the Suburban to within a few feet of the Ram, and the other men store their weapons in it. The chief orders them not to take anything from the dead men, not their guns, phones, money, anything. They have just removed the first crate from the truck bed when they hear a pulsing buzz from the Ram cab. They recognize it as an incoming phone call on what has to be a satellite unit, as no cell tower is in range.

They know the truck stopped, one of them says.

Don't piss your pants, the chief says. By the time they get here we'll be long gone.

Still, they step up their tempo, panting with effort, sopping with sweat, faces itching and bloated with mosquito bites. In another few minutes they shove the last crate into the Suburban, shut and lock the rear doors, scramble into the vehicle, and drive away.

RODRIGO AND MATEO AND CHARLIE

In a large room on the highest floor of a towering Mexico City building whose blazing neon sign reads Zuma Electrónicas, S.A., a young technician called a screener sits before a row of computers, intermittently shifting his gaze between the monitors and the sports magazine in his lap. It is dull duty but pays well. Like the majority of employees of Zuma Electrónicas, the screener has a university degree in computer engineering. And like everyone else who works on the top floor of the building, he has a top security clearance and knows that the company has commercial ties – mostly clandestine – to numerous other business organizations and that its true ownership is a secret protected by many buffering layers of corporate law.

The monitors keep track of company transport vehicles equipped with encrypted GPS senders and appearing as yellow blips on a green geographic grid. On this slow evening there are only two blips to keep an eye on. Alpha vehicle is delivering a shipment from Mexico City to Acapulco, and Beta vehicle is collecting a shipment at a transfer point on the Laguna Madre and relaying it to a recipient in Irapuato. The screener does not know what kind of cargo either vehicle is carrying or any of the names of its crew. His data sheets tell him only the type of vehicle each one is and its schedule, including the cargo's point of collection if the delivery did not originate from Mexico City. His responsibility is strictly to keep track of a vehicle's progress and confirm that its cargo arrives on time.

Both vehicles are holding to schedule. Alpha is only two hours from its destination, and Beta collected its cargo and left the lagoon twenty-three minutes ago, its crew chief phoning in on arrival there and again on departure. The Beta is moving at a snail's pace on what the screener knows is a difficult and circuitous backcountry trail that terminates at a junction road, but once the Beta arrives at that junction its progress will speed up and it will easily make the Irapuato delivery on schedule.

But now the Beta stops moving.

The screener looks at his wristwatch and enters the time on a clipboard form. An unscheduled stop by a company vehicle on business is always a matter for immediate attention. A flat tire or engine trouble can throw a delivery far off schedule, and a crew chief is obliged to call the screener about any such problem at once so that the company can dispatch speedy assistance if required and inform the awaiting party of the delay – and to dispel any worry about a hijacking. However, a crew chief isn't required to call if he's making an unscheduled stop shorter than three minutes, as for a roadside piss. The screener shifts his attention by turns from the unmoving blip to his wristwatch to the data sheet, which tells him the Beta vehicle is a new Dodge Ram pickup with less than four thousand miles on the odometer when it left the capital early this morning. When the third minute elapses he calls the crew chief's satellite phone. He lets it buzz and buzz without an answer for almost a full minute before he picks up another phone and calls the tracking manager to notify him of the stalled truck and its lack of response.

The manager says to keep trying to connect with the crew and to advise him right away if he makes contact or if the Beta resumes movement without having replied. Then the manager makes a phone call of his own. Within minutes of receiving it, a fire team of five armed men in a Ford F-250 truck races out of Ciudad Victoria, almost a hundred miles from the Ram's location but the company's nearest station to it.

* * *

Two hours later the fire team leader phones the tracking manager from the scene of the attack and tells him of the shot-up truck, the slaughtered crew, the stolen cargo. The hijackers must've made it back to the main highway before the fire team exited from it because the team spotted no vehicles on the dirt road. The manager tells the team leader to hold on while he relays the finding to the Director.

Awakened by the call, the Director, Rodrigo Wolfe – whose standing order is that he be notified without delay of any hijack, never mind the hour – listens to the manager's report without interrupting him, not even on hearing that the ambushed crew was that of his young cousin Alberto Delmonte. He commends the manager for his prompt action and concise account and instructs him to tell the fire team at the scene to convey the bodies to the Nuestra Señora del Cielo medical clinic in Mexico City and to have the Ram towed to the nearest junkyard and converted to scrap. The manager knows that the medical clinic is owned by the company and it will see to the proper but covert disposition of the deceased.

Tell the fire team to say nothing about the hijacking, not to anyone, Rodrigo adds. And tell the screener nothing other than he was right to call you and everything has been taken care of.

Using a different phone, Rodrigo then calls his brother Mateo, the chief of security, and tells him what's happened.

You notified the Zetas? Mateo asks.

Not yet. They're going to be unhappy.

Has to be an inside job, Mateo says. Somebody tipped the hijackers to the transfer. Somebody of ours or somebody with Charlie, but somebody who knew about tonight's run *and* who's familiar with the trail to Boca Larga.

Rodrigo sighs and says. The only people of ours who knew those things are you and me, Alberto and his crew, the tracking manager, and the screener. Neither the screener nor the manager knew what the load was. But as you know, Alberto always told his crew what they were carrying.

Yeah. Showed he trusts them, he always said. Makes them even more loyal. Can't say I entirely agreed with him, but I let him run his crew his own way.

On the Texas side, Rodrigo says, the only ones who knew about the run are Charlie Fortune and the delivery crew. At least that's the way he's always operated. I'll find out if he did anything different this time. Still, the odds are that the inside guy is one of ours.

Either somebody in Alberto's crew, Mateo says, or somebody who used to work the Boca Larga run in the past and who found out about Alberto's run tonight. Whoever he is, you think he tipped the Zetas? They steal their own buy, and when we tell them it's been ripped they act all pissed and demand their money back?

No. Scheme like that's beneath them. There are a lot easier ways for them to get money than by risking a breach with their best supplier of weapons. For damn sure, though, it was a professional crew. The fire team said the vehicle was shot to hell, every man in it with multiple wounds and every pistol still in its holster, that's how quick and hard they got hit. Automatic weapons, 5.56 black-tip rounds, diagonal enfilade from both sides. Fast and slick. They did the hit, ripped the cargo, got the fuck out. And as far as the Zetas are concerned, I can tell you that they're not going to want their money back, they're going to want what they paid for. We either recover that cargo for them very damn soon or order a replacement of it from Charlie and eat the cost.

Yeah, that's how it's looking, Mateo says. I'll start nosing around about the other pickup crews right away. There can't be too many guys among them who've worked Boca Larga before Alberto's crew took it over. If the tip to the hijackers was from one of our guys, I'll know his name before the sun comes up. On the off chance he's a Texan, Charlie will root him out pretty fast, too. We find the insider, we'll find out who did the hijack, I'll run their asses down and get the goods back. If they still got them.

There's a plan. Get on it. I'll call Charlie.

* * *

Charlie Fortune Wolfe awakens to the vibration of the cellphone under the corner of his pillow. The riverside night is still and clammy, ringing with frogs, the screened windows are black under the dense overhang of trees. The red numerals of the bedside clock radio read 1:46. He sees that the caller is his cousin Rodrigo Wolfe.

'Rigo. What is it?'

Rodrigo tells him, speaking in English.

'Alberto?' Charlie says. 'Ah, Jesus...'

In response to Rigo's question, Charlie tells him the only ones who knew about the run's cargo or schedule were himself and the crew.

'Who's the chief on it?'

'Eddie Gato.'

'I still haven't met him,' Rodrigo says. 'Frank and Rudy I know, but Eddie not at all. Alberto mentioned him many times. Close cousin, right?'

'Right. Been working with me three years and been my Boca Larga man since last year. I broke him in on that run myself. Listen, Rigo, I know what you're wondering, so I'll tell you right now – Eddie wouldn't sell us. Neither would any of his crew. Those guys have been with me for years. And there couldn't have been anything odd about the transfer or Eddie would've clued me, but he called in an all clear after the drop. If somebody'd been holding a gun on him, he would've used a different code to tip us off.'

'Hey, Charlie, you vouch for them, that's it. Man, if I stopped trusting you, who the hell *could* I trust? Lot more likely the inside rat is somebody on our end. Mateo's out there right now trying to ID him. We have to find the son of a bitch and get the cargo back before it ends up who the fuck knows where.'

'Let us help, Rigo. Frank and Rudy are on the body run your guys gave us, but they'll be back tomorrow… hell, it *is* tomorrow. They'll be back this afternoon and I'll keep them on hand. Hey, man, I want those bastards as much as you do. It was *my* shipment and Alberto was my blood and bone, too. Just give the word and we're on the way.'

'I know it, Charlie. I'll be in touch as soon as Mateo has something.'

* * *

His name's Donasio Corona and he was in Alberto's crew, Mateo says. Twenty-six years old. Came to us three years ago after doing two and a half at Veracruz state for robbery. We put him on various small duties the first couple of years – runner, street lookout, driver – some of those jobs for Alberto, which is how they got to know each other. Last year one of Alberto's crewmen got killed in a bar fight and he took Corona on in his place. Anyway, he's our guy. No doubt about it.

It is nearing dawn. Mateo arrived at Rodrigo's estate in the city's Chapultepec district a short while ago. They're taking coffee in the softly lit courtyard gazebo, well distanced from the house and all servants' ears.

I'm impressed you ran him down so fast, Rodrigo says.

All it takes is talking to the right person, Mateo says, but you never know who the right person is till you talk to him. I been going around all night to see those of our people who know about Boca Larga, asking them all the same question and doing a lot of tap dancing to avoid telling any of them about the hijack. I think it's best we don't let word of it get out just now. Might put the guys who did it on sharper guard.

I agree. So who was the right person to talk to?

Ignacio Verdes, another of our crew chiefs. He said it was odd I should ask if he'd heard or seen anything out of the ordinary about any of the guys in the transport crews. Said Alberto called him yesterday morning before he left on the Boca Larga run and asked if he could borrow a man. One of his guys, Donasio Corona, had called him before sunup saying he was sick as hell, shitting and puking since three in the morning, probably because of some bad menudo he had for supper. Alberto told him to see the company doctor as soon as the office opened, then called Ignacio, who let him have Neto Valles, one of his best men. Like some of the others I talked to, Ignacio was curious about why I was asking, and I told him I couldn't say at this time. He's going to be awful damn pissed about losing Valles.

And Donasio Corona has of course disappeared, Rodrigo says.

Wasn't at home. Didn't go see the doctor. Isn't in any hospital or jail. I sent his picture and prints to our network guys with connections to the passport office and access twenty-four seven, and they reported that the prints aren't in the files, so he's never been issued a passport under any name. I ordered our border crews to post lookouts with all the wetback smugglers in case he should try crossing with one of them. On the off chance he's still in town, I have people keeping watch on all the joints where he's known to hang out. My guess is he got out of Mexico City but will stay in the country.

And Corona knows the Larga run pretty good?

The whole crew did. Alberto's been collecting all of Charlie's deliveries there for about two years steady now and mostly with the same guys the whole time, except for Corona just the past year. They were a good crew and he had no reason to mistrust any of them. They knew that guns are the only cargo ever delivered there, and the load's usually American military rifles and pistols and that every so often it includes machine guns, sometimes foreign subs. Since Corona's been with the crew, and not counting last night's pickup, they've made seven collections at Boca Larga. That's enough for him to have learned that run real good. He knew the exact distance from the junction road exit to the trail entry, which is impossible to spot at night unless you know just where to look. He knew the best spot to hit the crew on its way out. He knew there's no room on the trail to hide a vehicle and that there's only one spot just wide enough to make a U-turn without getting stuck. He knew everything you'd need to know for a hijack plan, and he laid it on somebody looking for weapons. And *those* motherfuckers took out our guys and stole our goods.

What's your read on them? Rodrigo asks.

I figure a young bunch. They're very good and they're full of themselves. Probably looking to make their mark in weapons retailing but not flush enough yet to invest in top-grade guns. But even if they could afford a load like this one, they might be the kind who think stolen fruit is sweeter than bought fruit. A lot more satisfying to rip a load than buy it. Not a very smart outlook as a long-term business practice, but not uncommon in young guys with big balls. You're not so old yet you can't remember what that kind of cockiness is like.

I'm not so old yet I can't still kick your ass. And Corona?

Hell, he's just a dumb shit who thinks whatever they paid him was worth it. The big question is who *they* are, but the pressing question is where *he* is. I figure hiding out with a relative, a pal, a woman, somebody. Thinking to hole up till things blow over. It's what all the stupid ones do. Don't understand some things never blow over.

So what are we doing? Rodrigo says.

I've alerted our intelligence people. Gave them the full jacket on him. They've put spiders out everywhere. We'll find him.

Has to be fast, brother.

I know, Mateo says.

Rodrigo calls Charlie Fortune to relay what he's learned.

RUDY

It's a pleasant Saturday afternoon on the Gulf. We're bearing south along the Texas coast, about a mile and a half off Padre Island. The sky is bright and nearly cloudless. On the distant eastern horizon a freighter is trailing a thin plume of dark smoke. There's no other vessel in view except a small boat a quarter mile ahead of us and off to starboard.

My brother, Frank, and I are on the bridge of the *Salty Girl*, a thirty-five-foot customized sportfisher belonging to one of our uncles, Harry Morgan Wolfe, who normally uses it for fishing charters, but it sometimes serves other purposes as well. Frank's at the wheel and I'm astraddle the swivel stool beside him.

Out on the foredeck, Rayo Luna and Jessie Juliet are lying side by side on their tummies, sunning their exquisite butts in string bikinis and talking about God knows what. Thick as thieves, those two – Rayo of the caramel skin and short black shag, Jessie a tanned strawberry blonde, her long hair loosely knotted in a bunch at the back of her head. They know we're enjoying the view and that our pleasure isn't hindered a bit by the fact they're our cousins. Like Frank and me, Jessie is part of our family's Texas side and is only a couple of branches removed from us. Rayo's from the Mexico City half of the family, which originated from the same paternal root and is also surnamed Wolfe, but it places her further out from us on the genealogical tree. For the fun of it we sometimes refer to the two sides of the family in unison as the House of Wolfe. Over the generations, the Mexican Wolfes acquired a touch of mestizo strain through marriage, and most of them have the same light brown complexion and black hair as Rayo. In contrast, we on the Texas side of the house largely reflect the original family's Anglo-Irish origin, almost all of us fair-haired and light-skinned. Frank and I are the only American Wolfes with a wee drop of mestizo blood, gained by way of a grandaunt whose father was Rodolfo Fierro, Pancho Villa's right-hand man, and for whom I am first-named and Frank middle-named. For whatever reason, though, Frank tans more readily and darkly than I do, and given his black hair and bandido mustache, when nut-brown in high summer he bears a strong likeness to the Fierro we've seen in historical photos. The rest of the Texas clan could be taken for typical natives anywhere in Western Europe.

Rayo hollers, 'Look!' and points at a bounding bunch of dolphins that's surfaced on the port side and is keeping pace with the boat. Frank and I and Jessie grew up around here and have been familiar with boats and the sea since we were children, but Rayo had never even been to a seacoast before she made her first visit here eleven years ago when she and Jessie were sixteen. She grew to love the beach even more during her years at the University of Miami, but ski boats and day sailers were the only kinds of watercraft she was familiar with until she came to live with us two years ago and we took her out on deepwater boats. By now she must've seen dolphins on dozens of occasions, and she still gets excited as a kid every time. She still marvels at *everything* about the sea.

'You know what?' she says, looking up at me and Frank. 'I been thinking about how great it'd be to *live* on this boat. Never go ashore for anything but supplies, a little barhopping and dancing.'

'Well, you better give it plenty of thought before you take up a cruising life,' Frank says. 'There's an old saying – it's better to be on shore wishing you were at sea than it is to be at sea wishing you were on shore. Lot of downsides to boat life.'

'There are a lot of downsides to *any* life,' Jessie says.

'Such bleak perspective from one so young and fair,' Frank says in the professorial mode he at times assumes for the fun of it and has enjoyed doing since we were in college. The truth is he could've been a professor. 'I suppose,' he says, 'it stems from a frequency of journalistic exposure to a surfeit of human woe.'

Jessie's a reporter for the local paper. She makes a face at him.

'Actually, some good arguments can be made for boat living,' I say, 'and the best of them was made by the Phoenicians. They believed that no day spent on the ocean was deducted from a man's life.'

'What about for a woman?' Rayo says.

'They didn't say.'

'Of *course* not,' she says, tossing her head in disgust. 'Well, I'll tell *you* something, Rudy boy,' Jessie says, pointing at me. 'Back in the Middle Ages it was widely believed that every time a man had sex it *shortened* his life by a day. And *they* didn't say anything about a woman, either!'

'Yeah!' Rayo says. She and Jessie trade high fives.

'Well now, that's just rank nonsense,' Frank says. 'Because if it were true, I would've been dead a *long* time ago!'

The girls whoop. 'Listen to him!' Jessie says. 'Frankie Casanova. Sex probably hasn't taken *two weeks* off his life!'

'Unless self-abuse counts,' Rayo says. 'In that case he could kick the bucket any minute.'

They laugh it up some more.

'*Self-abuse?*' Franks says in an injured tone.

'Spanking the monkey, waxing the tent pole, shaking

hands with the bishop,' Rayo says. 'All those cutesy clever phrases guys have for it.'

'Massaging the midget!' Jessie adds. 'Strangling Mister Johnson!'

Those really get them howling, and Frank and I can't help grinning. They can always give as good as they get.

'I must say, brother,' Frank loudly declares, 'I am aghast to hear this sort of talk from women of allegedly proper upbringing.'

'Words cannot describe the depth of my own distress,' I say. 'Yeah, yeah,' Rayo says. 'Listen, if I were you boys I'd play it safe from now on and never have sex, not even with just yourself, *except* on a boat.'

She gives me an exaggerated wink, then laughs when I point my forefinger at her and flick my thumb like I'm shooting her. Ever since she's come to live with us, she and I have had some lovely times together, but she's made it abundantly clear she's not my 'girlfriend,' a word she enunciates like it's been soaked in sour milk. What she and I are, she's also made quite clear, is good-buddy distant cousins who like to get it on with each other. Quote, unquote. She's like that. Direct as an arrow. At the University of Miami she got her degree in theater arts and lettered in track, tennis, and swimming – and was a regional collegiate swim champ. When she went back to Mexico she got into stunt work in movies and TV. Some of the stunts she's done are unreal, but the worst she's ever been hurt in any of the 'bits,' as she calls them, was a sprained thumb. One Sunday morning we were strolling by a schoolyard playground and she jumped the fence and hopped up on a set of monkey bars and went through a workout routine worthy of a spot in the Olympics. She was wearing a loose short skirt, and it wasn't the first time she'd simultaneously shown me her gymnastic skills and her scanty underwear. She once said she was almost ashamed of herself for teasing me like that, because, as she put it, 'It's so *girly*.' From up in the wheelhouse, her so-called tramp stamp – a little red tattoo inscription just above the thong strap and between her sacral dimples – is scarcely discernible, but I've many a time read it up close. *FACTA NON VERBA*.

We're on our way home from Louisiana, where we delivered two men and a woman, all three using the name Aguirre, and perhaps they were truly related, we didn't ask. We had been contacted about them by our Mexico City relations, our usual source of clients in desperate need of a stealthy exit from Mexico and a new identity in the States. They sent us the necessary photos and pertinent physical data, then kept the Aguirres in a safe house down there while we arranged their relocation. Two weeks later when the Aguirres were transferred to the *Salty Girl* from a boat we rendezvoused with just a few miles off the Tamaulipas coast, we presented each of them with an American birth certificate, a duly issued Social Security card to match it, and a bona fide Texas driver's license showing the address of a rooming house we own in Harlingen. At a Mississippi River boatyard a few days later and some thirty miles below New Orleans, we turned them over to some associates – kinfolk of ours named Youngblood – who escorted them the rest of the way to their new home. Because they had expressed a desire to live in a beachside community, a spacious apartment had been leased for them in Panama City, Florida.

A body run is what we call that sort of smuggle. Rayo Luna has been on a few of them with us before, all of them to Corpus Christi, Galveston, or Houston. She thinks they're pretty dull and they usually are. But when she heard we were making a run up near New Orleans and would be spending the night there, she asked if she could come along, and when we said okay, she asked if Jessie could come, too. Neither of them had been to New Orleans since Mardi Gras in their senior year of college. But unlike Rayo, Jessie isn't in our line of work and has never wanted to be, and Frank and I make it a rule not to take anyone on a run who isn't in the trade. We don't need anything more than the cargo to safeguard or worry about. Then again, a body run is the least likely sort to encounter trouble, and we knew that even if things should for any reason get a little dicey, Jessie would be no liability. Like the rest of us she learned how to use a gun when she was a kid, and a couple of years ago down in Mexico City she proved beyond question she can handle herself pretty well. So we made an exception and took both of them along, and after the conclusion of business in the boatyard we treated them to a night in the French Quarter before starting for home the next morning.

All in all, it was a satisfying trip.

* * *

It's what we do, we Wolfes: we smuggle. Mostly into and out of Mexico, now and then Cuba or Central America. Been doing it for over a hundred years, ever since we settled in Brownsville, Texas, which is on the Rio Grande, about twenty-five miles upriver from the Gulf. We began by smuggling booze from Mexico into the States, then started running guns down there before the outbreak of the Revolution. During Prohibition we ran more booze than ever until repeal killed that gold-egg goose. Over the generations we've expanded into high-tech military gear and today we carry everything from infrared and thermal-imaging optical instruments to portable radar units to a wide range of explosive-device components. The only things we don't smuggle are drugs and wetbacks. The drug biz is unarguably a money river, but it attracts too many crazies. Smuggling is chancy enough without having to transact with such impulsive personalities. Besides, except for alcohol, we take a dim view of drugs. Ruinous stuff. As for dealing in wetbacks, the process entails too many stages and too many agents and too many people overall for too little reward. We like to keep every operation as uncomplicated as we can and restrict its number of participants to the fewest necessary. We do smuggle people every so often but usually carry only one or two individuals and never more than three, and what they all have in common is that they're running from mortal danger and can afford to buy a sure escape from it. Ours is a costly service but worth every dime, considering the official documents we include in the package. The federal government can't hide you better than we can. The fact is ID documents in general are selling better than ever, and not just to those on the run. Lots of people have something to hide that can best be hidden by way of various certifiable identities, and that's become truer than ever in our worldwide digital age. We can supply as many identities as anybody might want, each one supported by authentic documents registered in the files of the relevant agency. A certificate of birth or baptism or naturalization, a Social Security account, a military service record – whatever paper or set of papers a client requests, we can produce it. Some of our clients have asked how we do it. Our stock answer is that we have our ways. The simple truth is that the world turns on greed, and greed slavers at an ample bribe. Our insiders at official agencies, bureaus, and record departments have long prospered by way of our incentives.

Among the family, our extralegal pursuits are known collectively as the shade trade, and its main constituent has always been gun smuggling, guns being an article of commerce that, unlike drugs, we very much favor. Nothing else in the world so ably and indisputably accords physical equality between human beings as a gun. A 250-pound man has no advantage over a 90-pound woman if both of them are armed. As we see it, self defense is the most elemental of all natural rights and includes the right to possess the same means to defend yourself as might be used to assault you. Absent that right, you have to rely on agents of the state for protection, but you can't count on such an agent being at hand when you find yourself at the mercy of an armed antagonist. We choose not to depend on someone else to safeguard us or to rely on anyone's mercy. We're aware that many people of intelligence and good intention would disapprove of our outlook and deem it sophistic, cynical, self-serving, pick your righteous reproof. That's okay. Sticks and stones. Other people have their ways of looking at things, we have ours.

The family also owns a variety of legitimate and profitable enterprises – a law firm, a real estate company, a tech instruments and graphics store, a marine salvage and repair boatyard, a gun shop, plus a few others. The majority of those businesses are in Brownsville, all of them gainful and, not altogether coincidentally, most of them of advantage to the shade trade. As a matter of record, Frank and I are employed as 'field agents' by Wolfe Associates, one of the most respected law firms in South Texas. So are Rayo Luna and two other of our cousins. The firm's three partners are our uncles Harry McElroy Wolfe – Harry Mack to those who know him – and his close cousins Peck and Forrest. The position of field agent requires that we be state-licensed investigators, a hugely valuable sanction. The most routine duties in our formal job description – serving papers, conducting background checks, searching police records, and so on – are carried out by lower level hires. What *we* mainly do is track down essential witnesses who deliberately or against their will have gone missing. We're as good at finding people as we are at helping them to get lost. I love everything about the work – tracking them down, keeping them under wraps for as long as the firm requires, and all the while staying alert for whoever might be trying to get them back from us or simply wanting to prevent them from appearing in court or making a deposition. Rayo's been on several such assignments with me and Frank. She's got all the right instincts for the trade.

When we're not on a job for the Associates, we work for our cousin Charlie Fortune, the chief of shade trade operations. He's big-muscled but limber as a fly rod, and with his close-cut dirty-blond hair, a scar through one eyebrow, and the beard he keeps at a five o'clock growth, his countenance is as daunting as his physique. His only boss is his daddy, Harry Mack. Frank and I have been Charlie's main smugglers since graduating from college, though for the past year or so he's been letting one of our field agent cousins, Eddie Gato, do gun runs, too. Rayo has gone with me and Frank on a few such runs and enjoyed it, but not as much as tracking down people. She doesn't find it as satisfying. 'Not as much juice,' she says.

Most of our arms shipments go to our Mexican kin, who in turn sell them to their clients. Like us, the Mexican Wolfes are a large family of social standing who own and operate an assortment of lawful and profitable businesses in addition to engaging in various unlawful pursuits. And like us, they have always trafficked in such activities primarily for the satisfaction of asserting their independence from the horde of bastards who own the government and devise laws that first and foremost serve their own interests. It's a matter of self-respect, of a pride that's bred in our bones. Our Mexican cousins don't like being played for saps any more than we do. Unlike us, however, they conduct their illicit dealings by means of a small outfit of their own creation called Los Jaguaros. To this day, not the Mexican government, the police, nor the press is conclusively certain the Jaguaros even exist, notwithstanding the pervasive rumors that they're the principal suppliers of arms to some of the country's largest criminal societies. It has long been alleged by much of the news media and by political enemies of the current administration that the Jaguaros are a fabrication of the federal government, intended to cover up many of its own misdeeds. Over the years a number of captured cartel operatives have said that much of their armament came from the Jaguaros, but none of them knew where that organization is headquartered or could name any of its members. Some government critics insist that such prisoner allegations of the Jaguaros' existence are outright lies intended to conceal the true sources of cartel arms. Despite all such conjectures and suppositions, the Jaguaros' tie to the Mexico City Wolfes remains an impenetrable secret. Even the cartel chiefs who do business with the Jaguaros don't know of the connection to the family. Not even most Jaguaros know of it – except, of course, for their Wolfe crew chiefs, all of whom use false surnames.

Also, unlike ours, the Jaguaros' primary stock-in-trade isn't guns but information, and the cartels are their foremost market for that commodity, too. They sell military intelligence, police records, names of informants. They sell blueprints of banks, jewelry stores, art museums, prisons – of any venue someone might want to break into or out of. Much of that information comes from insiders at government bureaucracies, police and military agencies, corporate offices, construction companies, et cetera. But almost as much of it originates from the Jaguaros' squads of ace hackers. Their access to so many sources of information also serves the Jaguaros very well in finding people who may or may not want to be found. Their boundless web of informants – whom they call 'spiders' – reaches to every region of the country and every level of society, from shoeshine boys, house maids, whores, and gardeners to hotel staff, media reporters, cops, and politicians. Not even the federal police have such a comprehensive network of eyes and ears as the Jaguaros do, or as secure a system for transmitting, sifting, cataloging, and storing the data they amass. And even while the cartels are their primary buyers of information, the Jaguaros have compiled vast files of data on each of them as well. *That* knowledge, however, is not for sale. It's maintained by the Jaguaros solely for their own purposes. They of course also have a security unit, and it says something about Rayo Luna that she was a member of it before she came to live with us and joined the shade trade.

It's a rock-hard rule in the Texas family that no member of it can work in its unlawful trades without first earning a college degree, which can be in any major except phys ed or one that ends in the word *studies.* Charlie got his BA in history at A&M. Frank and I both got ours in English at UT Austin. He's a Hemingway man, Frank, and his senior thesis contended that Stephen Crane's influence on Hem's short works was even more significant than had been previously recognized. His mentor thought that with a few minor tweaks the paper could get published in an academic journal, but Frank shrugged it off. My thesis was on Alexander Pope, who could express more insight in a heroic couplet than most poets can muster in an entire poem. The department offered Frank a graduate fellowship, but he turned it down. And even though he'd told the baseball scouts he wasn't interested in a pro career – he had a rifle-shot fastball, plus a changeup that made a hitter swing like a drunk, and he came within four strikeouts of breaking the conference strikeout record in his senior year – the Orioles picked him in the third round anyway, hoping to change his mind with a big-bucks offer, but he nixed that, too. I was a good-field, good-hit third baseman and got a few offers myself, but the scouts didn't swarm me like they did him. We've now been in the shade trade about fourteen years, and I can't speak for Frank, but I think it's safe to say that, like me, he hasn't any regrets about his college major or career.

* * *

This time it's Jessie who shouts, '*Look!*' She's pointing at a fish hawk that's appeared to our left, circling, on the hunt. It's a beautiful thing, its breast and shoulders bright white against the gray-and-white checkering of its underwings and tail.

'Osprey!' Frank tells the girls. 'Name comes from the Latin *ossifraga*. Means "bone-breaker"!'

'*Bone-breaker!*' Rayo says. 'That's so perfect!'

I wouldn't say Frank's a showoff, but he does like to impress women every now and again with his erudition, and I have to admit most of them get a kick out of it. Just a few nights ago, Rayo and I were at a bar with him and a girlfriend of his, a nursing instructor at UTB, who got riled at the bartender for some reason and said to Frank, 'Hit him with an English major put-down, baby.' So Frank said to the guy, 'You, sir, are the terminus of an alimentary canal.' We all laughed, even the bartender, who admitted he didn't know what Frank called him but thought it sounded funny.

Now the osprey spies a fish and wings around to the east before turning back again.

'He's coming into the sun so the fish won't see his shadow,' I tell the girls. Frank's not the only one on the boat who knows stuff.

The osprey's gliding now as it starts angling into a descending trajectory and picking up speed, tucking its wings back as it swoops down. It's just a few feet above the water when it slings its legs forward with the talons spread and *wham*, it hits the surface with a terrific splash and flies up with a sea trout in its grip.

We all cheer and watch the hawk rise and start angling off to wherever its nest is. Then it jerks sideways a split second before we hear the gunshot, and it drops into the water about twenty yards from us, still holding the fish. It's trying to fly but is just splashing around in a small circle.

'Son of a *bitch*!' Frank shouts, slowing the boat and turning it toward the hawk.

'It was them,' Rayo says, pointing at the small boat we'd noted earlier.

I pick up the big field glasses and home in on it, a little over a hundred yards off and bobbing at anchor. A bowrider, twenty-two, twenty-three feet, stern drive, its Bimini top furled. Two guys standing in it, long-billed fishing caps, dark glasses, looking this way. One holding a scoped rifle with one hand, muzzle up, the butt resting on his hip.

We draw up beside the hawk, and Frank tells me to take the wheel and hold us in place, then gets his SIG nine from the bridge locker and goes down and around to the fishing cockpit, where the girls are discussing how to get the hawk out of the water. It's beating one wing in a spread of blood, and even from the bridge I can see the other wing's crippled and the chest torn. No way it can be saved. Frank picks up a long gaff and Jessie says, 'Not with *that*, you'll hurt it worse.' Then she sees the pistol in his other hand and says, 'Ah, hell.'

Frank steps around them and starts to take aim at the hawk, but it abruptly goes still. Before it can sink, he gaffs it out of the water, the fish still in its clutch, and lays it on the deck. He looks up at me and points at the other boat, and I start us toward it, then reach down and take my Beretta nine out of the locker and slip it into my waistband.

Frank detaches the trout from the osprey and lobs it overboard, then places the hawk at the foot of the cockpit's starboard gunwale. He goes up close to Jessie and says something to her, glancing over at the bowrider as he talks. She looks out at it, too, then nods and goes up to the bow and stands by the rail. He beckons Rayo to him and furtively hands her the SIG as he speaks to her. She listens, then moves back to the stern, holding the pistol out of sight behind her leg. Frank looks up at me, his back to the bowrider, and shows me with his hands how he wants me to position our boat in respect to theirs. It's pretty much what I had anticipated, and I show him a fist to let him know I got it.

The two guys watch us close in on them, and I draw up alongside, our deck several feet higher than theirs. I align our cockpit right next to their open bow, where the one with the rifle, the bigger and older of the two men – mid forties, I'd guess – is standing with the rifle barrel now propped against his shoulder, his finger on the trigger guard. It's an M1 Garand out of the Second World War and a fine weapon to this day. The other guy's in the cockpit, a kid of eighteen or nineteen, his thumbs hooked into the front of his cargo shorts to either side of the .38 revolver tucked there. Four fishing rods, their lines out, are in rod holders affixed to the stern. Both guys take off their shades for a better look at the girls and keep smiling from one of them to the other at either end of the boat.

'Y'all come over here to tell me what a helluva shot that was?' the big man says.

'It was something, all right,' Frank says. 'Damn bold, too, seeing as it's against both state and federal law to shoot a hawk.'

The big man shrugs. 'I don't reckon you for no game warden.'

'Oh, hell no. Thought you might want your prize, though.' Frank picks up the osprey and lobs it down near the big man's feet.

'Hey, fellas!' Jessie shouts. The two men both look over at her, and she yanks her top up to show her tits.

In the moment they're gawking, Frank vaults over the gunwale and drops into their boat, grabs the M1 with both hands, and wrenches it away as he shoulders the big man backward – and Rayo whips up the SIG and fires a round through the bowrider windshield and yells, 'Hands high, boy!' and the kid's hands fly up. Frank drives the rifle's steel butt plate into the big man's mouth with a crack of teeth I hear in the wheelhouse, knocking him on his ass, blood gushing over his chin. He tosses the rifle into the water and kicks the guy onto his back and straddles his chest, pinning his arms with his knees, then picks up the hawk by one of its feet and rakes the talons down one side of the guy's face and then the other side, the guy just screaming and screaming. Frank gets off him, hauls him to his feet, and pushes him over the side, then turns to the kid, who can't raise his hands any higher. 'Hey, man, hey, *I* didn't do nothin! I didn't *do* nothin'!' the kid screeches. Frank takes the revolver from the kid's pants and backhands him with the barrel, cracking his cheek and dropping him to his knees, then flings the gun away and yanks the kid up and shoves him overboard, too. The two guys tread water clumsily, gasping and moaning, blood running off their faces.

'I don't know where you shitheels are from and don't care!' Frank shouts. 'But I ever see either of you around here again, I'll cut your face *off*!'

He picks up the hawk and hands it up to Jessie, who's got her top back in place, then pulls himself aboard and signals me to move out. Rayo's draped a beach towel over the transom to hide the boat's name from the two guys – playing it safe despite the unlikelihood they would ever try tracking us down.

About a half mile farther on, Frank has me stop again. By then the two shitheels have managed to get back into the bowrider and are just a speck heading off in the other direction. Frank hooks the transom ladder to the stern and lowers himself into the water until it's up to his chest, then Rayo hands him the hawk. He holds it below the surface for about half a minute before letting go of it, and we watch it slowly sink. Then he climbs back up on deck and gives me a hand sign and I head us for home.

I'm not saying Frank's a softy or anything, but in truth he's always been prone to get a little upset when he witnesses mistreatment of an animal.

* * *

It's after dark when we come off the Gulf and into the seventeen mile ship channel leading to the Port of Brownsville. Near the channel's halfway point we turn off into a short canal that ends at the entry to Wolfe Marine & Salvage, a south-bank boatyard owned and operated by Harry Morgan Wolfe, known to everyone in the family as Captain Harry. The yard contains two long docks, one for local boats undergoing maintenance or repair, the other reserved for fishing and family vessels.

We tie up next to a trawler rig we know Eddie Gato used for a run to Boca Larga last night. A painter working at its transom by lamplight is putting the finishing touches on the name *Gringa* and, just below it, 'Brownsville.' He's already restored the true hull numbers. It's good work in that there's nothing fresh-looking about it. Frank and I used to do the Boca Larga run, but it became so rote it was starting to get boring, and when Charlie said Eddie wanted it, we said by all means.

The night manager, Dario Benítez, informs us that Captain Harry's already gone but left word he'd meet us at the Doghouse Cantina. Frank and I get cleaned up and into fresh clothes, but the girls plead tiredness and say they'll take a pass on the crowd and racket of a Doghouse weekend night, and they head for home in Rayo's pickup. We hop into Frank's restored '68 Mustang GT named 'Stevie' and follow a well-graded dirt road through the scrubs to State Highway 4, known locally as the Boca Chica Road. A few miles east, roughly halfway between Brownsville and the sea, we exit onto a sand trail where a low roadside marker reads wolfe landing just above the arrow pointing toward the river and a grove of tall palms mingled with hardwoods hung with Spanish moss. The grove's an extraordinary geographic incongruity out here, where most of the countryside consists of marsh grass, scrub brush, and mudflats. Once upon a time, however, much of this low stretch of the Rio Grande was lined with palm trees as tall as the masts of the Spanish ships that landed here – Rio de las Palmas, those first Europeans called it. Now the only other local palm grove besides ours is one in Brownsville that's been a nature preserve for a lot of years. The trail to the Landing is just wide enough for two vehicles to pass each other, and our headlights sweep from one side to the other along the winding route through the high brush before a final eastward curve brings us into the Landing's glow.

Our ancestors established Wolfe Landing in the early 1890s, and in 1911 they somehow managed to get it chartered as a town, even though to this day it's no more than a village covering about 60 acres in the middle of the 450-acre grove. Only for a few short periods in the past has the Landing's population exceeded a hundred residents. The most recent census put the number at seventy-something. It's a place of perpetual shadows, its air always dank and heavy with the odors of fecund vegetation, its nights loud with frogs and cats and owls. From an airplane, the river all along the border of Cameron County looks like a tangled string, so closely bunched are the serpentine loops and crooks of its meanders, a feature that over time has formed numerous resacas on both sides of the river – what they call 'bayous' or 'oxbows' in the Deep South and other regions. There are several resacas in the palm grove, and the biggest of them, Resaca Mala, is in the gloomiest and most remote part of the property. It has been home to a small colony of alligators since the first Wolfes settled the place, though nobody knows about them except for a few of us in the shade trade. Charlie's house is the only one back in there.

All of the Landing's streets and trails are narrow and packed with crushed shell except for Main Street and Gator Lane, which are paved with tar and gravel. The trail off the highway melds into Main Street, on which stands the community's only stone building – the single-story town hall, comprising the mayor's office, the police department, and a two-cell jail. Charlie Fortune is both Wolfe Landing's mayor – now many times re-elected – and the chief of its police force, which at present consists of only himself and has never had more than one deputy. Also on Main are the Republic Arms gun shop and shooting range, Mario's Grocery, Riverside Motors & Garage, Get Screwed Hardware, and Lolita's, a little place that sells secondhand clothes. Main ends at a trail that curves northward past a couple of piling homes – one of them Frank's, the other mine – and up into the grove's higher ground, where you'll find the graveyard and main residential area, composed of a scattering of cabins and mobile homes. Many of the Landing's inhabitants are in the employ of Charlie Fortune in one way or another, while others operate businesses of their own but only with his approval.

Branching off Main, just opposite the Republic Arms, is Gator Lane. It runs straight to the river and ends at the Doghouse Cantina, with Big Joe's Bait & Tackle store just across the lane. Big Joe is Joseph Stilder, who showed up last year in a banged-up old Buick with expired New York plates, saw the for sale sign in the store window, gave the place a quick look-over, and bought it from Charlie for cash. He's a burly guy with thick white hair and could be anywhere from fifty to seventy. Highly sociable dude and a talented teller of tales, a much-revered gift in a community where even skillfully wrought bullshit is highly prized. Like almost everybody else who lives here, he's not big on personal disclosure, but he became a hell of a good bartender somewhere along the line and is always willing to fill in at the Doghouse. He's also a voracious reader, and in addition to everything you might expect to find in a bait-and-tackle store, the place sells used books – fiction, histories, travel guides, sex manuals, name it. People would be surprised at the number of readers in the Landing, and they much appreciate Big Joe's sideline.

The Doghouse is owned by Charlie Fortune and is the largest building in the village. Its short-order grill serves breakfast, lunch, and supper, and its spacious bar fronts a dance floor flanked by dining booths along three walls. There's a side room with pool tables, and the office in the rear is the base of operations from which Charlie runs the shade trade – a fact of course known solely to those of us in the trade. The only Wolfes who live at the Landing are Charlie, Frank, me, and a cousin named Jimmy Quick, who manages the Republic Arms, also owned by Charlie. Jessie and Rayo live at the beach, way back in the dunes, in a stilt house they rent from Captain Harry. The rest of the family lives 'in town,' which to everyone in the Landing means Brownsville – or, as Frank likes to refer to it, the Paris of Cameron County. Big Joe once heard him call it that and he said *that* was why he had decided to settle here. He'd always wanted to live in Paris.

* * *

As on every Saturday evening the Doghouse parking lot is jammed. Most of the vehicles belong to Brownsville regulars who come out every weekend for the supper specials of seafood gumbo on Friday night and barbecued ribs on Saturday. During the week Charlie will work the grill at the end of the back bar for about two hours every morning and then for another hour around midday. He's a superb short-order cook and sandwich maker. The backroom kitchen he mostly leaves to Concha and Juana, a mother-daughter team that can handily accommodate the Friday night crowd by making large kettles of gumbo well ahead of the supper hour. But grilling the Saturday ribs is a nonstop task, and Charlie always assists them with it. There aren't any waitresses. You pay for your order at the bar and receive a card with a number, which you take to the little kitchen window at the end of the bar and give to Charlie or one of the other cooks, then sit and wait for the number to be called. Signs in each booth say clean your table, and the big garbage barrels along the walls are labeled either non-food or scraps. Charlie employs a balding graybeard known only as the Professor to keep an eye out for patrons who neglect to bus their table or who empty their trays into the wrong barrel. To commit either of those transgressions is to get barred from the Doghouse for a month. Runs a tight joint, Charlie does. Every Sunday afternoon a couple of us will load the weekend scraps barrels into a truck and take them to Resaca Mala and feed them to the gators. Those brutes have long been useful for disposing of all sorts of organic matter.

The place is boisterous, and the ceiling fans are whirling with minor effect against the concentration of body heat. The dining booths are full, and at the bar every stool is taken and the spaces between them packed with standees, keeping the weekend trio of barmaids on their toes. Even though the jukebox is turned way up against the laughter and loud conversation, Charlie's kitchen bellow of '*Eighty-two and eighty-three!*' carries through the din and a guy scoots out of a booth and over to the window to collect his ready plastic plates of ribs.

The Doghouse juke is renowned for the variety of its musical selections. It holds everything from Tex Ritter to Sinatra to Elvis to Los Tigres del Norte. About a third of its content, though, is 'swing music,' 1930s and '40s big band tunes by Glenn Miller and Benny Goodman and their ilk, even though Charlie and Frank and I and the Professor are just about the only ones who ever play it. Actually, the dances of that era are a lot of fun. Our mother – who had learned them from her mother – taught Frank and me how to do the Lindy Hop, fox-trot, jitterbug, and other such dances when we were still in grammar school, and it's a rare girl who doesn't get a kick out of learning them from us. Sometimes a patron will complain about all the big band stuff, but Charlie says anybody who doesn't want to hear it can go somewhere else. A guy once told him he should put some hip-hop in the juke, and Charlie said he'd sooner hire an idiot child to sit in the corner and bang pots and pans together.

Captain Harry and Eddie Gato are standing at the far end of the bar, leaning close in conversation. We go over and press up beside them, the nearest standees making room when they see who we are, and I signal Lila for a couple of Shiner Bocks. She's Charlie's only full-time bartender and is in charge of the two part-timers who assist her on weekends. On her days off or a busy weeknight, Charlie or Big Joe will help her out. As she heads for the beer cooler, her brown ponytail swings above a delectable butt snugged into faded jeans that cling to it like pale blue skin. It's shaped like a perfect upside-down Valentine's heart, and when she bends over into the cooler, the heart turns rightside up. She and Eddie have had an on-again, off-again thing for the past few years.

Frank claps Captain Harry on the shoulder and says, 'What's the good word, Unc?'

'Evening, fellas,' Harry says. But his smile's a puny thing and Eddie's looking grim.

'What the hell, guys?' Frank says. 'You look like somebody let the air out of your sex dolls.'

'*Sex dolls?*' Lila says as she sets our beers on the counter. 'That's what I love best about this place, the highbrow conversation.' She goes off to attend to other customers, pert ass and ponytail swinging.

Talking just loud enough for us to hear, Eddie tells us that Alberto Delmonte and his crew were bushwhacked last night as they were heading back on the Boca Larga trail. 'Every man of them dead and the load jacked,' Eddie says. 'Charlie told me as soon as I got back. He got it from Rigo himself.'

'We know who did it?' Frank says.

'Not yet. Charlie said don't discuss it out here, but I thought you oughta at least know. He wants to see us all in the office after closing.'

* * *

The Doghouse shuts down at midnight, and at twenty till there's nearly two dozen people still here when Lila yells, 'Last call!' rousing the usual groans of protest. She goes over to the juke and hits the kill switch, prompting more grousing, but she just shrugs and smiles.

As she's passing by the other end of the bar to go back behind the counter, a tall, rangy guy in a western shirt and cowboy boots gives her ass a swat and loudly says, 'Yo! That is *fine*, mama!' I've never seen him before, or the two men with him, all of them grinning.

Lila spins around with a glare. She puts her finger in the guy's face and says, 'Don't ever do that again. I mean *ever*!'

'Ah, now, sugar, I was *admiring* is all.'

'You've been warned,' she says.

He draws closer, looming over her. 'But what if I just can't *help* myself, darlin'?'

'Then you'll have to deal with them.' She points at us at the end of the counter, where Frank and Eddie and I have stepped away from the bar in readiness to engage with the three of them, Frank putting a hand to Captain Harry's chest to keep him out of it. But when the rangy guy turns his head to look our way, Lila does a nimble little move with her feet and drives her knee up between his legs. He hunches forward and his mouth drops open, and she stiff-arms him hard in the chest with both hands, propelling him backward into one of his pals, who tries to support him by the underarms, but the rangy one's legs quit him and he sags in the man's grip and almost pulls his pal down with him.

Onlookers cheer and laugh, and a woman shouts, 'All *right*, girl!'

'Get him out,' Lila tells the rangy one's buds. 'He chucks up in here, you'll clean the mess.'

They half carry, half drag him out the door. In keeping with his duty, the Professor goes to a front window to make sure they go away. Whenever somebody gets booted from a bar, and especially if he's drunk, there's always a tense interval afterward because there's no telling if he's one of those guys who's coming right back with a gun. The Professor stands watch at the window for a minute, then looks at Frank and gives him a thumbs-up. He'll continue to keep an eye out for a while in case their vehicle returns.

Lila goes behind the bar and is grinning big when she comes over to us. Captain Harry tells her he's never seen man nor woman deliver a knee to the cojones with such grace and asks if it was pure luck or what.

'Pure *execution*, Captain,' she says. 'Rayo taught me. It's all distraction, timing, and speed.' She points off to the side as she says, 'Distract, set, *do* it,' fluidly shifting her feet and whipping up her knee.

'Be damned if the women around here aren't getting downright dangerous,' Frank says. He tells Eddie he better never piss off Lila again unless he's wearing a cup.

Our laughter's strained. But still, it's a minor respite from the bad tidings about Alberto and his guys.

* * *

A half hour later, Lila and the other barmaids have gone home and the only ones still in the Doghouse are Frank and me, Uncle Harry, Eddie, and Charlie. We're in Charlie's office, and he's given us the details about the ambush and hijacking and told us about Donasio Corona and the all-out search for him by the Jaguaros' army of informants.

'I've promised Rigo that, if necessary, I can have a replacement load ready in five days. He's talked to the Zetas and they said okay, but if they have to wait longer than that they'll demand a late-delivery fine of twenty percent of what they paid for the original load. Rigo didn't have any choice but to agree, and if we end up having to pay the fine he and I will split it. He's pretty sure, though, that Mateo will find the rat quick, and as soon as he does, they'll let us know. When the word comes, you two' – he looks at me and Frank – 'are going down there. I want you with the Jaguaros when they brace the bastard and find out who jacked our load, and I want you with them when they get it back and into the Zetas' hands in less than five days. If it's a close call in timing and the Zees give Mateo any shit about a late delivery of just a few hours, I want you to remind them who sells the Jaguaros the guns they sell to the Zetas. They should be made to understand that any disagreement they have with the Jaguaros could become a problem with us and therefore a problem with one of their main lines of arms supply.'

'Maybe we should call them motherfuckers while we're at it,' Frank says, deadpan. 'Just to make *extra* sure we piss them off enough to kill us on the spot.'

***

The word comes from Mateo the following afternoon. He tells us the rat's in Monterrey, holed up at his brother's house. Mateo's taking off from the capital in twenty minutes with a three-man team in a company Learjet. He gives us the coordinates and code letters of a private airfield on the outskirts of Monterrey. He'll take care of our landing clearance, but he won't wait there for us longer than an hour.

Frank and I have been ready to go since last night. We've got our Mexican documents – passports, driver's licenses, gun carry permits, and ID badges as employees of Toltec Seguridad, a private security business owned by the Mexican Wolfes and headquartered in Cuernavaca, its high-powered legal department always prepared to render whatever assistance we might require. We slip into shoulder holsters holding Beretta nines, put on ultralight waterproof windbreakers to conceal them, and grab our ever-ready gym bags holding short-trip essentials, three extra twenty-round magazines, and a pistol suppressor, what the movies like to call a 'silencer.' We call ours a 'Quickster' because it's custom-made for us by Jimmy Quick, who is a firearms genius. Though it's only three and a half inches long, roughly half the length of most suppressors, it muffles a gunshot better than the bigger ones. And it's a lot easier to carry a Quickster-equipped pistol on your person than one with a standard-sized suppressor.

A driver takes us out to the Spur Aviation Company's airstrip and hangars, where Wolfe Associates keeps its two twinprop aircraft, one a four-passenger model, one that carries six. Harry Mack's provided us with the smaller one. The pilot is Jimmy Ray Matson, an amiable, red-haired young man out of Mississippi who claims to be twenty-six but doesn't look old enough to drive a car. He's an ace pilot and has ferried us before, and he's already got the engines running when we climb aboard. The cockpit's in open view of the cabin, and Jimmy Ray – dressed as usual in denim shirt and pants, hiking boots, and a gray Confederate army cap – greets us with 'How do, fellers, good to see ya.' He puts on his earphones, tells the tower we're ready, and in minutes we're airborne.

Mexico City is about three times farther from Monterrey than we are, but a twin-prop is no Learjet and Mateo got the jump on us. He'll get there before we do.

* * *

The sun has just begun to settle behind the mountains when the little airfield appears below us, Monterrey spread out in the near distance beyond it. There are two runways, three hangars, and a two-story building containing the control tower. A Learjet is on the apron, four men standing next to the plane. The only other people in sight are two guys in mechanic overalls at the entrance to one of the hangars. We touch down and taxi up close to the apron. Three of the men get into the Lear and one starts toward us. I recognize him as Mateo. Officially, he's chief of security for various of the Mexican Wolfes' legitimate businesses. Under the name of Mateo Dos Santos, he's also the operations chief of the Jaguaros.

We lower the cabin stairs, and as we exit the plane Mateo calls out, 'Tell your pilot he can refuel at that truck by the far hangar, then go home! His flight's cleared!' He has to shout for us to hear him over the rumbling idle of our plane's engines and the high whine of the Learjet as it turns about on the apron to face the runway. Frank leans into the cabin and relays the instructions to Jimmy Ray, who yells back, 'Okeydoke!'

We each embrace Mateo in turn and he says, 'Excellent timing! We haven't been here half an hour! Soon as you guys started making your approach, I told my pilot to fire up the jet again! Come on, let's get aboard! I'll tell you everything on the way!'

* * *

As the Learjet levels off at cruising altitude, the last of the day's light is deep red along the mountain ridges on our left and the black earth below is showing small clusters of town lights. In Spanish, Mateo has introduced us to his three-man team as Francisco and Rodolfo. His guys are a big black dude unimaginatively nicknamed El Negro, small and bucktoothed Conejo, and burly Gancho, whose name indubitably derives from the chrome hook he has in lieu of a left hand. El Negro carries a zippered bag strapped across his chest. Mateo sees me looking at it and says in English, 'Mufflers, flex cuffs, duct tape, other essentials.'

He tells us that the Jaguaros' intelligence people searched through Donasio Corona's prison files, then through the civic records of every place he's ever lived or been jailed, then looked up every relative or friend of his mentioned in any of those records. They came up with only four known friends who aren't dead. Three of them are in prison, the fourth's a paraplegic who lives with his mother.

'Donasio's only living kin,' Mateo says, 'are a sister in Oaxaca – she's a deaf widow with several children – and a brother, Luis, who's been arrested for robbery a few times but only been in prison once, a two-year fall. He got out about four months ago. Lives in a run-down barrio just outside Monterrey. Holds the registration on an old Chevy pickup. All that information came to me this morning. I had a spider stake out Luis's place, and he wasn't on lookout three hours before he calls and tells me he saw Donasio come out of the house and get something from the truck. Talk about shit for brains, hiding at his *brother's*, like that wouldn't be one of the first places we'd look. I called a couple of my Monterrey guys and gave them Luis's address and truck plate number and told them to go there and hold both the fuckers till I arrive. In the interest of time, I also told them what I wanted to know from Donasio and how to radio the plane if they got that information while I was still in the air. Promised them a bonus if they did. Well, they don't waste time, these guys, and we were making our descent into Monterrey when they called me with their report. They'd gone to Luis's place, showed him police ID, and went inside just as Donasio came out of the kitchen with a beer in his hand. *Wham-bam*, they get them both on the floor and handcuffed. They ask Donasio who jacked the arms shipment at Laguna Madre the night before last, and he says he doesn't know what they're talking about. So they drag him into the kitchen and get a cleaver and hack off his thumb, then roll a hand towel for him to bite on and stifle his howling, and they wrap up his wound with another one. They ask him again who did the hijack and he starts blabbing nonstop. His brother, too. Didn't take long to get the whole story, which is short and simple. Not long before Luis got out of prison, he met a guy who's a member of Los Sangreros, a street gang working out of Juárez and El Paso, bunch of young bucks with a rep as up-and-coming. To impress the guy, Luis brags to him about his brother who makes gun-smuggling pickups for some big league Mexico City gang, and the guy says he'll pass that on to his boss, who's always in the market. A week or two after Luis gets out of the pen, the Sangrero boss, guy named Miguel Soto, gets in touch with him. Says he'd like to talk to Luis's brother about a gun deal, and Luis arranges a meet in Mexico City. Donasio tells Soto he works for a band of smugglers he won't name but that mainly deals in U.S. Army weapons, and Soto says that's good. Thing is, he tells Donasio, he's convinced that most gun smugglers are greedy bastards who gouge their buyers, and he'd rather rip *them* off than let them fuck him over. He offers Donasio ten grand American for nothing more than a solid lead on a smuggle transfer. Donasio says he'll be in touch, and then a couple of days before the Boca Larga run he calls Soto and says he's got something good for him. They meet again and

Donasio tells him he wants *fifteen* grand, ten up front. *And*, because he knows we're going to find out pretty fast it was him who sold us out, he wants a job with the Sangreros, plus some fake ID and a place to live in El Paso. Soto says yeah, sure, no sweat. He sends one of his guys out to the car and he comes back with a money belt holding ten gees. Soto tells Donasio he'll get the other five right after the hijack when they pick him up at Luis's place on their way back to the border. In exchange, Donasio gives Soto a packet of information – descriptions of Boca Larga and of the little trail to it, hand-drawn maps, an estimated timetable of the drop – all the necessary details. Soto tells him welcome to the Sangreros and they'll see him at Luis's in two days.'

'And Donasio swallowed it?' Frank says. 'They'd pick him up at Luis's and pay him another five? Take him into the gang? Hide him in El Paso?'

'I tell you, cousin, the number of dumb shits in the world is doubling by the day. And get this. The ten grand was counterfeit. And very poorly made, as Donasio found out when he tried to exchange some of the Bennies for Mexican currency. The bank teller did a little chem test on a couple of the bills right in front of him and Donasio saw the smears and knew that wasn't good. The teller told him to wait just a minute and went to the manager's desk. The manager took a look at the bills and over at Donasio, then picked up a phone. Donasio figured the money's queer and the cops are coming and he hauls ass. He went to another bank and told a teller he'd received a gringo hundred in payment of a gambling debt and wanted to be sure it was good. The teller tested it and laughed. So there he was, with all these hundreds not worth the cheap-ass ink and paper it took to print them *and* with us about to start hunting for him. And what's he do? Goes to hide at his *brother's*. Told my guys he thought it'd be a safe place because his brother didn't have anything to do with the hijack so why would anybody look for *him*.

My guys laughed in his face. I told them they'll get the bonus.'

'And Donasio?' I say.

'Yeah. Well, he and Luis got relocated to another hiding place.'

'Another hiding place?' Frank says.

'Underground hideout.'

We get it. A grave.

'And we're going to the border?' I say.

'Juárez. Our web guys ran down Soto and got an address. No picture, but we have a description.' He takes a little notebook from his jacket and flips a few pages. 'Twenty-four years old. Five-nine, one-forty-five. Crew cut, clean-shaven, got a white scar down one side of his mouth. I've notified Charlie we're on the way to brace the son of a bitch.'

* * *

We touch down at a regional airport just south of the city. The night's hot. We go through the little terminal and find a pair of dark green Durango SUVs with drivers standing by parked one behind the other at the curb. Mateo dismisses the drivers and he and Frank and I get in the lead Durango, Mateo driving, and head into town, the other Durango staying close behind us. A green-lit dashboard screen shows a street map of Juárez with a yellow route laid out on it, courtesy of the Jaguaros' info web. When the techs got Soto's address, they drew up the route to it from the airport and downloaded it as a superimposition over the vehicle's city map. The traffic is heavy, the going slow.

'It's a nice house, nice neighborhood, but way below the security of the big chiefs,' Mateo says. 'Soto's not big enough yet to have to live on high alert or anyway not rich enough to do it. He doesn't have guards or dogs, so we won't have to cowboy our way in. Besides a maid, the only ones who live with him are his brother Julio, who's in the gang, too, and both their girlfriends. Lot of trees along the street, plenty of shadow cover. Front gate's got a pushbutton lock and our guys got the code from the contractor records. Same for the front-door lock. The maid's quarters are just off the kitchen but, lucky for us and luckier for her, she always gets Sunday off to visit her family and won't be back till tomorrow morning. The four bedrooms are all in a row on the second floor, all the light switches on the wall just inside the door and on the left. We'll park at the sidewalk in front of the house. Gancho will cover the front gate and courtyard. Conejo's got the lower floor. Me, Negro, and the two of you will take the upstairs.'

We attach suppressors to our pistols.

* * *

Soto's property is protected by a high stone wall topped with glass shards fixed in cement. The walkway entrance gate is fashioned of steel bars with spear points. Mateo taps the numerical code into the gate lock and there's a soft *click*. Guns out, we pass through the gate and follow the walkway across the courtyard and to the front door. A few touches to the door lock's keypad and we're in the house. The lower floor is softly lighted and the air-conditioning's going strong. We cross the living room and pause at the bottom of the stairs. There are muffled sounds from the second floor – recorded voices, snatches of sound track music. They're watching TV, maybe a video. We go up the stairway as cautiously as cats.

The TV's louder now and emitting sounds of gunfire and Spanish dialogue. They're coming from the room at the end of the hall, its doorway fully open but only faintly and flickeringly lit, the TV probably the only light within. We take a look into each of the first three rooms by turn, silently opening each door, switching on the light, guns ready, and find all of them unoccupied. We come to the open door and Mateo very slowly leans into it for a peek, then backs us down the hall a little way before whispering that there's four of them in there, two guys, two women, all in one bed against the far left side of the room, watching a big TV on the opposite wall. He tells us how we'll work it, then leads us back to the room. He takes another look inside, then Frank and I follow him in, all of us holding close to the wall. El Negro brings up the rear and stays by the light switch. The glow of the TV is sufficient for us to see that the two guys are wearing only boxer shorts, the girls only panties. I recognize the Spanish-dubbed movie they're watching. *Heat.* De Niro and Pacino. Good flick.

Halfway to the bed, Mateo pauses and taps his gun against the wall, and Negro clicks on the lights. The girls let out short shrieks, and we dart out from the wall to form a firing line facing the bed as they all jerk around to gape big-eyed at the row of us pointing pistols at them. The girls are nicely hootered, and there's no mistaking Miguel Soto with that mouth scar. He says, What the fuck – but Mateo tells him to shut up and orders them all to put their hands on top of their heads and they do. Julio looks as scared as the girls. Frank goes to the TV wall and yanks out a plug, and the screen goes dark and silent. If you're curious about the ending, he says to the couples on the bed, the cop kills the robber.

Mateo tells the girls to push the covers and all the pillows to the floor, and they do it. He stirs the bedclothes with his foot to assure there are no weapons in them, then asks Soto if there are any firearms in the room and he says in the closet. Negro opens it and collects the two shoulder holsters hanging on door hooks, each one holding a large revolver. Mateo opens the window and sticks his head out and looks down, then tells Negro to drop the guns into the bushes below.

We flex-cuff the four of them with their hands at their

backs, then gag and blindfold the girls and Julio with duct tape, but not Soto. We place Julio in an easy chair and tape his ankles to the forelegs. Mateo tells Negro to take the girls into the adjoining bedroom, put them on the bed, and tape their hands and feet to the bedposts. Negro hustles them away.

Mateo walks around the room, looking it over like he's thinking of buying the place. He picks up a wad of currency from atop the dresser, seems to weigh it with his hand, then puts it back. He holsters his pistol and takes out a switchblade and snicks out the blade. Where's the Boca Larga shipment? he says. If I have to ask you again, it'll be after your dick's on the floor.

Soto stares at him. Then at me and Frank. He looks like he's considering every possible lie as fast as he can and not finding any of them propitious. Corona ratted, huh? he says. I shoulda shot the whoreson.

Mateo starts toward him with the blade brandished.

In the Suburban in the garage, Soto blurts out.

What garage? Where?

My garage. Soto juts his chin toward the rear of the house. We look around at each other and smile. Sometimes it's this easy.

Mateo puts away the knife. You and your brother and who else did the hijack? he asks.

Oh, hell... Cheto and Gaspar.

Frank casually looks at Mateo and strokes his mustache, his sign that he thinks Soto's lying about the names. He's the best I know at perceiving a lie. The best Mateo knows, too. Calls him a human polygraph.

Where are they? Mateo asks. Cheto and Gaspar.

Across the river in El Paso somewhere. I don't know where they live, exactly. They don't want me to know. Those fuckers don't trust anybody, not even their own chief.

Another mustache stroke from Frank. Soto's protecting

his other two guys. He's a loyal chief. There's that to say for him.

El Negro returns, and Mateo takes him aside and whispers to him and they take out their phones. Mateo taps a button on his phone and Negro's buzzes and he swipes the screen and nods. Keep it open, Mateo tells him, and they pocket the phones. Negro remains in the room with Julio as Mateo, Frank, and I take Soto, still cuffed and in his underwear, downstairs and out the back door.

We cross the high-walled rear patio to the garage, and Soto tells us the numbers to tap into the garage door lock. We go in and turn on the interior light to reveal a mud-smeared black Suburban with dusty black glass. Been driven hard over rough country and not cleaned up. We go around to its rear and I open the lift gate and there it all is – the unopened crates of carbines, machine guns, ammo. Plus a pair of loose M4s. I eject the magazine from one of them, make sure there's no round in the chamber, take a whiff of its muzzle, and nod at Mateo that it's recently been fired. Then I give the other one the nose test and say, 'This one, too.' There's also a small package, a carton wrapped in brown paper and sealed with packing tape and without any markings on it. It's of a size to hold a few trade paperback books but feels lighter than that.

Mateo asks what's in it and Soto says, Movies. DVDs. The chief likes movies. I was gonna give them to him.

Chief? Mateo says. I thought *you* were the chief of this bunch.

I am. I meant the chief of the Sinas. You know. El Chubasco.

We all trade looks again, and Soto shows a little smile at our response. 'Sinas' is a common nickname for the Sinaloa crime cartel. It dominates most of Mexico west and south of Juárez to a point about halfway down the Pacific coast, though control of some of the area's prime smuggling routes into the U.S. – a span of border ranging from El Paso to Tijuana – is in chronic contention. And as everybody knows, the chief of the Sinaloa organization is Jaime Montón Delacruz, more widely known as El Chubasco. The Stormy One. By way of the extensive media attention he's received over the years, everybody knows of his impoverished childhood on the backstreets of Culiacán, his admission to the Sina cartel when he was a teenager, his early reputation as one of its most proficient killers, and his rapid ascension through the ranks. And that six years ago he took over the organization after engineering the assassination of the previous Sina chieftain – a badass called La Navaja – by way of a rocket grenade ambush in downtown Culiacán that obliterated Navaja's vehicle and everybody in it. Made front pages and TV screens everywhere. The Jaguaros have been selling guns – most of them procured through Charlie Fortune – to the Sinaloa outfit since before Chubasco became its chief. But they've always made the deals and deliveries through Sina subchiefs or intermediaries, and no Wolfe has ever met Chubasco himself.

Mateo asks what the Sinaloa chief has to do with any of this.

That's kind of a story, Soto says. But, hey, man, my hands are getting numb. Can you –?

No, Mateo says. What about Chubasco?

Well… I stole your guns because I needed to arm some new guys I wanted to recruit. Then when I saw that two of the crates had machine guns, I thought I hit the jackpot. And *then* I thought, hey, I'll make a present of them to Chubasco, show him what the Sangreros are capable of getting for him, you see? I figured he might appreciate it so much he'd take us into the Sinas as a subgang. Big step up, no? I was gonna take the guns to him next week, surprise him. And, believe me, there was a good chance he'd take us in. He likes me.

Likes you? Mateo says. You know him?

Oh, yeah. Well, I mean... I met him once. At a party in Ensenada two, three months ago. He's got a big fancy ranch just outside town where he likes to throw parties for his border chiefs and some of their guys. They say he's got a big meth factory somewhere around there, too, but I can't swear to that. A good pal of mine told me. Tico Ruíz. He's the subchief of a Sina gang in Hermosillo. Well, I mean, he *was*. His girlfriend found out he was fucking around on her and she cut his throat while he was asleep. Pretty low-down, huh? Kill a guy while he's sleeping? She told some of her friends she –

Back to Chubasco, Mateo says.

Yeah, right. So Tico, he's the one invited me to the Ensenada fiesta and introduced me to him. It was great. He's a really good guy, the chief. Said he was glad to meet me. Told me he could use all the friends he can get in Juárez, especially if they come up with some good smuggling routes around there. Asked me did I deal in guns, and I said yeah, I got some good connections. He wanted to know could I get submachine guns and I said sometimes but they can be hard to come by. He said he was interested in only the best and from now on whenever I got some good submachines to sell I should offer them to him ahead of anybody else. He tells his segundo, a big dude called El Puño, tells him to give me his number so I could call whenever I had machine guns for sale. He's a good guy, too, Puño.

Frank's glance says he can't tell if the kid's lying. But Mateo's told us about El Puño – the Fist – Chubasco's second in command. All the gun deals Mateo makes with the Sinas he arranges through Puño. He's never met the man in person, but the Jaguaros who've made deliveries to him say he's a big bald dude with fists the size of grapefruits.

Soto's been talking faster and faster. He's hoping he might luck out and hit on something that'll interest us enough to let him live a little longer, even if it's just another day or two, just another few minutes. They all get like this when they know it's the end.

Now his expression brightens and he says, Hey, hey listen, I got a really great idea. I can *introduce* you to him! To *Chubasco*! What do you say to *that*? Could mean a lot of really good business for you, right? You could probably make some pretty good deals with him, no? I mean, if –

What's any of this got to do with the fucking movies? Mateo says.

Hey, man, it's funny you call them fucking movies, because that's what they are. They're *fuck* movies. Porno. At this party I'm talking about, a big downstairs room was showing them one after another on this big screen, and the chief kept going in there for a look. I heard him telling some of the guys they were the best he'd ever seen, way better than most stuff on the internet. Kinda funny, though, going in a room to look at fuck movies when all over the place are all these fine-looking women who are there to *be* fucked. I had two of them myself that night, no lie. Really great-looking girls. I mean, I've had some nice stuff before, but *these* –

The movies, Mateo says.

Yeah, right. Well, like I said, at this party the chief kept going in there, in the room showing the movies. Even after I saw him go upstairs with a girl, as soon as he came back down he went into the movie room again. So I got kinda curious and went in for a look, and, man, I gotta admit, what was showing was really damn good. It was in English, but who cares what they're *saying*, right? Then I get this idea. I go to the guy who's running the DVD player from the back of the room and ask him can I write down the names of some of the movies he's showing. You see, I know this guy in Saltillo runs a business that deals in nothing *but* sex DVDs, the best stuff, gets it from everywhere, and I thought he might have some as good as the ones on my list. But I didn't get a chance to go to Saltillo for a while, not till day before yesterday, when I was on my way back from, ah, you know... Laguna Madre. So anyway, I go to the store in Saltillo and I showed the guy my list and asked did he have any movies as good as them but even newer – I didn't want to give the chief any movies he already had, right? – and my pal said, yeah, sure, he has the best ones on the market and some of them just a few months old. So I bought six or seven of his newest and he packed them in that little box. I thought the chief might like them, you see. Together with... you know... the machine guns. Be a nice little extra for him and, who knows, maybe give us a boost up the ladder.

He's almost breathless now, and the mention of Laguna Madre and the machine guns has brought him back to square one. There's nothing left to tell. Nothing left to stretch out with more talk. His eyes move from Mateo's to mine to Frank's, searching for some sign of hope, no matter how small. He won't find it. He killed Mateo's crew. He killed Alberto. He was good as dead as soon as we set out for him. He could ask for mercy, but he knows he won't get it. My bet is he won't ask. Despite his fear, I peg him for a tough kid who won't piss on his pride by begging.

But he does say, Hey, man, the girls upstairs, they don't have nothing to do with this. They don't know *anything*, they really don't. You don't have to, you know... worry about them.

They know what we look like, Mateo says. He takes out his phone, its connection still open to Negro's, and says into it, Do it, and then get Gancho and Conejo out to the vehicles. He turns off the phone and puts it in his jacket.

I think the kid's telling the truth about the girls and I want to say something to Mateo, talk him out of popping them. But I don't. It's his show.

From the second-floor window comes the suppressed

discharge of Negro's Beretta. That's it for brother Julio. I can tell by Soto's face he's waiting for another shot. Two more. So am I and Frank.

Mateo chuckles and says, Quit worrying, guys. The girls are all right. Negro's cutting them loose and giving them money to get out of town. Yeah, they know what we look like, but so what? You think they want to talk to the cops about keeping company with gangsters? About the bodies the maid's gonna report in the morning? And even if they *did* talk to cops, what could they give them? Descriptions? There's a million guys look like us except for El Negro, and *black* is all the description they can give of him. They don't even know any part of our names. By sunup they'll be long gone with a wad of cash in their purse.

Thanks, man, Soto says.

Mateo nods and unholsters his pistol. Face the wall, he says.

Soto does it. I'm standing off to one side of him, Frank on the other. Mateo raises the gun, holding the suppressor muzzle a few inches from the back of Soto's head. The muffled shot is fairly loud in the close confines of the garage but not enough to carry to neighboring homes. It jars Soto's head and he crumples to the floor, a bloody splatter of brain and skull fragments oozing down the wall.

Mateo phones Rodrigo and says, We got it. All of it. And got rid of the prick who took it. He listens, then says, Yeah, sure, go ahead.

Keeping the phone to his ear, he tells us in English, 'Rigo's calling the Zetas. Those guys are gonna love this. *Major* points for us with them. A reminder that nobody fucks with us or our clients and gets away with it.'

A long couple of minutes pass, then Mateo says, Yeah, into the phone. He listens intently. Okay, give it to me… Got it, he says. Call you when it's done.

'We're taking the load to Nuevo Laredo,' he tells us. 'To

number thirty-two on Calle Rio Montez. Don't forget that address, in case I do.'

Nuevo Laredo is the Zetas' home base.

* * *

With Frank driving and Mateo in the shotgun seat, the Suburban leads the way to the border bridge. Negro and I are behind them with me at the wheel of one of the Durangos, and Conejo and Gancho trail us in the other. We cross into El Paso and get on I-10 East. At Fort Stockton we gas up, take a piss, grab some snacks and six-packs, then cut south for Del Rio. Traffic is meager. The moon's a low sliver in the west, and we're enclosed in the immensity of desert darkness under what looks like an arrested explosion of stars. Only way the hell out at sea are the stars as spectacular as in the desert. In Del Rio we refuel again, then cross back into Mexico.

We get to Nuevo Laredo not long after sunrise. Our windows are down and the air's heavy with the wet-dust smell of freshly hosed sidewalks and the aromas of coffee, chorizo sausage, corn tortillas.

The address turns out to be that of an auto junkyard that takes up the whole block on one side of a rutted one-way street fronted by narrow broken sidewalks. The yard gate is unchained and wide open, and Frank pulls into the short driveway in front of it and stops. I park against the curb and Conejo pulls in behind me.

A dapper mustached man wearing aviator shades and a very much out-of-place white suit comes out through a door marked oficina that flanks the vehicle gate. He talks to Mateo, then takes a look in the back of the Suburban, then peers over at us. A Zeta. They have a certain manner, those guys – like they're always assessing the threat level of everybody in view. He again says something, and Mateo gets out and Frank drives into the junkyard and out of sight. Mateo and the white suit go in the office.

A short while later, Frank drives partway out of the yard gate and summons me with a head motion. Negro and I say so long, and I slide out and head for the Suburban just as Mateo exits the office. He tells me he's called Rodrigo and informed him the Zetas are pleased with the shipment and, of course, there's no late-delivery fee. We embrace and he says it was good working with me again. Until next time, I say. He gets in the Durango, Negro now in the driver's seat, and the two SUVs depart.

I climb into the Suburban and Frank tells me Mateo said we could have it. 'Flip you for it,' I say, and take a nickel out of my pocket. I flip it, catch it, smack it on the back of my hand. He calls heads, and heads it is. He laughs and says he doesn't want the damn thing, I can have it. But I'm no fan of SUVs, either – I love my stick-and-Hemi Challenger – and we decide to let Charlie have it. The shade trade can always use another big set of wheels.

We're in no hurry and both of us ravenous, so we stop at a café and order platters of huevos rancheros – refried beans layered with shredded white cheese, topped with fried eggs, doused with a tomato salsa thick with minced peppers and cilantro, and served with a stack of corn tortillas. Delectable. But if I *had* to choose I'd go with the huevos rancheros Charlie Fortune makes. His salsa is unsurpassable and its recipe a tightly guarded secret.

* * *

We get back to Wolfe Landing in late afternoon. We turn off into Riverside Motors & Garage, go past the double row of vehicles for sale in the front lot, park behind the garage, and go in to talk to Jesus McGee, the owner and manager. Jesus is a first-rate mechanic and does a steady business with customers who drive out from Brownsville for his tune-up and repair service. But his real profit comes from the sale of stolen vehicles, almost all of them taken from the hubs of Dallas, Austin, San Antonio, or Houston. He pays low cash for them, works up new papers and tags – he's got contacts in a half dozen DMV offices in South Texas – and sells them to Mexican buyers as far south as Monterrey, to American car lots as far up the coast as Port O'Connor, and to dealers on both sides of the river all the way up to the two Laredos. He tells us that by the day after tomorrow he can have a title for the Suburban in Charlie's name, with a new VIN, registration, and tag to match.

It's a steamer of a day. In the nineties and with the humidity way up there as well. Rain's predicted for this evening and it can't come soon enough. We're already sweat-soaked as we head out on foot for the Doghouse. At this hour the streets are deserted, everyone being sensible enough to stay indoors with oscillating floor fans or window air conditioners. The housing types out here are pretty simple – stilt houses, trailers, cabins, that's about it – none of them structured for central air, which neither Frank nor I would choose even if we could, because we can't stand to have the windows shut. Same goes for Charlie. Strictly window and ceiling fans for us. From the corner of Gator Lane we can see our adjacent houses at the far end of Main Street. The look on Frank's face tells me he's wishing the same thing I am – that we could go straight home, take a badly needed shower and a much-desired nap. But even though Rodrigo has certainly told Charlie all the details about the shipment recovery, we know he's waiting to hear the story from us as well.

There's only a handful of patrons in the place at this hour. Three guys at the bar are laughing with Lila. She gives us a little wave as we cross toward Charlie's office and says, 'He's been expecting you.'

* * *

Nearly an hour later we're still in the office, Charlie behind his desk, Frank and I seated across from him, all of us drinking beer. The floor's now almost completely in shadow, the ceiling fans are doing a passable job. Charlie's so pleased about the way everything turned out, and by our gift of the Suburban, that the beer's on him, a circumstance of which we're taking full advantage. Because Frank and I are both in that dopey sort of high spirit you sometimes get when you're sleep-deprived but still juiced from a job well done, we're slurping the beer at a pretty good pace. Charlie's keeping up with us to be polite.

Charlie told us that Rodrigo's happy, too. They both approve of Mateo settling the scores the way he did with the Coronas and the Sotos, and they're in accord with his decision to let the two girls go. Like Rigo, Charlie's intrigued by Soto's allegation of having met El Chubasco, but like us he suspects the guy was lying through his ass, trying to stay alive by way of a phony connection to him.

Charlie calls Lila on the bar phone once again and says, 'We require additional hops posthaste.' He's a touch tight, and Frank and I are enjoying seeing him cut loose a little. She brings in three more bottles and sets them on the desk and collects the dead soldiers, sweeping a reproachful eye over the three of us before stalking off. She's a funny one, Lila. Very open-minded about most things but she frowns on Charlie getting even slightly tipsy in the Doghouse, never mind how rarely he does. She thinks it looks bad for patrons to see the proprietor the least bit under the influence.

We're not halfway into the fresh beers before she's back, this time with a small carton wrapped in brown paper. 'McGee just dropped this off,' she says brusquely, putting it on the desk. 'Said you guys left it in some vehicle.' Then she's gone again.

'What's that?' Charlie asks.

'DVDs,' Frank says. 'Porn movies. Soto bought them for Chubasco. Was gonna give them to him as a present to try to score some points because, according to *him*, Chubasco's a big fan of skin flicks and thinks productions by these particular companies are the best of their kind. The box was in the Suburban with the shipment. The guys who did the unloading in Nuevo Laredo must've thought it was ours.'

'The best of their kind?' Charlie says. 'Rather a categorical assessment, wouldn't you say? I'm inclined to put it to the test. Might you gents be of similar inclination?'

Frank and I say we're of similar inclination.

Charlie turns on the desk lamp and slits open the carton with a penknife and takes out its contents, six DVDs. He shows us the top one, which displays the title, *The Love Tutors*, directly above a photo of three dazzling young women in nurse uniforms skimpier than any ever beheld in an actual hospital – a blonde with long straight hair, a pigtailed redhead, and a ponytailed brunette who's either nicely tanned or blessed with a natural cinnamon complexion. They're standing side by side, smiling archly, each with one hand on a cocked hip and the other pointing a finger at the viewer as if in admonition to him to be sure to take his medication. Charlie turns the case over and skims the text, then takes out the disc and slides the case to us. The back of it carries a terse summary of the action – 'By way of their specialized skills, the love tutors help troubled men regain the capacity for sensual intimacy.' The case text also informs that the actresses, the blonde, redhead, and brunette, are, respectively, Sunny Diamond, Ginger Snapper, and Kitty Quick. There are also three male actors listed – Jack Rocker, Buck Toole, and Mitch DeMann. The director is Dick Stone. The film is but thirty-nine minutes long and, with a copyright date of 2010, can't be more than eight months old. It was made by Mount of Venus Productions, Inc., whose address is a post office box in Tucson, Arizona. The price and shipping cost of the DVD are displayed in an info box in a corner of the case, together with a notice that credit card or debit card payment is acceptable but not cash or check. And that's it. No email address, no phone number, no other contact information.

Charlie's gone over to the DVD player under the big-screen TV against the wall and inserted the disc. 'I think it would be sage of us to have the next couple of rounds at hand before we begin the entertainment,' he says. 'That way we won't need to call for more beer in the midst of the movie and have to turn the thing off to keep Lila from getting an eyeful and denouncing us for libertines.' As he rings her up and orders six more beers – 'That is correct, my dear, six,' he says – Frank and I scan the cases of the other five DVDs. Two of them are also made by Mount of Venus but by directors other than Dick Stone, and neither of them uses any of the *Tutors* actresses. Each of the other three was produced by a different company.

'Major resupply is en route,' Charlie says, hanging up the phone.

When Lila comes in with the loaded tray of beers, I casually cover up the DVDs with a handy section of newspaper. Charlie's right about not needing to give her more reason to be miffed at us. Still, her eyes narrow when she sees we still haven't finished the last round. She sets out the six bottles, thunking each one down on the desk, and leaves without a word.

'Is there anything sadder,' Frank says, staring at the door she closed behind her, 'than a pretty girl with a truly fine ass and a great big bug way up it?'

Even though the room is now in deep shadow, we lower the blinds to achieve a more proper movie-watching darkness, then shift our chairs around to face the screen. The remote in hand, Charlie turns off the desk lamp and says, 'Well now, compadres, let's just see if Señor Chubasco's aptitude for film criticism is worth a goddamn.'

The opening credits offer no more information than the DVD case – just the logo of Mount of Venus, the title, the names of the actors and the director. But within the first few minutes the movie's production qualities are indisputable. Not only are the actresses uncommonly pretty – though we're willing to bet the brunette can't possibly be the lawful age of eighteen and that the blonde might be a close legal call as well – every technical facet is first class. The directing, editing, camera work, lighting, everything. Even the sound track, a frisky soft jazz number, is pretty good. The plot, such as it is, consists of a series of vignettes, each one dealing with a different patient who, for one reason or another, has been having trouble pleasing his sex partners and, desperate for help, has come to the Spire of Power clinic, wherein the tutors are employed. The vignettes rotate from tutor to tutor, each girl treating a different patient each time, teaching him some technique guaranteed to curl a woman's toes, and during which instruction the patient receives bounteous pleasures of his own. Each of the male actors plays several different parts, every character made physically distinct from the others by some minor guise – a mustache or beard, a wig, eyeglasses. Not surprisingly, all three dudes are impressively equipped, especially Mitch DeMann, whom we're soon referring to as Jumbo. The dialogue is a high cut above most that you hear in this genre and all the players are adept in their delivery of it. What's more, Sunny Diamond and Ginger Snapper both have southern accents that add to their appeal, while Kitty Quick's voice has a huskiness that reminds me of Lauren Bacall.

Halfway through the movie, Charlie says that if the other flicks in Chubasco's collection are of equal quality to this one, the man's opinion of them is on the money.

* * *

With about ten minutes left in the movie – in the midst of a scene in which Ginger Snapper and Kitty Quick are double-teaming Jumbo, whose particular problem this time is a profound fear of submitting to oral sex because he's afraid to let teeth come anywhere near his manly treasure – the office door opens, admitting a bright shaft of light from the outer room and provoking snarls of objection from all of us. Charlie hits the pause button, and we turn to glare at a couple of silhouetted figures in the brightly lit doorframe.

'Oh… my… *gawwwd*!' Jessie Juliet's voice.

Then Rayo Luna's laugh, and *she* says, 'That hombre up there must be making you boys feel *sooo* inferior!'

She's referring to the freeze frame, in which Jumbo is lying on his back while Ginger Snapper is proving beyond all question that he's no longer fearful of receiving fellatio, and Kitty Quick is observing the action from very close range, smiling in approval of her colleague's artistry.

'*Out!*' Charlie says. 'Both of you! *Out!*'

'Not a chance, boss man,' Rayo says. She directs Jessie onto the divan next to the doorway, then shuts the door and sits beside her. 'If you guys are uncomfortable about watching such racy stuff in mixed company, that's your problem. But we wanna see.'

'What're you doing here, anyway?' Charlie says.

'We heard these two mavericks were back from Mexico and we wanted to know what they've been up to, buy them a welcome-home beer,' Rayo says. 'But first let's see the rest of this. Looks pretty good.'

'What the hell?' Frank says. 'They wanna watch, let 'em watch. Who cares?'

'A man can't watch this kinda thing in front of his *niece*,' Charlie says.

He turns on the desk lamp and I see that Jessie's transfixed by the paused screen image. Then she looks at Charlie and says, 'For pity's sake, I'm twenty-seven years old! Play the damn thing!'

Charlie cusses under his breath and switches off the desk lamp and plays the damn thing.

But it's not possible to ignore the women's presence, and not a man of us says anything during the remainder of the flick while Jessie and Rayo – mostly Rayo – laugh and cheer and make remarks about the action or dialogue as the impulse moves them, cracking themselves up. Then it's over. The end. No closing credits.

Charlie hits the stop button and switches on the lamp, and Rayo flicks the wall switch to turn on the ceiling fluorescents. I make for the door, saying, 'Didn't somebody mention something about buying me and my brother some beers?'

Rayo comes up beside me and says with exaggerated sultriness, 'That would be me, sailor. But given all this visual stimulation, could be you'd rather we go straight to your place and see what that leads to.'

'I don't recall the beer offer having anything to do with other options,' Frank says, right behind us.

'The man's right,' I say to her. 'Beers first.' The truth is the movie's got me so jazzed up I'm ready to do her bent over Charlie's desk if she'd let me.

She makes a moue and says, 'Yeah, yeah, beer first. Always the priority with you buckaroos.'

At the door Jessie asks Charlie if he can spare a minute. He says sure and tells us they'll catch up, and we go on.

No telling what Jess wants to see him about. Their relationship goes much deeper than uncle and niece. She was only two years old and Frank and I were in grammar school when her daddy, Axel, Charlie's older and only brother, went to prison for aggravated robbery and assault. A year later her mother ran out on her and none of us knows what became of her. Axel never saw Jessie again except in photos of her that Charlie would take to him on visits as the years went by, and she was too young to have any real memory of him. He'd been locked up for over twenty years when he and another convict broke out of a West Texas unit two years ago, and despite a hell of a manhunt that covered most of the western half of the state, neither of them was found. The authorities had reason to assume they had drowned in the Rio Grande rapids below the Big Bend. We all thought they were probably right, because Axel and Charlie were closer to each other than to anybody else on earth, and if Axel had survived he would've let Charlie know it. But who knows – there could be some other reason he hasn't come around or made contact, and we keep thinking that one of these days he might. Whatever the case, ever since Axel's been gone, Charlie's practically been a father to Jessie.

JESSIE AND CHARLIE

'I need a favor but you can't question me about it,' she says. She looks so serious Charlie can't hold back a smile. 'If you want somebody killed, why not just ask Rayo?'

'I'm serious, Uncle Charlie.'

Whenever she calls him *Uncle* Charlie he knows she's in earnest. 'Okay, sorry. What?'

'You promise no questions?'

'Yes, if that's what you want. So what is it? Oops, a question.'

'You gonna keep it up, or can we get serious?'

He moves an open hand down past his face, assuming a serious look, and says, 'Okay. All serious. No questions. What's the favor?'

'There's a girl in that movie. The black-haired one?'

'Kitty Quick by professional appellation,' Charlie says.

Jessie rolls her eyes. 'Why the hell not? Anyway, I'd like two still frames of her from the movie. You can do that, right?'

'Still frames? What for?'

'*No* questions. Look, it's just… it has to do with something personal to somebody I know and that's all I can tell you. If you will just please make the stills for me, I'll be ever so grateful.'

'A girl in this flick is linked in some personal way to somebody you know?'

'You *said*…'

He expels a hard breath and flings his hands up. 'Yeah, yeah, all right. You have specific frames in mind? That's a *technical* question. I have to ask that.'

'That's okay. One of them can be any directly frontal close-up of her face. Serious, no smile. The other one *is* specific. It's in the last part of the movie. The swimming pool scene. Near the end of it.'

She stands beside him as he sits at the desk and takes up the remote and turns on the TV and the DVD player. 'Bad enough I let you watch as much of this as you did.'

'You can't imagine my shock. I pray I haven't been traumatized.'

'Keep it up, smart mouth.'

The disc does not offer such amenities as scene selections or a skip-to-next-scene function, but it does allow fast-forward and reverse and permits display of elapsed time at the bottom of the screen. Charlie starts the movie from the beginning and fast-forwards it, saying, 'Tell me where to stop.'

'There!' Jessie says. 'That one you just passed. It's a perfect close-up!' He pauses the video, then reverses it in short jumps until it's at the shot she wanted and she says, 'Right *there*.' He hits the pause again and makes a note of the elapsed time.

He then fast-forwards toward the swimming pool sequence at the tail end of the movie and says he can't believe he's doing this – even as he laughs along with Jessie at the passing sequence of comically rapid sexual romps. When they reach the pool scene he resets the video's speed back to normal.

'Yeah,' Jessie says. 'Somewhere in this section. A little further along. Almost at the end of the movie.'

Sunny Diamond and Kitty Quick are skinny-dipping with two guys, and Charlie now advances the film in short jumps until Jessie says, 'That's it!' and he again pauses the video. The two guys have exited the scene, and Sunny and Kitty, their hair plastered to their scalps, are in the pool and clinging to its near side in a medium close-up, smiling at the camera, nothing of them showing but their heads, shoulders, and hands.

Charlie again jots down the elapsed time.

'Cut the blonde out of it,' Jessie says. 'Crop it around the Kitty one, okay?'

'Sure. What size you want? *Tech* question.'

She mulls a moment. 'Six-by-eight?'

'Does the resolution have to be first-rate?'

'Well, *yeah*. I mean, the better the resolution the more helpful. And, oh… make them in black-and-white, okay?'

He puffs out a soft breath. 'Black-and-white?'

'*Don't* ask.'

'Okay, here's the thing. Color *or* black-and-white, I'm not sure I can cut pictures of that size with the best resolution possible. But what I *can* do is get somebody better than me to do it.'

He picks up his phone, thumbs through the roster of contacts, and taps his finger on one. He listens, then says, 'Good evening, Aunt Laurel, Charlie here… Real good, ma'am, and you?… Good, that's good, glad to hear it. Say, if I'm interrupting your supper, I can call back… Really? You sure now?… Okay then, but I'll make it short. I just called to ask if I could borrow Louie-Louie from you sometime tomorrow. Won't take long. Need a first-class pair of black-and-white prints extracted from a color video… Oh, yes, ma'am, that'd be great, just perfect, thank you… No, really, Aunt Laurel, nothing else. You're an angel… Yes, ma'am, you, too. Bye now.'

Louie-Louie is the ace 'visuals technician' for Delta Instruments & Graphics, a Brownsville company owned and operated by Laurel Eve Wolfe. The company sells and services a broad assortment of electronic and digital equipment but specializes in print and photographic instruments. In addition, it has many wildcat suppliers of state-of-the-art military technology, such as IED triggering mechanisms, night-vision optical tools, surreptitious listening devices, and other surveillance gear of sundry types, much of which it acquires at Charlie's request and which he then smuggles to his buyers. Delta Instruments & Graphics is also capable of producing masterful forgeries or counterfeits of anything printed on paper.

'The techie will be here sometime between noon and two tomorrow,' Charlie says. 'He's fast and highly skilled, but to ensure he has enough leeway, I'd say hold off on picking up the prints until about three.'

She leans down and hugs him around the neck and kisses his ear and cheek. 'My handsomest, smartest uncle can do anything!'

'Yeah, yeah, right. Come on, let's get out there with the others before they drink the place dry.'

* * *

Charlie's at his desk and the prints are ready when she shows up at three o'clock the next day. She takes them out of a manila envelope and studies them with such absorption that he can't refrain from asking, 'You *know* her, this Kitty Quick?'

She sighs. 'No questions.'

'You can't even say if you know her?'

'No.'

'No, you don't know her, or no, you can't say if –'

'Will you *quit*?'

She puts the prints back in the envelope and gives him a kiss on top of the head. 'Thank you, Charlie. I love you.'

She goes out to her Jeep Liberty, parked in the shade of an oak on the far side of the Doghouse lot, and starts it up to engage the air-conditioning. She then takes an envelope from under her seat and withdraws two black-and-white photographs from it.

When she and Charlie joined the others at the bar last night, she could see they were all going to make a late night of it, and after one beer she took her leave on the pretext that she had to finish a report her editor expected the next morning. She'd then gone home to the beach house she shares with Rayo, and from a bulky carton in her closet she took a shoebox of old photographs and searched through the pictures until she found the two she wanted, the two that had come to mind during the tail-end part she'd seen of *The Love Tutors*. One photo is a six-by-eight-inch studio close-up portrait of a girl named Sandra Little, taken in San Luis Potosí, Mexico, in 1909 to memorialize her quinceañera, the traditional celebration of a girl's fifteenth birthday. The other picture, a four-by-six, was taken the following year at a country estate not far from San Luis Potosí, by an itinerant photographer who must have been a wizard at every element of his art to have produced a picture whose clarity has so well withstood the passage of a hundred years. Like the studio picture, it is black-and-white. It depicts two girls in medium close-up, huddled side by side in a darkwater pool that Jessie recognizes as a stone watering tank for ranch stock. They are holding to the tank's rim and smiling at the camera, only their sodden-haired heads, their hands, and their bathing-suit-strapped shoulders visible above the rim of the tank. One of the girls is Sandra Little; the other, her younger sister, Catalina. They are Jessie Juliet's great-great-grandaunts.

She puts the two pictures on the passenger seat and then alongside them sets the two Kitty Quick prints made by Louie-Louie. She looks from one pair of pictures to the other several times and whispers, '*Damn.*' The moment she'd seen the Kitty girl on the screen last night she'd been flabbergasted by the resemblance between her and Sandra Little. Then the poolside scene near the end of the movie – with the Kitty girl posed so much like Sandra in the stock tank picture – really brought home their surreal similitude. She'd wanted the Kitty girl's prints in black-and-white in order to make the comparison with the older pictures as much on a par as possible. She checks her watch, then scoops up the pictures, puts them all in one envelope, and gets rolling out of Wolfe Landing.

She had phoned Aunt Catalina late this morning, said she had something she wanted to show her, and asked if it would be all right to drop by her house around four. Catalina said of course. Jessie's certain that Aunt Cat, the family grande dame – and, at the age of 115, very likely the oldest living person on earth – will be as awed as she herself is by the seemingly impossible similarity between Sandra Little and Kitty Quick. It isn't easy to present Catalina with some sort of surprise anymore, but Jessie's always on alert for anything that might do the trick. She can't wait to see Aunt Cat's face when she gets an eyeful of this girl.

II

THE GIRL

CATALINA

It is long past dispute that Catalina Luisiana Little Wolfe is a preternatural wonder of longevity. If any other person who has achieved the age of one hundred years or more was possessed of a vitality equal to hers, no one has uncovered evidence of it. Judging strictly by her appearance and bearing and acuteness of mind, one might guess her to be, at the most, an unusually energetic eighty. It's as though when she turned seventy she ceased to grow old at the same rate as the rest of the human race. She is still lean and of erect carriage and, owing to the Celtic-Irish origins of her paternal line – a long-boned clan incongruously surnamed Little – taller than most women of the family she married into. Her silver hair is cut close and trimmed at the nape. Her face is the envy of women half her age, its crow's-feet and other creases but lightly etched. Her blue eyes are bright with intelligence and curiosity and very often the suggestion of some private amusement. Even now she needs spectacles only for reading and sewing, which together with tending to her garden are her preferred recreations. She still maintains the routine of a morning stroll around the block, although the walking stick she once carried solely to ward off overly frolicsome dogs now serves to some extent the purpose for which it was made. Her hearing remains so keen that the rest of the family are careful of what they say about her when she's under the same roof. It has been frequently remarked among them that such singular aural acuity well warrants their nickname for her in both English and Spanish – the Cat and La Gata. None of them, however, would ever presume to address her by either soubriquet.

The local community largely views her with civic pride, although no one outside the Wolfe family has made her acquaintance in the last forty years except for the sequence of live-in maids Catalina has employed over the decades and her next-door neighbor Señora Villareal, who moved in eighteen years ago. Ever since her one-hundredth birthday, journalists, historians, anthropologists, and various stripes of medical specialists have repeatedly requested interviews with her and have repeatedly been turned down, at first with polite refusals, then with more assertive insistence that they stop annoying her, and finally with cold disregard. A sign on the front gate of the chain-link fence enclosing her yard reads trespassers will be prosecuted. Charlie Fortune put it there at the behest of Harry Mack in an effort to dissuade petitioners who sometimes showed up at her door in hope that she might relent to a direct personal plea to answer just a few questions. But the other residents on her street are also highly protective of her, and more than one importunate interview seeker has been run off from Catalina's gate by a neighbor's bellowed threat to call for the police with a report of elder abuse.

A few years ago a young professor at the university learned of her daily walk and one morning intercepted her at its midway point, curbing his car and jumping out, beseeching a few minutes of her time. Unbeknownst to him, the troop of dogs that trailed her by a few yards – having learned from swipes of her stick not to follow too closely – were her customary retinue, and on seeing her accosted by a stranger, they attacked the man in a snarling fury. He barely made it back into the car, his trousers in shreds and both legs bloodied, but managed to drive himself to the emergency room. Fortunately, as Catalina liked to point out in retelling the adventure at family gatherings, all the dogs had been duly vaccinated and hence were in no danger of contracting some professorial disease. The episode caught the attention of the local news media, and public reaction was almost unanimously in support of Catalina Wolfe's right to be left alone and in favor of the dogs that defended her. In consequence of the incident, the university's faculty senate passed a resolution prohibiting its members from any further solicitations of her except by way of the postal service.

While her age is the most awesome of the few public facts about her – and the record of her marriage into the Wolfe family in 1915 the most mundane – the most sensational is that she shot her husband dead at a party in 1931, was sentenced to thirty years in prison, and served thirteen before she was granted parole. The shooting made all the major Texas newspapers, but none of the reporters was able to elicit information about her from any member of the family other than those who worked for Wolfe Associates and represented her at trial, and they limited their statements to matters of the case. The family has always rigorously safeguarded even the most basic details of her life.

* * *

Her mother died giving birth to her on New Year's Day 1895, at Patria Chica, the Little family's sprawling ranch in Central Mexico, where she spent her first sixteen years and where most of her blood kin still reside. Her father was an officer in the Guardia Rural – the national police force that patrolled the countryside – and was killed in the line of duty when she was still a young child. Her godfather was Porfirio Díaz, who ruled Mexico with iron resoluteness for over thirty years until the Revolution of 1910 put an end to his dictatorship. But no one has ever heard her speak of anyone with higher admiration than she has always expressed for her great-grandfather, an American named Edward Little, who was a close personal friend to Díaz and the chief of his secret police. She has often said that the most important things she knows about the ways of the world were taught to her in childhood by her great-grandfather Edward.

Yet much about her life remains unknown even to the Wolfes – except perhaps to Jessie. Catalina has always openly favored Jessie Juliet and Eddie Gato over all her other kin, and she assumed a third pet when Rayo Luna came to live with the Texas side of the family two years ago. But as fond as she is of Eddie and Rayo, they know that Jessie is her only true confidante. Seven years ago she agreed to let Jessie write her biography on the strict condition that she promise not to publish the book or reveal any detail of it to anyone until after, as she put it, 'they stick me in the ground.' In full collaboration with the project, Catalina not only submitted to innumerable hours of taped interviews but also granted Jessie access to her store of personal letters, plus a collection of photographs of herself and many of the people central to her life. She would not, however, allow any of the tapes or letters to leave her house for fear that they might get lost or stolen, and so most of Jessie's work on the book had to be done at a desk in the corner of Catalina's living room. The only resource material she was permitted to take home were the pictures, though again only on the promise of not showing or even speaking of any of them to anyone else while Catalina still lived.

Despite these exacting conditions, and notwithstanding her full-time duties with the newspaper, Jessie completed the book three years ago. She told Aunt Cat that it was really an autobiography because most of it consisted of Catalina's own words from the tapes. Except for segments of historical background and other bits of exposition that Jessie inserted here and there, Catalina had created the book. 'You told the whole thing in your own way,' she told Catalina. 'All I did was write it down.'

When she asked Aunt Cat to read the manuscript and see if she wanted to make any changes, she said no. Then said, 'But tell me truthfully, child, what do *you* think of it?'

Jessie told her she thought it was a hell of a tale. Catalina smiled and said, 'Yes. I suppose it is.'

Ever since they first heard that Jessie was writing Aunt Catalina's life story and learned of the conditions imposed on its publication, the family has enjoyed the running joke that the book will never see print for the simple reason that Catalina will never die.

CATALINA AND JESSIE AND CHARLIE

She stares at the four photographs Jessie has laid out on the coffee table. Her intense blue eyes shift from one picture to another and back again.

'Isn't it *amazing*?' Jessie says. 'I mean, really, señora, a century apart and they look like twins, don't they? I thought you'd get a real kick out of it.'

'Yes. The similarity is very hard to believe,' Catalina says. 'You say this young woman is an actress and these pictures came from a movie?'

'Yes, ma'am, some silly thing on DVD. Something about nurses or some such. I dropped in on some friends and they were watching it and I only saw the last part. I told the fellow who owned it that I just couldn't believe the likeness between one of the girls in the movie and a distant cousin of mine and how I wished I had a picture of the actress, and he was good enough to offer to make some prints off the video for me. I specifically asked that one of those prints be this swimming pool one because the minute I saw it I remembered this picture of you and Aunt Sandra in the tank. I thought you'd want to see for yourself just how incredibly alike they look and… I don't know. I just thought it would tickle you.'

'What is her name, this actress?'

'Oh, God, you're gonna laugh. Kitty Quick. An acting name, of course. Who knows what her real name is.'

Catalina looks up from the photos. 'And who is the friend who made the pictures for you?'

Only now does it occur to Jessie that in her eagerness to surprise and delight Aunt Cat she's neglected her own common sense. How could she not have anticipated that Catalina might ask for specific details about the source of the prints, and that if she did, there would be no way to keep them from her? Lying is out of the question. She can sometimes shade the truth a wee bit with her, as she's done so far with the Kitty pictures, but only once, years ago, has she ever told her an outright lie, and Catalina easily recognized it as such.

'You're blushing, my dear, and the cat seems to have stolen your tongue. Why?'

Jessie tells her everything. That she and Rayo walked in on Charlie and Frank and Rudy watching a pornographic movie in the Doghouse office last night. That she'd been stunned by the Kitty girl's resemblance to Sandra and was sure Catalina would be, too. That Charlie had called on an expert technician to make the two stills – and *no*, she did *not* tell Charlie why she wanted them, nor has she spoken of them to anyone else, not even to Rayo Luna, not yet. She concludes with an admission that she is *totally* embarrassed about confessing to *her*, the person she most respects in the whole world, that she and Rayo viewed a porn movie with an uncle and two male cousins.

Catalina laughs. 'My dear Jessica,' she says, 'why on earth should you be embarrassed? Am I of such frail sensibilities? Can you possibly have forgotten the things I've told you about my own escapades with males from the time I was a girl? Things that I have confessed to you in such shameless detail? Of course, I'll be dead before anyone reads the book, but have I seemed to you to be terribly concerned about what anyone will think of me after reading it? For you to believe I would be offended because you and Rayo watched a sex movie in the company of males, well, don't you see the silliness of that notion?'

'When you put it that way, ma'am, yes, I do.'

They both laugh, and Catalina reaches out and pats her hand. 'Thank you for the pictures, querida. They're *very* interesting. But I must ask you something more. This actress, this Kitty person, does she have a voice a little deeper than most women?'

Jessie stares at her. 'Well, yes... *yes*, ma'am, she does. Why –? Oh, God, don't tell me Aunt Sandra had a deep voice.'

Catalina smiles. 'An astonishing coincidence, no? *Another* astonishing coincidence, I should say.'

'Yes, ma'am, it most certainly is.'

'I would like to hear her voice. Where is this video now?'

'I guess in Charlie's office. It's where the tech made the stills.' Catalina takes out her phone and asks the title of the video and makes a face when Jessie tells her.

'He'll know I told you,' Jessie says.

Do not fret, daughter, Catalina says in Spanish. She scrolls through her phone contacts to the Doghouse number and taps on it.

Charlie answers. 'My esteemed Tía Catalina. I nearly swooned at seeing your name gracing my phone screen. How wonderful to receive a call from you. It's been far too –'

'Cease the foolishness, Charles. You have in your possession a DVD entitled *The Love Tutors*. I would like to see it. Have someone bring it to me right away.'

'*The Love Tutors*,' Charlie says. He clears his throat. 'I hardly know what to say, señora. Why would, ah... how do you even know about such a... an entertainment?'

'That is no one's concern but my own. Nor why I want to see it. I need only to know that you'll send it to me at once or I will contact Harry McElroy and have him give you a call.'

'That won't be necessary, ma'am,' Charlie says. He's baffled by her demand and he needs a moment to ponder things. 'Just hold on a second while I make sure I still have it. Sometimes a tech will take a DVD home to make a copy for himself. I don't want to say yes and then find out it's not here.'

'Do not trifle with me, Charles.'

'No trifling intended, señora. Won't take a minute. Hold on.'

His thoughts speed. This is Jessie's doing. That's why she wanted those frames. To show to the old woman. He can't think of any reason she'd want to do that, but how else would the Cat have come to know about the video? But why would she want to *see* it? Christ, who the hell knows the why of anything with that unkillable crone. He'd love nothing better than to hang up on her without another word and then not answer any more calls she might make, which would really piss her off. But either he gives her the disc or his father will order him to do it and be irked at having to be involved. Harry Mack has many times told him that no battle of wills with Catalina can be won. Well, whatever that ancient grimalkin and Jessie are up to, it can't be anything major or they'd need his help. The hell with the old bone bag. But Jessie's got some things to explain.

'It's here, señora,' he tells her. 'I'll send it right away.'

'I want it in my hands within thirty minutes,' she says.

* * *

Twenty-three minutes later, there is tinkling from the little array of chimes mounted on the wall next to the front door. Jessie answers the door and greets Ricardo, one of Charlie's runners, who doffs his cap and says, Good evening, miss, and hands her the encased disc, wrapped in newspaper and sealed with tape.

Catalina dismisses the maids and instructs them not to come into the living room during the rest of the evening. She permits Jessie to operate the DVD player, and because her interest is strictly in Kitty Quick, she agrees with Jessie's suggestion of fast-forwarding past any scene that does not include Kitty. They thereby run through the movie in less than twenty minutes, Jessie feeling keenly uncomfortable the whole while about watching such a thing in the company of her great-great-grandaunt, never mind that Catalina is totally enrapt in each of Kitty's scenes.

At the video's conclusion, Catalina excuses herself and goes into the bathroom. When she returns, her face has been freshly washed and her eyes are mildly red. She remains standing as she tells Jessie that the girl looks *exactly* as Sandi looked the very last time she saw her. Then she smiles weakly and adds, 'Except, of course, Sandi was wearing clothes. She was not yet seventeen, and I don't believe this one is, either. And her voice... it is the same as Sandra's. The very same. It is very hard to believe.'

'She doesn't look anywhere near legal age,' Jessie says. 'Neither does the blonde, for that matter. But hey, I knew a girl in college who in her senior year looked like she should be in junior high. With some, you never know.'

Catalina opens her arms to her and they hug.

'Thank you, my dear girl. Now go home and rest.'

'You rest, too, Aunt Cat. It's been a tough night.'

'Yes, I will.'

She sees Jessie to the door and waits there until she's in the Jeep and leaves, then shuts the door and locks it. Then goes back to the sofa and the photos on the coffee table. She mulls them for some time before at last going to bed.

She sleeps later than usual the next morning. Then has a light breakfast. Then once more studies the pictures of

Sandra and the Kitty girl and resumes her deliberations of the night before.

It is late afternoon when she phones Harry McElroy.

RUDY

After getting to bed late the night before, I was hoping that the next morning I'd be able to catch up on the sleep I'd missed out on during the shipment recovery. But Rayo pretty well sabotaged the effort by doing a lot of wriggling against me, pretending to be half asleep and simply making herself more comfortable and not really trying to get me worked up, which she managed to do deep in the night and then again shortly after daybreak. The girl's unreal. I finally gave up the try for more sleep, and we went to the Doghouse for a brunch of egg-bacon-cheese-and-tomato sandwiches. Frank was already there and had called up a girlfriend named Marisa to see if she wanted to come out and join us for a lazy day of pitchers, a bite to eat, a bit of eight-ball, a lot of dancing. She did. Turned out she had the next day off, so we stayed up pretty late again, and it was close to noon today when the four of us got together for breakfast at the Doghouse. Frank and I told Charlie about the splendid huevos rancheros we'd had in Nuevo Laredo, so he worked up four plates of his own recipe, then waited with hands on hips for us to make the taste test. Marisa said, 'Wow,' and Rayo blew him a kiss. Frank smiled and nodded, and I gave Charlie the 'okay' sign. He grinned and shook his joined hands over his head like an old-time boxing champ.

Now it's half past four and we're playing Wild Wolfe draw

poker – two-bit ante, dollar-limit bets, deuces and jokers wild – and telling stories about some of the more memorable residents of the Landing who are no longer with us. Big Joe's tending the bar and looking on from behind the counter.

Charlie's cell sounds the opening notes of 'Tuxedo Junction.' He takes it from his shirt pocket, glances at the screen, puts it to his ear, and says, 'Yessir?' I figure it's his daddy on the horn, since Charlie rarely says 'yessir' to anyone else. Like the rest of us, he refers to his father as Harry Mack, but he never addresses him directly as anything other than 'sir.' If he's ever called him 'Dad' or 'Father' or any such thing, nobody I know has ever heard it. He looks over at us and says, 'Yessir, they are.'

He listens, then says, 'I'll tell them... Yessir, you, too.'

'You'll tell *who* what?' I ask him when he puts up the phone. 'I'll tell you boys that the uncounted wonder of the world, the antediluvian silver Cat herself, wants you to go see her. She said right now would be fine, so perhaps you best not dawdle.'

'What is it this time?' Frank says. 'Toilet stopped up? Oven on the blink? Water heater?'

'Harry Mack didn't say, but I can hardly wait for you to get back and tell me.'

Because Catalina never permits strangers to enter her home, any household problems that crop up – plumbing, electrical, whatever – can be attended to only by somebody in the family. Most often that's me and Frank. The last time we were in her place was a few months ago, when we picked up a new refrigerator she'd ordered and then installed it for her. Jessie and Eddie and Rayo visit her at home a lot more often than we do, but she's never asked any of them to do a repair more challenging than a leaky faucet Rayo once fixed. And though Charlie's as much a handyman as Frank and I, she'd never ask him for help. The whole family's aware of their reciprocally irritant relationship. He has a tendency to get sardonic with her, which she deems impertinent, and he doesn't care for her 'royal-ass manner,' as he calls it.

* * *

She lives on Levee Street in a small, well-kept two-bedroom house. Built in the early twentieth century, it has withstood every hurricane since then with no more damage than a cracked window or two and a few blown roof tiles. The place is as hardy as she is.

We park next to the fence gate and let ourselves in and wave at Señora Villareal next door, who smiles and waves back from her porch rocker. Aunt Catalina detests door knocking of any kind as well as the sound of most doorbells, and to announce ourselves we jiggle a little door-side chain that sounds a small set of chimes inside. Anna, the younger of the two live-in maids, admits us into the living room, where Catalina is seated on the sofa, a long coffee table before her. On the other side of the table and facing her are two armchairs. She smiles at the sight of us.

'Francis. Rudolf.' She leans forward, and we each in turn bend down to kiss her on the cheek. She extends a hand toward the chairs. 'Please, nephews, be seated. Would you care for something to eat? Anna makes wonderful sandwiches.'

We assure her we're not hungry

Just the beer, Anna, she says. The girl says, Yes, madam, and vanishes into the kitchen.

'I'm grateful to you for coming,' Catalina says. 'I know how busy you are.'

When we come on a repair job, she usually speaks Spanish. That she's addressing us in English is a clear indication she doesn't want the maids to comprehend anything they might overhear. She has never hired a maid who knows English, and she has ways of determining during an interview how much of the language, if any, a prospective employee understands. The armchairs are positioned close to each other so that she can study both of us with only slight shifts of her eyes. Knows a lot of tricks, the old Cat. I'm watching her as closely as I can without being obvious, but there's nothing about her that suggests disquiet.

Anna returns with a tray holding three bottles of Dos Equis and sets it on the low table. Aunt Catalina tells her that will be all and the girl goes.

'I have taken up your preference for drinking from the bottle rather than a glass,' she says. 'Let it be a lesson to you. You're never too old to acquire unrefined habits.' She smiles as she says it, and we smile at her jest. The thing is, she doesn't really drink, but she's a decorous hostess and always goes through the motions of joining her guests in a libation, though never actually taking but a few wee sips of beer or wine.

She raises her beer to us and we clink our bottles against hers, then pull deep swallows as she takes a tiny taste.

'Now,' she says, setting her beer aside. 'You're wondering why I have asked to see you.' She opens the wide, shallow drawer beneath the tabletop and withdraws a manila envelope. 'As you know, I once had a brother and a sister, Eduardo and Sandra, but they were lost to me a very long time ago.'

'Yes, ma'am,' Frank says.

The whole family knows the story, but as commonly happens with a story that is told and retold through generations, it has been modified into slightly differing versions. What is known for certain is that in the spring of 1911, during the first year of the uprising against the regime of Porfirio Díaz, when Catalina was sixteen years old and rebel troops were closing in on the Little family's ranch, Patria Chica, her great-grandfather Edward Little put her and her sister and their older brother on a train to the border and the safety of their Wolfe relations in Texas. But the train was derailed en route by bandits, Eduardo was killed and Sandra kidnapped. According to one account, Catalina was raped, but nobody of the living family has ever claimed to have heard *her* say so and no one has ever had the nerve to ask her if it's true. Nor has anyone ever asked her if, as some versions attest, she killed one of the bandits. Whatever the full details, Catalina was the only survivor of the attack, and when the bandits left she set out to follow the train tracks the rest of the way to the border, which was still almost two hundred miles away over rugged open country. She would never have made it if a detachment of Pancho Villa's men hadn't come upon her and taken her the remaining distance to Matamoros, just across the river from Brownsville. The Villistas' rescue of her was an ironic turn, given that such men were the danger from which Edward Little had wanted to distance the children. On arriving among her Wolfe kin, Catalina told them about the train attack, but who knows how much she withheld? If she's ever told the full truth about the incident to anyone, it would be Jessie, who has faithfully held to her promise not to disclose any details of her book as long as the Cat's still alive. In any event, when word of what happened got back to Edward Little, he dispatched search parties and private investigators all over northern Mexico and all along the border in quest of Sandra or information about her. But none of them would ever uncover anything of promise, and the family at length had to accept the hard fact that, dead or alive, she was lost to them forever. A few weeks after the train incident, the revolutionary forces triumphed and Porfirio Díaz went into exile in Paris. And not two weeks after that, Edward Little was killed in the Mexico City earthquake that preceded by only a few hours the rebels' victorious entrance into the capital.

What any of that might have to do with us being here I can't begin to guess.

She takes a black-and-white photograph out of the envelope, places it on the table, and rotates it so we can see it right-side up. It's of two girls in a stock tank. Aunt Catalina puts a finger to one of them and says, 'That is Sandi at age sixteen. The other is me.'

It's a stunner of a moment to see Catalina as she looked a hundred years ago. Then my gaze shifts back to Sandra. There's something vaguely familiar about her. Frank's staring at the picture like he might be sensing the same thing.

Catalina takes a larger black-and-white photo from the envelope and lays it beside the first.

'That is Sandra almost a year earlier.'

It's a studio close-up, and it doesn't take five seconds for me to realize she's the spitting image of one of the girls in the sex video we watched in the Doghouse the other night. Frank and I cut a look at each other.

'Ah,' the Cat says, 'She reminds you of someone, yes?'

Oh, man. You can't tell your great-great-grandaunt her sister looks like somebody you just saw in a porn movie.

'Well, señora,' Frank says, 'I have to confess that, for a second there, I thought she looked a lot like a girl I once knew, but... naw.'

'I know the one you mean, though, Frankie,' I say. 'You dated her in high school. Aleana or Elena, something like that.'

'Oh, stop it, both of you,' she says. 'If that's the best you can lie, it's a miracle you have survived for as long as you have.'

She takes another photo from the envelope and sets it down beside the studio shot. The pictures are the same size and this one, too, is a black-and-white close-up, but even so, there's no doubt whatever it's the black-haired girl in *The Love Tutors*.

'Where did *that* come from?' Frank says.

She ignores the question and says, 'Her dubious name, as you may recall, is Kitty Quick. Look at her and Sandra. Just *look* at them. Have you ever seen two people who looked more alike?'

I shake my head. Franks mumbles, 'No, ma'am, can't say I have.'

'And her *voice*. It is identical to Sandra's.'

'Her voice?' I say. 'But, señora, how can you possibly know that?' And hastily add, 'With all due respect.'

She reaches into the drawer again and this time takes out a DVD of *The Love Tutors* and sets it beside the pictures. 'Please return that to Charles at your convenience.'

'Charlie gave you that?' Frank says.

'He did. At my request.'

'Señora,' I say, 'why… *how* do you even know about this thing? This movie?'

'How do you suppose?'

'How else?' Frank says. 'Jessie or Rayo or both of them, right? They thought it'd be real funny to tell you about busting in on us at the Doghouse when we were watching a… an adult movie. But why would they want *you* to see it?'

'I know why,' I say. 'I'll lay odds Jessie has seen pictures of your sister. When she was writing her book about you. Right? I'll bet anything you showed her pictures of Sandra Little.'

'Very good, Rudolf,' she says. 'Yes, she has seen pictures of Sandra.'

'Of course!' Frank says. 'Then Jessie sees the movie and the girl's resemblance to Sandra and she wants you to see it, too. And then *you* want to see… no, then you want to *hear* the girl, and so you get Charlie to hand over the movie.'

'Yes, yes, *yes*,' the Cat says, raising her hands shoulderhigh as if in surrender. 'It is such a joy to observe clever minds at work. You have surmised it all correctly.'

'What about the prints?' I ask Frank. 'Where'd *they* come from? How'd Jessie –' I fake a dummy slap at my forehead. 'Well, who's got the video? Charlie. Had to be he made them for her. So now the question is did Jessie tell him *why* she wanted them? Because if she did –'

'She did not,' the Cat says. 'She has always had a way with Charles, as you know. Without revealing her purpose she was able to persuade him to make the pictures for her. But enough!

You are… what is the word?… masterminds. You understand everything. The only point of importance now is that this girl and my sister are mirror reflections of each other. You can both see that. You have admitted it. And if you had ever heard Sandi speak, you would not be able to distinguish between their voices, believe me. There are millions of *twins* in the world who are less alike than these two.'

She raises her beer to her lips, and Frank and I jump at the chance to take a pull off our bottles, swapping a look as we do. She catches the exchange and says, 'My dear nephews, I know that their similarity of appearance and voice is likely no more than an incredible coincidence. But will you grant me that it is also possible, *possible* and nothing more, that this girl is a descendant of my sister?'

I now know where this is heading and I can tell Frank does, too.

'Well, ma'am, as you know, *possible* covers an awful lot of ground,' Frank says. 'There are countless things that might be possible but are not at all probable.'

'Are you saying you do not believe there is *any* possibility, *none at all*, that the girl is related to Sandra?'

'Well, ma'am, I can't say there's no possibility *at all*. But I don't think it's probable.'

'I see. You don't believe it's probable but you think it might be *possible*?'

'Ma'am, there's no way of knowing –'

'Forgive me for interrupting, Francis, but a simple yes or no will suffice. Do you think it might... *might* be possible they are related?'

Frank lets out a long breath and half raises his hands in surrender. 'Yes, ma'am, it *might* be.'

'And you, Rudolf?'

'I have to agree with Frank, señora.'

'What exactly is it you agree with?'

She holds her stare on me, waiting for me to say it.

'I think it might be possible.'

She smiles at each of us. 'Excellent. So then, because all three of us believe it *might* be possible that this girl is descended from my sister, I want to see her with my own eyes. If that can be made to happen, if I can simply see her before me and hear her voice, I'll know if she is or is not descended of Sandi. I'll know it *in my bones*. And this is something I must know.'

There it is.

She affects a sip from her bottle, allowing us the opportunity to finish off ours.

'Would you care for another?' she says.

'No, thank you, señora,' I say. 'I'm good.'

'Me, too, ma'am,' Frank says.

'Very well then,' she says. 'I want you to bring this girl to me. Nothing very difficult, you see? I have already asked Harry McElroy if I could borrow the two of you to locate someone for me and he said yes. He of course asked whom I wanted found and said that Charles would also want to know because he is your operations chief. I said I would not reveal that information to anyone except the two of you, and he did not ask me again, nor will he. He also granted my request that you be permitted to borrow one of his airplanes and a pilot to take you wherever you may need to go. He asks only that you call the airfield this evening and tell them your destination and what time you wish to leave so that they can make a… what-do-you-call-it.'

'Flight plan,' Frank says.

'Yes. Now then, I don't believe you will have any trouble finding her, but I told him the search might take ten days or so, perhaps two weeks, and that if he thought it necessary he could inform Charles that you might be gone that long. Do you agree that two weeks should be far more than enough time for you to find the girl and bring her here?'

'Well, ma'am, that's just really hard to say,' Frank says.

'Not only that,' I say, 'but suppose we do find her and –'

'Suppose?' she says. 'What is there to *suppose*? Finding people is your principal proficiency. Of course you will find her. After all, she is not even in hiding, is she? Why would she be? She has committed no crime.'

'Well, ma'am, what I mean is suppose that *when* we find her she doesn't want to come with us? That could present a problem.'

'That could present a lot of problems,' Frank says.

'If she's not of a mind to accompany you, then you will have to change her mind. She cannot be more than sixteen years old. A child. Are you no match for a *child*? And do not forget for a minute that for someone so young to be exploited for such purpose as this degrading sort of… *entertainment* is a criminal offense. Whatever else she is, she is a victim. She requires rescue from such mistreatment and you will provide it. Tell her whatever you must to make her come back with you. Give her money.'

I can't help thinking that the kid sure didn't look like she required rescue. She looked like she was having a damn good time.

Catalina suddenly sits back and smiles shyly, a most unusual expression for her. 'I cannot believe I am instructing you in your own profession. How terribly presumptuous of me.'

'No, ma'am, not at all,' Frank says. 'You're speaking frankly, making suggestions. Nothing presumptuous about that.'

'I'm relieved to hear it,' she says. 'Because I would not like to seem presumptuous in suggesting that Rayo Luna go with you. She has better comprehension of a young girl's mind and emotions than either of you and is better suited to persuade her to accompany you. Do you for any reason object to having her go with you?'

'Not me,' I say, and look at Frank.

'Me neither,' he says.

'Good. Harry McElroy has said I may send her with you.'

We can't hold back smiling side glances at how far ahead of us the old girl is.

'One thing more. Harry McElroy has probably already informed Charles that I am sending the three of you to seek someone for me. In spite of his insolent manner, Charles is not a stupid man, and because of my request of the video from him after he made the Kitty girl's pictures for Jessica, I suspect that he has already guessed whom I want you to find. He is certain to ask you if he is correct, but you are not to confirm it for him. You are not to tell him *any* details of your task. The more he finds out about it, the more likely he will want to be involved in it and probably even try to assume control of it on the basis of being your chief. But I do not want his assistance and you do not need it. The only ones to know the specifics of what you are doing are we three and Rayo Luna. And Jessica, of course. As soon as we complete our business here, I will inform both of them of the situation. I have told Harry McElroy that Jessica is also involved in this matter, even though she will not be going with you, and that I do not want Charles to harass her about it in any way. I will instruct Jessica that if he should try to bully information from her, she is to come and live with me until your return. So. Only the five of us are to know what you are doing. No one else. Am I understood?'

'Yes, ma'am,' Frank says.

She looks at me.

'Yes, ma'am.'

'Good.' She picks up the DVD and hands it to me. 'Do not neglect to return that to Charles. Now go and get her. Tell her what you must. *Do* what you must. But bring her back here and directly to me so I can see her in the flesh. That is the only way... Oh, dear.' She puts a hand to her mouth, then removes it from her small smile and points at the DVD. 'Please believe me, I did not intend to make a joke at the girl's expense.'

Frank and I grin anyway. Because in a manner of speaking, all of us have already seen Kitty Quick very much in the flesh.

***

We stop at a diner that knows us well and we're given the private corner table we request. We order filets and a pitcher of Negra Modelo, and while we wait for the steaks we start on the beer and begin forming a game plan.

'I'll have Rayo dig up whatever online information she can on anybody connected to the tutors video,' I say. 'I've got a hunch there won't be a website for the company. If there was, the DVD case cover information would likely have included it. There might not be much for her to find. If so, then what? Tucson?'

'No other selection,' Frank says. 'The PO box is all we got. And yeah, sure, there are legal ways to get such confidential information as the name of a box holder, but most of them take a while, and we don't wanna sit around twiddling our thumbs all that time. We go to Tucson and either keep watch on the box till a key holder shows up and we front him, or we find out who the key holder is and where he lives and we pay him a visit. I'm for choice number two.'

'So am I. We need somebody with an inside line who can get us the box holder's name pronto.'

'Mateo,' Frank says.

'Who else? As close to the border as Tucson is, the Jaguaro network probably has a contact of some kind who can come up with the name.'

'Right. But first call Spur and get us a flight to the García ranch tomorrow morning. Then call Félix and tell him what time we'll be there and that we'll be needing a vehicle to go to Tucson. A proper one.'

Félix García is the present patriarch of our kin in El Paso. The Garcías have been linked to our family by marriage since the early 1920s. They're good people and we've done each other plenty of favors over the years. As for a 'proper vehicle,' that's our phrase for one that's almost totally bulletproof, except that its ballistic glass is resistant only one way. Its outer side resists a bullet's entry, but a round fired from inside the vehicle easily passes through the glass, even the windshield. Another marvel of modern engineering. I don't have to ask why he wants such a vehicle. We're only slightly acquainted with that stretch of the border, and it's one of our basic rules that whenever you enter unfamiliar territory it's best to be prepared for all possibilities.

I call Rayo and get a recording and tell her to call back as soon as she hears this. Then I ring up the operations manager at the airfield and tell him there are three of us who need to go to El Paso tomorrow, more specifically to the Half-Moon Ranch and its private airstrip just north of the city. He puts me on hold for a moment, then comes back and asks how a nine fifteen takeoff sounds. We'd arrive at the Half-Moon sometime around noon, depending on the in-flight weather. I say that's fine and he says we're on.

I next connect with Félix. I hasten through the amenities and then tell him we're flying up to his place tomorrow morning and give him our ETA. Our pilot will radio the ranch landing field when we're a half hour from arrival. When I tell him we need a proper vehicle for a trip to Tucson, he says that's fine, we'll have it.

I'm about to phone Charlie when Rayo gets back to me and says she's just talked to Catalina, who told her what was happening and that she would be going with us. She's being cool about it, but I'm pretty good at reading her tones and can tell she's excited by the assignment. I tell her our takeoff time in the morning, then instruct her to search the net for anything she can find on Kitty Quick, the other actors in *The Love Tutors*, the director Dick Stone, and Mount of Venus Productions.

'I'm on it,' she says.

My call to Mateo catches him having supper at a restaurant, too. Like ours, his phone – and every other shade trade and Jaguaro phone – has an encryption-plus security system second to none. I give him the Mount of Venus PO box information and tell him what we want. He says the Jaguaro intelligence web has a station in Nogales – the Mexican Nogales, a far more populous town than the neighboring Nogales on the U.S. side – and it's got all sorts of law enforcement contacts in Arizona. He's pretty sure they can come up with something as simple as the name of whoever's renting a particular PO box in Tucson. 'Might take a while, though,' he adds. 'Maybe till tomorrow afternoon.'

I smile at his notion of 'a while' and I tell him that by tomorrow afternoon would be real good. 'We'll be getting into Tucson around five.'

'Oh, hell, you'll have it by then. One of my guys will call you with the info. Take care, cuz.'

'Always do, primo. Thanks.'

I'm just about to call Charlie when the phone buzzes in my hand, and it's him, saying he's been trying to get me for the past ten minutes. His father's told him about Aunt Catalina borrowing us and Rayo Luna for a week or two to go find somebody for her, and Charlie is majorly irate that she wouldn't tell Harry Mack who we're looking for. It pisses him off even more that we won't tell, either.

'Can't, man, we promised her,' I say.

'Tell you what I think,' he says. 'I think you're going to look for the Kitty Quick girl from the sex movie. First, Jessie wants me to make prints of her. Then the old Cat wants to see the flick. Then *you* guys are going to try to find somebody for her. Doesn't take a genius to put it together. Tell me I'm wrong. Or better still, tell me what the Cat woman wants with her. The Spur guys informed me Harry Mack's let you have a plane to El Paso. That where she is?'

'Come *on*, man. This is how the Cat wants it. One thing I can tell you is this job's no big deal, take my word for it.'

'That so?' he says. 'Well, if it's no big deal, what's the big fucking secret?' We both go silent for a few seconds before he says, 'Stop by on your way out in the morning. I'll have breakfast bagged and ready.' He cuts off before I can thank him.

'No big deal, eh?' Frank says. 'Try telling that to the Cat.'

'You know what? We'd be a hell of a lot better off if Charlie *was* in on this. He's got contacts everywhere and I bet some of them have ties to the skin flick business and could get some inside info on this girl.'

'Could be, little brother. But *you* know what?'

'Yeah. Try telling that to the Cat.'

'Even if we tried to use Charlie's help on the sly, she'd find out. You know she would. We would then be on her shit list for the rest of her life.'

'Oh, man, we don't want that,' I say. 'That would mean for the rest of *our* lives.'

We bust out laughing. And chuck the notion of asking for Charlie's covert assistance.

***

It's full night by the time we arrive at the Landing. Rayo's truck is parked next to the stairway to my house, and by the glow of light from the front window we can see her sitting in a deck chair on the veranda. She and Frank wave to each other as he heads up the stairs of his place. She's in jeans and a black T-shirt and custom-made running shoes that have metal toes and heels stitched into them. Frank and I will be wearing the same kind of shoes tomorrow. There's a travel bag at her feet, and I know it contains almost the same things as Frank's and mine – the Glock 17 she prefers to our Berettas, a Quickster suppressor, a shoulder holster, three extra fully loaded magazines, a few flex-cuffs, and very little in the way of clothes other than underwear, T-shirts, and a light windbreaker or something of the sort that can be tightly rolled and easily packed and whose chief purpose is to hide our shoulder holsters when we carry in public. Any other clothing we might require we'll buy as need arises. She, too, has a Mexican license and passport, a carry permit, and a Toltec Seguridad ID. The bag also makes clear that she has come to spend the night.

'Since we're leaving early,' she says, 'I thought I might as well sleep here rather than have to drive over from the beach in the morning.'

We go in the house and she tosses her bag on the sofa. I get two bottles of Carta Blanca from the fridge, uncap them, and give her one, and we go back out on the veranda.

She tells me she made a net search for Kitty Quick and found out there are scores of porn actresses named Kitty something-or-other, but 'Kitty Quick' came up only in reference to *The Love Tutors*. The movie itself came up only on sites that review porn films but offer little information on them beyond a cursory summation, an overall rating, and the names of the production company, director, and lead actors. It's been in release about three months. It has an excellent rating on every site, and the Kitty girl has reaped praise in all reviews.

'Got nothing but the same sites in my searches for Sunny Diamond, Ginger Snapper, Dick Stone, and the male actors,' she says. 'Either *The Love Tutors* is the only movie *any* of them have ever been involved in, or they've been in others but, for whatever reason, used other names in them, even the director.'

A breeze has kicked up off the Gulf and carries the wonderful smell of an imminent storm. It rains a lot in the summer around here, and the night storms are my favorite. The clouds are deepening the darkness. We finish our beers and go inside.

'Listen,' I say, 'I still haven't caught up on the sleep I lost out on in Mexico, and there's no telling how much sleep *this* gig is gonna cost us. I need all the snooze I can get tonight, but the only way that's gonna happen is if we crash in separate rooms.' Even as I'm saying this, I have to work hard at not picturing her with her clothes off and losing my resolve. I really do need the sleep.

She tilts her head sideways and gives me a look, as I open up the futon on the other side of the coffee table fronting the sofa and toss one of the sofa pillows on it. 'Take the bedroom,' I tell her. 'I'll crash out here.'

'Let me get this straight. You're saying that my, ah... unbridled passions, my... animalistic cravings have been depriving you of your proper rest these past few days?'

'I would've phrased it less poetically, but yeah. Only because I was already so ragged out when I got back.'

She issues a theatrical sigh. 'Come to bed, buster. I promise not to take advantage of you.'

'Yeah, I know how that goes. I'll stick with the futon.'

'*Bucka-bucka-bucka*,' she says, flapping her outthrust elbows like chicken wings, then picks up her bag and moseys off to the bedroom, putting a little extra swish in her butt.

* * *

I waken to the blasting thunder of the storm. The rain's drilling hard against the roof and windows, and every lightning flash illuminates the room with a shaky pale glow. The air's heavy with the smells of mud and ozone.

Then I comprehend that what actually woke me was the feel of Rayo's hands slipping under the waistband of my shorts. I'm lying on my side and she's on her knees behind me, and as I roll toward her, saying, 'For Christ's sake, girl –', she whisks the shorts down and off my legs as dexterously as one of those guys who can snatch a tablecloth from under a setting of dishware without upsetting so much as a teacup. Then her hand is on me and achieving its familiar and swift effect, and I can't keep from laughing as she says in a deep, old-time horror-movie intonation, 'I am the succubus Rayora, come to put you in my power and deplete you of your masculine vigor!' Then she's astraddle of me and her hips are in action and that's it, she's depleting my manly vigor, all right. I'm done before she is, and then her back arches like she's been punched in the spine and she gives a little quiver and slowly folds down onto my chest and laughs softly against my neck.

'I oughta press rape charges,' I say.

'Oh, no, sir, no. What you should do is thank me most earnestly. Because *now* you'll really sleep well, and your welfare is my utmost concern. My own base needs are of no matter whatever.'

'Medical studies have shown that excessive and inexpert sarcasm can wither a tongue.'

'Oh, dear God, what a deprivation to you if I lost my tongue.' She gives me a peck on the forehead. 'And by the way, sailor, you're welcome.'

She detaches from me and sashays off to the bedroom.

She's pretty good at getting her way when she sets her mind to it. A lot like Aunt Catalina in that respect.

* * *

At dawn the storm has passed. The Landing smells fresh and cool and holds a thin layer of ground fog. I'm glad Rayo doesn't ask if I slept well after her nocturnal sortie on the futon, because in fact I slept like the proverbial log and I really don't want to hear her crow about it.

When we come down the stairs with our travel bags slung on our shoulders, Frank's already waiting in the Mustang, sipping from a plastic mug of coffee and reading a magazine. Like us, he's wearing a baggy, untucked chambray shirt over jeans – the easier to conceal a pistol in our waistband should we need to – and steel-toed and -heeled running shoes. Frank and I both have white name tags stitched in red over the left pockets of our shirts, Frank's reading jake, mine nick. We've made use of these shirts many times before. I tell him of Charles's takeaway breakfast offer, so we swing over to the Doghouse and they wait in the car while I go in, holding *The Love Tutors* down against my leg. Only the usual early birds are there, having breakfast at the counter. Charlie's working the grill and sees me and brings over a pair of carryout orders in plastic bags.

'Egg-sausage-cheese burritos in one,' he says. 'Coffee and cuernos in the other.' A typical cuerno is a croissant-shaped pastry lightly coated with a sugar crust, but his cuernos include a cream filling. He knows I love them.

'Thanks, cuz,' I say. I slide the DVD across the counter.

He picks it up, gives me a two-finger 'Up yours,' and says, 'I hope the cuernos rot your teeth out.'

I show a pained smile and head for the door.

* * *

When we get to the airfield the runway's still hazed with a residual mist. Our plane is the same one that took us to Monterrey, and Jimmy Ray Matson is once again our pilot. We take off on schedule, and as we climb to cruising altitude, Jimmy Ray says, 'I gotta tell you folks we might have to deal with a touch of headwinds for some of the trip. A little mild turbulence is all, nothing to be scared of and won't slow us but about fifteen minutes. Now, I don't mean to scare nobody, but I have to tell yall that a twin-engine plane runs double the possibility of engine failure, that's the plain and simple truth of it. I mean, *two* engines, double the chance, right? But the *good* news is, if one of the engines *does* quit, the other one is still totally and fully capable, all on its own, of getting the plane all the way, and I mean *all the way*... to the crash site.' He guffaws without giving us a glance, and I strongly suspect this isn't the first time he's entertained himself with that one.

'Thank you for that comforting information,' Rayo says. Jimmy Ray laughs louder.

We open the breakfast sacks and extract the food and coffee.

'Why's Charlie being so nice, giving us breakfast?' Rayo says. 'I thought he was mad at us.'

'He is,' Frank says. 'But why be a dick about it?'

'No thanks, I done ate,' Jimmy Ray says, though nobody offered. 'But I gotta say, that coffee smells good.'

'Got a cup?' I ask him.

He stretches an arm into the cabin to hand me a white plastic mug emblazoned with a Jolly Roger. We each pour some of our coffee into it – mine and Frank's black, Rayo's with cream and sugar, making the mix in Jimmy's cup the color of weak mud – and I hand it back to him. He makes a face at the look of it but says, 'Much obliged.'

I tell him we have to talk business back here and would he mind giving us some privacy.

'Oh, yeah, sure thing. Got me a mix of my boys Kris, Willie, Waylon, and Johnny right here.' He takes off his hat and switches to a different set of headphones and starts moving his head in time to the music. He's got it turned up high enough that I faintly hear the strains of 'The Highwayman.'

* * *

The Garcías' ranch is just north of El Paso and about a dozen miles shy of the New Mexico line. We begin our approach toward its rudimentary runway alongside a range of pale gray mountains. Frank and I have been to El Paso a few times before, but this is Rayo's first visit to any desert region, and she's hunched up against her window, gawking down at the craggy panorama of the Franklin range.

'It's so desolate it's beautiful,' she says. 'Most of the mountains around Mexico City are way bigger, but these look a little spookier somehow. All those dark canyons.'

Jimmy Ray touches us down as lightly as a leaf and taxis toward the far end of the strip, where two large black SUVs and an aviation fuel truck are parked. We stop a short way from the SUVs, and a pair of men emerge from one of them as Jimmy cuts the engines. The truck then drives up close enough to the plane to access the fuel ports.

Jimmy's informed us the El Paso temperature stands at 100.6, and I feel every gradation of it as we alight.

'*Good lord!*' Rayo says as she steps off the plane. Having grown up in Mexico City's generally cool climate, she'd had to get used to Miami's heat and humidity during her college years, and when she moved to Brownsville she found its summers of clammy swelter little different from Florida's. But desert heat is something else. The air can get so drily hot it'll cause your nose to bleed spontaneously. It can evaporate sweat almost as fast as you exude any, a phenomenon that fools some people into thinking they're not really *that* hot. Then suddenly everything's looking a little pink around the edges and, next thing they know, they're flat on their back.

The two men coming toward us are our cousins Félix García and his youngest son, Cayetano. Félix is in his sixties and is an underboss for an organization that specializes in smuggling wetbacks over to this side and American motor vehicles into Mexico. Cayetano's in his early twenties, a fast learner and reliable as they come. They greet me and Frank with hugs. When we introduce them to Rayo Luna, Félix looks her up and down and says to Frank, 'I've never understood why your family has all the best-looking women.'

Rayo smiles and says, 'Well, it's easy to see *your* family has the best-looking men.' She hugs and cheek-kisses Cayetano, who responds with a blush. When she hugs Félix, he pulls her tighter against him and runs his hand over her butt. She draws her head back and grins. 'Well, now I guess we know who the *real* wolf in this family is.'

He releases her and gives her a crooked smile. 'I beg your pardon, señorita. I'm just an old fool who doesn't get many chances anymore to hold a beautiful woman. My hand could not control itself.'

'No offense taken,' she says – and kisses her forefinger and taps it on his lips. His grin looks like it might break his face.

'Let's get going,' Frank says to me, starting off toward the SUVs, 'before these two run off and get a room.'

Both vehicles are Grand Cherokees, both with armored bodies and ballistic dark glass. Félix says the brakes felt a little spongy on the one he drove out here and we should take the other. 'Keys are in it, maps in the console,' Cayetano says. He tells us the Chihuahua license plates and the registration paper in the glove box are in the name of José García, probably the most common name in Mexico as well as that of a recently deceased uncle. A cardboard box in the back seat contains three burner phones he bought in Juárez, should we for some reason need to get rid of our own cells. There are also two pairs of high-power binoculars, bottles of water, sunglasses, and adjustable-headband baseball caps of different colors. Under the rug in the cargo space there are three sets of stick-on business signs, each of them two and a half by three feet. They go on the front doors, easy stick-on, easy peel-off. A plumbing business, a carpet business, a cabinet business – the kinds of companies people are used to seeing in residential neighborhoods. No addresses on the signs, just fake phone numbers except for the Tucson area code. 'I thought the signs might be good to have,' Cayetano says. 'Never know when they might come in handy, you know?'

'Good thinking,' Frank says, and pats the kid on the shoulder. Cayetano grins proudly.

Again there are hugs all around. This time when Félix hugs her, keeping his hands off her ass, Rayo gives him a deep kiss on the mouth and pulls away with a laugh, then jogs off to the Cherokee and hops into the back seat.

'Jesucristo,' he says, staring after her. 'What a woman!' Frank pats him on the back and says, 'See you when we see you.'

'Vayan con dios,' Cayetano says.

'You drive,' Frank tells me, and goes around to the passenger side.

We put our pistols under the seats.

* * *

In just a few minutes we're on I-10 and crossing the New Mexico border. At Las Cruces the interstate cuts west, and a few miles outside of town we turn off into a Border Patrol checkpoint to get a quick inspection from an agent before we're permitted to proceed. From there it's smooth sailing. We've reckoned we'll get to Tucson right around sundown if we hold to the speed limits and allow for stops to get fuel and a bite to eat. Rayo remains captivated by the desert, remarking on the bare mountains and mesas and buttes, the scrubby hills and sandy flatlands, the pale immensity of the sky.

We pass a road sign advising that dust storms may exist.

'Now *there's* a pronouncement whose logic cannot possibly be refuted,' Frank says. In a bad imitation of Aunt Catalina, he intones, 'Would you grant me *that*, Francis? That dust storms *may* exist?' and gets a laugh out of us.

* * *

We're closing on the Arizona line when my phone buzzes. I look at the screen and hand the phone to Frank, who says, 'Yeah,' into it, then turns to Rayo and mimes a writing motion. She's had a pen and small notebook close to hand in readiness for this call. 'Go ahead, I'll repeat it to my partner,' he says to the caller.

'Richard Moss. Lives alone,' he says, and in the rearview I see her write in the notebook. He says, 'Residence,' and repeats an address, then 'Phone,' and repeats a number. Then 'Tortuga Station Post Office,' and gives her another address.

'Get it all?' he asks her. She gives him a thumbs-up and starts tapping keys on her phone.

'Okay, man, many thanks,' Frank says to the caller, then deletes the call from his log.

'Here he is,' Rayo says, and passes her phone to Frank. I glance over and see a street map with a highlighted route on it.

'Our exit's on a main avenue at the southeast end of town, and it runs straight north to his neighborhood,' Frank says. 'Two turns off it and we're on his street. Piece of cake.'

Rayo unfolds a street map on her lap and runs a finger

over it. 'The Tortuga post office is only two blocks north of him,' she says. 'It's a small neighborhood. Nothing much east of it but open desert.'

Frank widens the scope of the map on her phone and says, 'Yeah. You can't live much closer to wilderness and still be in a town.'

At Lordsburg we stop for fuel and burgers and sodas, then get rolling again.

* * *

It's after six when we exit into Tucson and head for Moss's house. The sun's still above the western mountains, and looming over the north side of the city directly ahead are the imposing Santa Catalinas. Saguaro cactus, tall and stately with its multiple upraised arms, is everywhere, the first saguaro Rayo's seen outside western movies.

I pull into a minimart gas station at a commercial intersection and fill the tank, then Frank has me wheel into the shopping plaza just across the intersection, where he's spotted an office supply store that's given him an idea. We park at the far end of the lot, where we can attach business signs to the Cherokee's doors without attracting much attention. Frank chooses b&r carpeting, and I place them on the doors while he goes over to the office supply place. Before long he comes back with his purchases – a clipboard and a small ream of all-purpose requisition forms – and Rayo and I commend him for his cleverness. Together with the door signs, the clipboard should satisfy the curiosity of any neighbors who may take notice of us when we arrive at Moss's house.

He binds several of the forms to the clipboard, prints 'B&R Carpeting' in large letters in the blank block at the head of the top form, enters Richard Moss's name and address and phone number in the pertinent lines just below that, and then on some of the lower lines scribbles a few illegible words and some numbers with 'sq. ft.' after them.

* * *

The house shadows are almost to the street when we roll into Moss's neighborhood. It's clearly a new tract of houses whose most salient features are the largeness of the homes and the smallness of their lots – the tiny yards covered with gravel rather than grass – and a dearth of trees except for a few bony mesquites and a green-bark kind that Rayo identifies for us as paloverde. There's not a person in view, not another moving vehicle on the street, as we go down his block. Every garage door is closed, only a few cars parked on driveways. The drapes or blinds are drawn in most of the windows.

Moss's house is at the end of the street, his driveway bare, the garage door down. No telling if he's home. I park in the driveway, and Frank and I put on black Arizona Diamondback caps, get the Berettas from under the seats and the suppressors from the travel bags and attach them. We jack a round in the chamber, snick the safety on, stick the pistols in our waistbands and cover them with our shirts. Frank hands me the clipboard, and we get out. Rayo squirms over the console and slides into the driver's seat. She's attached a Quickster to her Glock and sets the pistol in the console, then covers it with a half-open map. She'll give us a horn toot if she spots any sign of possible trouble. If we hear the horn we'll zip out the back and come around the side of the house. Even for unlikely contingencies, it's best to have a plan.

We go up to the door and Frank presses the bell. I casually look down the street to see if anybody's checking us out, but there's nobody outside or at a door or window. He's about to ring the bell again when the door's opened by a lean but potbellied man who looks to be in his forties. Close-cut brown hair, Denver Broncos T-shirt, tan cargo shorts over very pale legs, tennis shoes but no socks.

'Yes?' he says, his watery brown eyes curious and wary.

'Mr Moss?' Frank asks him.

'Yes? Who are you?'

'My name is Jake Barnes, sir. This is my assistant, Nick. I apologize for being so terribly late. You're our last call and I know we were due more than an hour ago, but it's been one glitch after another today. Then to top it off, my phone went on the fritz and I couldn't call you about the delay. I'm really sorry about all that and I hope it hasn't inconvenienced you too much. It won't take but a few minutes to get the floor measurements and come up with the estimate.'

'*Estimate?*' Moss says. 'Who *are* you?'

'B&R Carpeting, sir. We had an appointment.'

He looks past us at the Cherokee. 'You've made a mistake. I don't need carpeting.'

'You don't? Well now, *that's* odd. We have an order form.' Frank turns to me and I hold the clipboard so that he and Moss can both see the name and address on the top lines. 'If that new secretary fouled things up again,' Frank says to me, 'I'm really going to let her have it.'

'Well, *somebody* goofed,' Moss says. 'I hope you straighten it out.'

He steps back and starts to close the door, but Frank moves up onto the threshold and offers him his hand. 'Our mistake, Mr Moss, and again, I'm *very* sorry to have disturbed you.'

The man gives him a puzzled look but mechanically accepts the handshake – and Frank clamps his other hand on Moss's upper arm and pushes him backward into the living room, Moss blurting out, '*Hey!* What… *hey!*'

I go in right behind them, my hand on the pistol under my shirt, and shut the door gently and stay beside it, scanning all around, seeing no one else.

'This is housebreaking!' Moss says. '*Assault!* I'll call the police!'

In one quick move, Frank shifts his grip to both of Moss's elbows and presses his thumbs into the crooks. Moss yelps and his knees buckle, but Frank holds him up by one arm and gives him a quick one-hand frisk, then steers him to the sofa and shoves him down on it. Moss massages his elbow tendons and stares up at Frank in wet-eyed terror. On each of the end tables is a lighted lamp, and the lit doorway on my right reveals the kitchen.

'Is there anyone else in the house?' Frank asks him.

Moss shakes his head. 'No. What… who *are* you? What do you want?… You gonna rob me? I don't have –'

'Easy does it, Mr Moss,' Frank says. 'Take a minute, catch your breath.' He gives me a hand sign to search the house, and I put down the clipboard and go to the main hallway, waiting until my back is to Moss before I draw the Beretta, not wanting to scare him any worse than we already have.

Tapping light switches on and off as I go, I make a quick check of the bedrooms, closets, bathrooms – keeps a tidy abode, the man does – then go into the kitchen and, by way of its door, into the garage. It holds a compact dark-green Toyota SUV. I take a peek to make sure nobody's in it, then put the pistol back under my shirt and return to the living room, show Frank a fist, retrieve the clipboard, and resume my post by the front door. He's pulled an easy chair over to the sofa and sits facing Moss, their knees almost touching. The guy's breathing a little better but is still very obviously scared.

'All right, Mr Moss,' Frank says. 'We're not here to harm you or rob you or anything of the sort. All we want is some information. You give it to us and *whoosh*, we're gone.'

'Information? About what?'

'Mount of Venus Productions.'

Moss looks from Frank to me and back at Frank. 'I don't know what you're talking about. Who *are* you?'

'We're a couple of guys who would like to complete our interaction with you as agreeably and quickly as possible,' Frank says. 'But that can't happen if you lie to us. Look, Mr Moss… Richard… we know the mailing address for Mount of Venus is a post office box just a couple of blocks from here. A box that's rented in your name. Of course you know what we're talking about. So cut the shit.'

'The post office doesn't give out… whoa, are you the *police*? Well, hey now, hey… there's nothing illegal about those movies and… anyway, you can't just break –'

'*Stop*, Richard,' Frank says. 'We're not cops and we don't give a rat's ass you're in the porn business. All we want is to find a certain actress who's appeared in a particular Mount of Venus production. Which is all you need to know about *us*. Tell us where she is and we're done here. But jack us around and we'll cause you pain you *will not believe*. But believe *this* – if you lie to me I'll know it.'

Frank has a talent for articulating such dire threats as convincingly as the kind of guys who genuinely enjoy dispensing pain. His stone-eye technique, I call it. I can't do it as well, which is why he usually conducts the critical interrogations.

Moss's cheeks are bright with tears. 'I *can't* tell you! Because *I don't know*. I'm not jacking you around, I'm *not*. I don't know the names of most of the actors and I don't know where *any* of them live. I don't have anything to do with making the movies and videos. I'm just the *mail* guy. I pick up the mail at the post office every day and take it to Lance in the evening. That's *all* I do, I swear to God.'

'Who's Lance?'

Moss wipes at his eyes. 'My brother-in-law. Ex-brother-in-law.'

'And he works for Mount of Venus, too?'

'Yeah, he... well, he owns it, runs it, the whole thing. Knows everything about the business. Never any trouble with the law. It's not illegal, you know, the kinda movies he makes. But all *I* do is take the mail to him. I'm *not* lying, I'm *not*.'

'Good. How long you been the mail guy?'

'Ah, jeez... around two years, I guess. The guy who had the job had to quit and Lance asked me did I want it. Said it's easy and doesn't take much time, and it pays pretty good for just a little work, so I said sure, yeah. But that's *it*. I deliver the mail. That's all, I *swear*.'

'Easy, Richard, I believe you. Tell me, you ever watch any of Lance's movies?'

'Yeah, now and then... I mean, it's not like I watch that kind of thing all the time or anything. I can take it or leave it. It's only, ah, some nights there's nothing good on TV and so –'

'I understand. You ever seen a movie with an actress named Kitty Quick?'

Even from where I'm standing I can tell by Moss's face he knows the name. 'Listen, mister,' he says, 'if Lance finds out I been running my mouth about his business, Christ, he'll be *really* pissed.'

'At this moment, Richard,' Frank says, 'Lance is a problem somewhere else and for a later time, but I'm a problem right here and now. Tell me everything you know about Kitty Quick or I'm going to use a hammer on your hands and feet.'

'*No, Jesus, no, don't!*' The tears gush again and he brushes at them with the heels of his hands. 'I've seen her in only one movie. I don't remember what it was called. It had to do with nurses... yeah, she played a nurse. But that's it, I mean it, that's *all* I know about her. I'm not lying.'

'And you have no idea where we might find her?'

'No, I *swear* to God I don't! If I knew where she was I'd tell you, believe me. All I know about her is the one movie.'

'Would Lance know where she is?'

'Yeah, I suppose. Maybe.'

'You picked up today's mail?'

'I already put the sack in the car. Not very much today.'

'You take it to him at a certain time?'

'Usually around eight, little after.'

Frank and I check our watches. Seven ten.

'Where's the company?'

'Up in the hills. Not too far but it's slow going.'

'What is it? Warehouse, office complex?'

'No, there's only houses up there. The company works in Lance's house.'

'Describe it.'

'Oh, jeez. It's a big place. Two-story, lot of rooms. Five bedrooms, I think, plus a little guesthouse around back. Great big front porch, sundecks on the sides and rear. Hot tubs. *Big* swimming pool. Christ, I can't imagine what it cost him to put in a pool up there. But, hell, all the houses up there are pretty ritzy, and the area where Lance lives – Raven Heights – it's about the ritziest. He's got something like fifteen acres near the top of a hill and his house is on a flat cut into the slope. He makes all his movies and videos there, but you'd never know any two of them were made in the same place, there's so many different kinds of rooms and patios and all. Privacy's a big thing with the people up there, so all the properties are big and far apart. All got big iron fences. Lance says they were all built between big curves and behind ridges so that none of them have a clear view of any of the others.'

'What security he have other than the fence?'

'There's a guard company that's under contract to most of the residents up there. It patrols the hills all night, keeps an eye on things.'

'What's the drill when you get there? How do you get in?'

'When I stop at the gate, a detector somewhere in the

driveway signals Judson's phone, which connects to a gate camera and intercom. There's a floodlight comes on automatically after dark. He sees it's me and he opens up.'

'Who's Judson?'

'Lance's bodyguard, I guess you'd call him.'

'He big? Carry a gun?'

'Yeah. Big. Has a gun.'

'Are there other guards on the place?'

'No. Only him.'

'Who else lives there?'

'Just Josefina the cook. Mexican. The maids and the gardeners are day help. When Lance is doing a project that takes more than a day to make, he has the cast and crew stay at the house till it's done.'

'Any movie people there now?'

'No, uh-uh. He just finished a movie last week.'

'Once you go through the gate, what then?'

'I drive up to the house and park. Go up to the front door, ring the bell, and Judson lets me in.' He cuts another look from Frank to me and back. 'You fellas are gonna go there, huh? Oh, man, he's gonna know you found him through me.'

'For sure, since you're gonna take us. Where are your car keys?'

'Bedroom,' Richard says gloomily.

Frank stands up and says, 'Let's go get them.' He looks at me and juts his chin at the door, and I head out to the Cherokee.

Rayo has the radio tuned to a rock station, the volume low, but she switches it off as I get in and toss the clipboard in back, then give her the rundown on things. I get a couple of ball gags out of my bag and hook them on my belt.

The garage door rolls up and the Toyota backs out onto the driveway and stops, Moss driving, Frank beside him. The door comes down again, and Moss backs into the street and gets going and we pull out and follow. We trail them onto the main avenue that brought us to this neighborhood and head north. A short way up the road we turn off at a large minimart, where we park the Cherokee in a far, dark corner of the lot. We quickly remove the signs from the doors and stuff them and the other business signs into a nearby dumpster, then lock the vehicle up tight. I open the Toyota's hatchback, and we huddle into the cramped space behind the rear seat, pushing aside the baggy sack of mail Moss loaded earlier, and I shut the hatch.

'Roll it, Richard,' Frank says.

* * *

The avenue ends at a T-junction with a two-lane road branching up into the hills in both directions. Moss turns west on it. The road climbs the hillside in loops large and small, our headlights slowly sweeping past rocky outcrops and creosote shrubs and eerily lofty saguaros. Moss was right about the properties up here being sizable and the residences few and far between. All of them stand well back from the twisting lane and are connected to it by long driveways, and all of them are enclosed by a high railed fence with a lighted front gate. The city below is a carpet of sparkling lights.

After a while, we come out of another bend in the road and Moss points off to the right. 'That's it there. His fence. Can't see the house from here, though.' He turns off onto a driveway that runs about fifty yards to the gate, which is lighted by a pair of small flood lamps. He's advised us that the camera-intercom combination is attached to the stone gatepost on the driver's side and several feet higher than the Toyota, the better to see into the open beds of incoming trucks. As we close in on the gate, Frank and Rayo and I hunker down and press ourselves close against the right side of the vehicle, out of the camera's line of vision.

We halt at the gate, in the full glow of its light. Moss lowers his window and juts his face out of it so the camera can get a good look at him.

The seconds drag by and then the intercom crackles lightly and a hoarse voice says, 'Running a little bit behind tonight, Richie.'

'Yeah, I know,' Moss says. 'I got caught up with –' But the intercom clicks off.

We hear an electric hum and the gate slides open with a low rattle. Moss puts his window up and drives us onto the property and out of range of the gate light, and we sit up for a look around. The driveway weaves a mostly uphill route through the scrub-and-stone landscape and ends at a paved parking lot abutting a two-story stone-and-tile house in front of the hillside. Directly ahead of us and past the house is an open carport that looks long enough to shelter a half dozen vehicles side by side but at the moment is housing only two, a large SUV and a small sports car. A railed porch runs the front length of the house. A recessed entryway casts a soft yellow light, and as we ease past it we see the set-back front door and the light just above it. Frank has Moss park well away from the porch steps and out of the door's sight line. When Moss cuts the engine, Frank pockets the keys and we get out and pull our pistols and I hand Moss the slack bag of mail. From around the side of the house comes the hum of a big AC unit.

Holding Moss by the back of his collar, Frank has him lead the way to the steps and onto the porch. The recessed entryway restricts the width of the cast of light from above the front door and leaves the walls to either side of the entry in deep shadow. Frank directs me and Rayo to positions on one side of the entrance, and he pulls Moss into the shadows on the other side. He whispers something to him, their figures vague, and then they come out into the light, Moss still holding the mailbag. He stands at the recessed threshold as Frank moves out near the porch steps, holding his pistol down against his leg, and faces the entrance. He nods at Moss, who goes into the recess and out of my view for a few seconds and then hurries back out to Frank, who pats him on the shoulder and then retreats into the darkness. I catch on that he had Moss ring the doorbell. Moss sets down the mail and faces the door and stands slightly hunched with one hand atop the other at his chest.

Nothing happens for about a half minute before I hear the door open and then a shaft of bright indoor light more starkly exposes Moss in his awkward stance, his face contorted.

'What the hell, Richie?' says a gravelly voice I recognize as Judson's. 'What're you... what's the matter?'

'Got a pain just all of a sudden. Hurts to breathe.'

'Having a heart attack or what?' Judson says, coming out toward him. Like Moss said, he's big. Heavy work boots, jeans, dark oversized T-shirt. But he's no seasoned pro, stepping out like this, empty-handed and without a look to left or right. Frank glides out of the darkness and puts the suppressor muzzle to the back of Judson's head. 'Stand fast and hands up!'

Judson halts, hands half raised in front of him. With his free hand, Frank pats all around Judson's torso and waist, finds a cellphone, drops it on the floor, and crunches it under his heel, then kicks it off the porch. 'Where's your piece?'

'Rec room.'

'Good place for it. Put your hands in your back pockets and keep them there. Show a hand, I'll shoot it.'

Judson stuffs his hands into the pockets and cuts a look at Moss, who's gaping at him in fear and says, 'They *made* me bring them.'

'Shut up, both you,' Frank says. He looks my way and I go to them.

'This a robbery or what?' Judson says.

Frank jabs him hard in the back of the head with the pistol muzzle and says, 'I said shut up.'

Frank draws him over to a darker spot on the porch and makes him sit down with his back against the rail, and I cuff his hands behind him and around one of the posts. Rayo's still hanging back in the shadows and keeping an eye on the entrance.

Frank squats down beside Judson and says, 'All right, we're gonna have a quick Q&A, you and I. And you have to understand two things – I don't have time to fuck around and I always know when someone's lying to me.' He takes out his buck knife and opens the blade. 'The first time you lie, I'm going to cut open your knee joints, plus cut your hamstrings and heel tendons. No matter what the surgeons do, walking without crutches will be nothing but a memory for the rest of your life. After that, every lie will make me do something *really* bad to you. And *I'm* not lying. We clear?'

'Fuck yeah, man, *yeah*.'

Frank works the interrogation swiftly and Judson affirms that he and Lance and Josefina the cook are the only ones in the house. Judson was in the rec room having a beer and watching a ball game on TV when the doorbell rang. Lance is working in the editing room, on the upper floor and in a rear corner of the house, and he would not have heard the bell, the room being soundproofed because he doesn't like to be distracted while he's working. The cook's only concern is the kitchen. She never pays heed to the doorbell or anything else. She's finished her duties for the night and retired to her room. There's no landline in the house, and the only cellphones are his and Lance's. 'Well, only Lance's now,' he corrects himself, giving Frank a look. The only room in the house with a door that locks is Lance's bedroom. If he has guns anywhere in the house, Judson doesn't know of them.

Frank asks Moss if he knows where the editing room is

and Moss says he does. 'Then we're set,' Frank says, and gives me a nod.

I take a ball gag off my belt and fit it into Judson's mouth and secure it behind his head. It's a scary gag and clearly a novel sensation for him, and his eyes enlarge in alarm. He tries to speak but manages only a grunt, and I tell him that trying to talk will make the ball feel bigger and probably make him feel like he's choking, and what he definitely does not want to do is freak out and throw up and drown on his own puke. I tell him he'll be able to breathe well enough if he just stays calm. Even if his nose stops up, there's sufficient leeway around the ball for him to breathe through his mouth as long as he doesn't panic. I ask if he can keep cool till we get back, and he nods jerkily, his eyes bulging.

'Good,' I say. 'Just relax and breathe easy, Judsie, and you'll be fine. We'll take it off on our way out.'

Frank again grips Moss by the collar, then beckons Rayo out of the darkness and we enter the house, pistols in hand.

* * *

The big living room has been done in Old West decor. Lots of dark wood and leather, Indian blankets and rugs, some Remington sculptures and paintings that could pass for originals and maybe are. Moss leads us to a wide stairway and up to the second floor, then down a long hallway and around a corner into a shorter one, before he stops in front of a closed door and nods at it. The editing room. Not a sound seeps from within.

Frank draws Moss away from the door and pushes him toward Rayo. She grips him by the collar the same way Frank did and backs up to the wall, holding Moss in front of her and the Glock barrel alongside his head. He looks like he's just been told he has cancer. Because the door opens inward and to our left, we stand on that side of it, me up against the jamb, Frank a little farther back and aiming his pistol at the door. I gingerly try the knob. It turns with ease and I slowly push the door forward, gradually revealing a large room, softly lighted, the walls lined with shelves holding a variety of photographic and sound equipment. The door's half open before we can see the blond man sitting at a table on the other side of the room with his back to us. Wearing headphones and dressed all in denim, sleeves rolled to the elbows, he's intent on a movie on the wall screen before him in which three naked young persons, a guy and two women, are cavorting on a bed. On the table is a bulky electronic instrument of some kind with a broad panel of levers and slides and connected to a computer equipped with an extra-large keyboard. At one end of the table are a big plastic ice chest and a large, lid-covered food tray, a short stack of paper plates and one of paper napkins. He's engrossed in the scene and working with the panel controls, bringing the action into close-up and then drawing back again into a wide shot of the trio in their writhing. The players are linked to each other in a configuration commonly called a daisy chain. He works a slide that softens the lighting of the scene just a touch.

Frank juts his chin forward and I advance into the room until I'm ten feet from Lance, who remains absorbed in his work. Frank comes up beside me, digs a quarter out of his pocket and lobs it toward the table in a high arc. It thunks next to Lance's hand and bounces high, and he recoils sharply – snatching off the headphones with one hand and flicking a switch with the other in what seems an instinctive move that freezes the screen action – and swivels halfway around to gape at us with our pistols pointed at him. He's bewildered, but I wouldn't call him terrified. Got a measure of cool. Judging by his incipient crow's feet and the few tinges of gray in his hair, I'd say he's early fifties.

Frank tells him to toss the headphones, then put his hands

on top of his head and stand up. Lance mutely complies. Taking care not to block my line of fire, Frank goes to him and pats him down with one hand, then tells him to sit again.

'Can I put my hands down?'

'Stick them in your front pockets and don't take them out again unless I say so. There any guns in the room?'

'No, hell no. Look, fellas, I don't keep a lot of cash in the house. I think there's around fourteen, fifteen grand. It's yours. If you're after drugs, there aren't any. I don't allow them on the place. There's some jewelry, not much, but –'

'What *is* it about us,' Frank says, cutting him off and looking at me, 'makes everybody so damn quick to think we're robbers?'

'Beats me,' I say. 'Makes me feel kinda lowdown.'

'*What?*' Lance says. 'If you're not robbers, who the hell are you and what do you want? How'd you get past the gate, anyway? By Judson? And –'

'First things first,' Frank says. 'Are you Lance?'

'Yeah. How you know *that*?'

Frank moves aside so Lance can see into the hall, where Moss is held by Rayo from behind, her gun muzzle pressed up under his chin.

'Ah, Christ,' Lance says, eyeing Moss. 'He in this with you?'

'Does it *look* like he's in with us?' Frank says. 'We ran him down through your PO box. And if you're wondering, Judson's all right, too, but for now he's restricted to the front porch.'

Frank nods at Rayo and she pushes Moss ahead of her into the room. Frank tells him to go sit down with his back against the near wall and his hands under his butt, then tells Rayo to cuff Lance's left hand to the back of the chair.

As she turns to hand me the Glock and takes a pair of flex cuffs from her belt, I see Lance getting his first good look at her and admiring what he sees. She goes over to him and he gives her his hand, saying, 'Hey, girl, you're really something.'

She laughs lightly and says, 'Really?' and slips the cuff onto his wrist. 'The kinda something that could make a go of it in your, ah… art form?'

'A go of it?' Lance says. 'Honey, you've got it all in spades – body, moves, everything.'

Frank gives me a look of 'Do you *believe* this?'

Lance cranes his head around to try to keep his eyes on her as she positions his arm behind the chair and crouches down to cuff it to the back brace.

'I'm a great judge of women's bodies, even with their clothes on,' he says, 'and unless you're covered with burn scars or something, yours is five-star stuff. Besides, I saw the way you looked at the screen when you came in. You *like* my art form. You should give it a try, make a picture with me. You could be a star, I mean it.'

She lets out another small laugh and checks the fit on his wrist and the tautness of the cuff's pull, making sure it won't cut off the circulation in his hand, then stands up. 'I'll think about it.'

'Do that,' he says. 'I'll give you my number. There's paper and pen right there.'

'Don't need it,' she says. 'I'll write you at the Venus PO address.'

She waggles her brow at me as I hand back her pistol, then returns to her post by the door, Lance watching her all the way.

Frank sidles over to block his view. 'If you're done promoting employment opportunity to my associate,' he says, 'I'll address your question of what we want. But first, I have to ask if you've ever heard of a man named Bad Eddie Roget.'

I have to fight down a smile. Bad Eddie is a persona Frank created when we were in college. We came home to our apartment complex one afternoon and found an unfamiliar car parked in our assigned space in the residents' lot. We assumed it belonged to some visitor who didn't feel like walking any farther than necessary and so parked in the nearest spot he could find. On a whim, Frank wrote a note I liked so much I can still recall it almost verbatim. 'My name is Bad Eddie. I'm called that because I do very bad things. You have parked in a space assigned to my friend. Should you do so again, you will soon afterward make my acquaintance and regret it evermore. I've made note of your license plate and can easily find you. Yours very truly, B.E.' He folded the note and put it under the driver-side windshield wiper. The car was gone a few hours later, and if its owner ever made a return visit to the complex, he didn't park anywhere near our spot again. In the years since, we've made referential use of Bad Eddie on various occasions.

Lance says he's never heard of him. 'Name like that, what's he, like some kinda criminal?'

'You need only know,' Frank says, 'that as his forenames imply, Mr Roget is not a man of meek nature or one to trifle with, and I advise you not to do so. Like you, he's an entrepreneur, and like you he prefers to conduct his operations with discretion and a minimum of disharmony. We're here because he wants us to locate a young woman who, under the name of Kitty Quick, appeared in a film of yours, *The Love Tutors*. Where can we find her?'

'*That's* what this is about? You're looking for *Kitty*? Why the hell not just say so? There's no call for *guns*, handcuffs, all this badass bullshit.'

'I'm pleased to hear it,' Frank says. 'Tell us where she is and our business here is concluded. However, if what you tell us turns out to be incorrect, you can count on seeing us again. And on *that* occasion we'll begin by breaking bones. So. Where is she?'

'Los Angeles, at least that's where she *said* she was going, last time I saw her, back to LA,' Lance says, his speech a little faster, most likely because of the mention of bones being broken. 'She'd come to me from there, you see. I wanted her to do another movie with me, but no dice. About two weeks after she split I called her to see if I could change her mind, but the mobile number she'd been using was no longer in service. I mean, she really cut the tie.'

'How long ago she leave?'

'Uh... three months, give or take a day or two.'

'Give it from the top. From the time you met her.'

He tells us she came to him around four months ago by way of Ben Steiner, a film agent pal of his in LA who specializes in great-looking young girls who want to be in the movies but don't have any experience beyond a high school play, if that much. Steiner's able to persuade many of them that the quickest way of getting professional experience and building a portfolio and earning good money all at the same time is in sex videos and film, and if they're willing to give it a go, he's willing to help them. Lance is just one of many adult-film producers in the western United States who have an arrangement with Steiner to refer aspiring actresses to them. His service doesn't come cheap but it's worth it because the girls are all truly good-looking and he guarantees that they have been medically examined and found to be free of STDs and drug use. Through police pals, he also makes certain that a girl he refers is not a law enforcement agent and is free of criminal convictions or pending warrants. The only things Steiner can't vouch for are a girl's true name and age. His producer clients are on their own in dealing with those aspects. So Steiner sent him this girl who said she was Katie Moore from Fresno and swore she was eighteen years old, but she had no official ID to verify any of it. Lance knew she was lying about both her name and her age and guessed her to be sixteen or seventeen. But she had a great face and body and such sassy confidence that he went ahead and gave her a test anyway. Turned out she could follow direction to a T, and the camera loved her and she had a gift for playing to it. 'One of those born naturals,' he said. He offered her a part in *The Love Tutors* and she grabbed it. To guard against the risk of a child-porn problem, he had his half-sister, who works for the DMV in Sun City, issue her a legit license in the name of Katherine Moore with a date of birth that made her eighteen. He photocopied it for his records in readiness against some agent of the law showing up and demanding proof she wasn't a minor. Whatever her actual age, she was one of the best newbies he'd ever worked with. She asked if she could be called Kitty Quick, and he liked the name and said why not. He put her in with two seasoned actresses and she stole the show, as most of the reviewers agreed.

'So many wannabes,' he tells us, 'think that taking their clothes off and having sex in front of a camera is all there is to being a porn actress. But there's a big difference between just *having* sex and *performing* sex. What so many of them don't seem to know is that the biggest sexual turn-on for most guys is enthusiasm. Am I right or am I right? Nothing stokes a guy more than a woman taking obvious pleasure in sex, whether it's a woman he's having sex with or one he's just watching have sex. And yeah, sure, a really good actress can fake that kind of, ah… *gusto* pretty good. But the real thing is unmistakable and better than any acting, and this kid you're looking for, her enthusiasm's the real thing. It comes across on the screen like gangbusters. I can understand why your Mr Roget wants to meet her.'

'I didn't say he wants to meet her,' Frank says. 'I said he wants us to locate her. You were saying?'

'Yeah, well, she told me she was going back to LA, and maybe she did, maybe she didn't, but *that's* what she told me she was gonna do. She lived here with me and the other actors and the crew while we made the tutor thing. When the shoot was done, I threw a two-day party like I always do when we wrap, and she hung around for that, then off she went. With a copy of the flick as per the actors' contracts.'

'So she was here maybe a month?'

'Yeah, about a month. I'd planned on a much shorter shooting schedule, but there were all kinds of glitches and... well, hell, it took a month to do it. When we finally wrapped, Kitty was ready to book. She'd had enough of Arizona and figured she could make more money back in LA. For sure they pay better out there, but the competition's cutthroat. Two dozen grade-A girls for every part that comes along. But like I told you, there's something really special about Kitty. And now she's been in a good feature she can show to producers, let them see how talented she is, what she can do. All things considered, I expect she's making out all right.'

'She from LA?' Frank says. 'She grow up there? Go to school there? Ever mention friends or family there?'

'She never said anything about any of that, not to me or to anybody else on the set. I *know*, because I asked them all the same questions when I was trying to run her down. Could be she was from LA, could be she was from East Bumfuck. Listen, most of the girls in this business leave home because they don't like any part of it. Where they're from is the last thing they want to talk about. I've worked with more girls than I can count and never knew where half of them came from or even their real names. Same goes for Kitty.'

'The LA guy who sent her to you... Steiner,' Frank says. 'You think she'll go see him? See if he can find her something? Wouldn't that be her best shot?'

'Yeah. Yeah, it would. And you want me to call him, right? Find out if he's seen her, knows where she is, who she's working with, whatever.'

'Very astute. Do it now.'

'And if he asks why I want to know?'

'Good question... Let's see... There's an entertainment company in Texas. New outfit called, ah... the Texas

Starlight Group. Hasn't got much publicity so far, but it's loaded with investment capital, and its biggest ambition is in adult-film production. A couple of its people saw Kitty in *The Love Tutors* and think she'd be perfect for a major part in a production they're putting together… an adult sword-and-sorcery thing. They're making it in partnership with a cable company that's heavy into pay-per-view, video on demand, hotel TV, et cetera. If she's interested, they're prepared to make her a very attractive offer. Her agent would be in for a nice piece of change.'

Lance grins big as he finishes up scribbling notes on a pad. 'Not bad for bullshit on demand. Some guys have a gift for it. No offense, it's a compliment. Phone's in that drawer.' He points and Frank goes over and takes it out and gives it to him, then releases his left hand from the cuff. Lance shakes and flexes the freed hand a few times, then makes the call, listens, then quickly taps the speaker button and holds out the phone so we can hear the recording saying to leave a message, name, and number and 'I'll get back to you.' Then he says into the phone, 'Bennie. Lance Furman. Give me a call ASAP. Got somebody here interested in an actress you might still be handling. It's a sweet deal. Be waiting to hear from you.'

He ends the call and says, 'He's pretty good about getting back when I say it's important, but if he's talking business with somebody it might be a while.'

'Whatever it takes,' Frank says.

Lance flaps a hand at the covered tray and the ice chest. 'Meanwhile, if anybody wants a beer or something to eat, just help yourself. Josefina always prepares a heap of chow for me when I expect to work late. Usually beef sandwiches and fried chicken, because that's what I like best, but she always makes way more than I can ever eat by myself. I know she overdoes it just so she can give the leftovers to the garden guys the next day. Thinks I don't know she's sweet on one of them.'

'Well, I, for one, am famished,' Rayo says. She goes to the table and takes the lid off the big tray, chooses a chicken breast, and puts it on a paper plate, then digs a bottle of Negra Modelo out of the ice-packed cooler and uncaps it. She looks over at Moss, still sitting on the floor, and says to him, 'Come have something to eat.' He looks at Frank, who tells him to go ahead. Moss shifts from one side of his ass to the other to free his hands, then works some feeling into them and struggles to his feet and joins Rayo at the table. Then we're all seated and Moss is noshing on chicken, too, while Frank and I and Lance dig into excellent roast beef sandwiches.

* * *

Almost an hour later, while we're all playing quarter-limit stud with a shabby deck Lance fished out of a drawer and I'm starting to wonder if the Steiner guy will call back anytime tonight, Lance's phone chirps. He picks it up and checks the screen and says, 'Our man.' He swipes it with a finger. 'Bennie, thanks for getting back.' With his notes at hand, he gives Steiner the story Frank laid out about the Texas Starlight Group and its interest in talking to an actress named Kitty Quick.

'Yeah, Katie Moore,' he says. 'That's the one. You still rep her?'

He listens and gives us a smiling nod.

'Because they figured she might still be working for Mount of Venus,' he says. 'So they nosed around in the right places and came up with my name and office number. This afternoon they gave me a call, said they were in town and had to be in Vegas day after tomorrow and wondered if we could meet this evening to talk about Kitty. I was curious so we got together at this club I know, and I tell you, they're *burning* for the kid! Talking nice figures. Your end would be juicy, and they've agreed to lay a finder's fee on me just for helping out. I mean, is this a great business or what? Give me a number and address on her and I'll pass it on to them.' He listens again, says, 'Ramhorn?' – and now looks a little agitated. He asks if she's still under contract to 'him,' whoever that is, and he stares at the floor as he listens. 'Christ's sake, Bennie, all they want to do is *talk* to her, see if she's interested. *If* she is, *then* they can go to him.' He listens, not looking at any of us. Then brightens and says, 'Oh, hell *yeah*! Hey, if Kitty says yes to their prop, I guaranfuckingtee you they'll go for that.' He gives us a wink. '*Will* you? That'd be great, Bennie, because that's all they want, the chance to pitch it to her… Hell, yeah… Okay, I'll be right here, man. Do it.'

He cuts off the phone and grins at us.

'I'm not the only one in the room who can come up with bullshit on demand,' Frank says.

Lance points at himself and makes a face like, 'Who, *me*?' Then tells us Kitty did go to see Bennie, who took a look at *The Love Tutors* and was so impressed with her work that he got her a contract with an old pal named Nolan Dolan. Dolan started out in porn production way back when and is now head man at Ramhorn Associates, an immensely successful Southern Cal consortium of film and video companies whose most gainful product is adult entertainment. In her first two months back in LA she was in two features made by Ramhorn affiliates and did both of them under the name Kitty Belle. The contract commits her to Ramhorn for one more movie, which was scheduled to start shooting two weeks ago but hasn't gotten under way yet. Steiner doesn't know why not, but whatever's holding it up could be something that might make Dolan willing to release her from the project outright or at least let us buy out the contract.

'Ben's calling him right now,' Lance says. 'Hell, man,

even if Dolan doesn't cut her loose but says you can buy the contract, he's gotta let you go talk to her, right? See if she's interested in what you got? You've *found* her, man, you're gonna *see* her, and then... what? You say your guy Roget doesn't want to hurt her, and I hope to hell you're not lying. I mean, I like the kid, I like her a *lot*, and I don't like Dolan worth a shit. I could tell you stories but... ah, what the hell. Doesn't matter. I just don't like the idea of her working for him is all.'

'As I've told you, you can rest easy about Mr Roget,' Frank says.

'Good, that's good,' says Lance. 'But let me tell *you*, you can't rest easy with Dolan. Listen, this kind of business involves a lot of companies working under so many different corporate partnerships that it's not real hard for a smart accountant to, ah, *obscure* a company's financial standing, know what I mean? The business lends itself to a kind of bookkeeping that's very attractive to certain sorts of cash investors.'

'You're telling us the porn biz is a good money laundry,' I say. 'Not exactly a profound revelation.'

'All right, no big news to you guys,' Lance says. 'But the word is that Ramhorn's one of the biggest such laundries in the business. *And* that one of its chief investors is an outfit down Mexico way. One of the big-time drug outfits, to be exact. Now, I'm not saying it's true, you understand, it's just the word. But I thought you should know that about him. He might be connected to some badass people.'

'Thanks for the tip,' Frank says.

* * *

Steiner calls back.

'Yo, Bennie,' Lance says. He listens for a while and what he hears makes him smile. 'All right, amigo! Nice going,' he says, then listens again. 'Well hell, Bernardo, that's just great. I'll give them a call and they'll take it from there. Thanks a ton, buddy. Yeah, you, too, my man. Take care.'

'You're on,' he tells us. 'He talked to Dolan and told him about Texas Starlight's interest in getting Kitty for some project and how you'd like to talk to her and, *if* she's interested, possibly work out a deal to buy out her contract from him before you go back to Texas. Dolan had him hold awhile as he ran it past one of his guys, then said he can meet with you at nine tomorrow morning but has to leave for the airport at nine thirty to catch a flight. He'll be in South America for the next few weeks, so unless you want to wait till he gets back, a half hour is all he can give you. But so what, right? All you want to know is where she is, and you won't need ten minutes to find out. Could be tough getting any kinda charter flight at this hour but ...' He checks his watch. 'To hell with a charter,' he says. 'You get going right now, and even with fuel and piss stops, you can drive it and be there under the wire with only minor risk of a speeding ticket.'

He tells us Arizona doesn't do daylight saving, so right now we're on the same clock as California. He works his phone, scrolls the screen, writes a few things on a note sheet, then tears the sheet off the pad and hands it to Frank. 'Ramhorn's address. Super easy to find. Follow those simple directions and you can't miss it.' He opens a table drawer and gets out a remote control for the gate and puts it on the table. 'You'll need this.' I tell him we'll leave it under the driver's seat of Moss's vehicle, together with its keys, at the minimart just south of the foothills avenue. Lance says he knows the place. Frank tells him to wait a couple of minutes for us to clear the grounds before going down to uncuff Judson, who's sure to be in ill temper and might be inclined to take a shot or two at us if he's got a weapon in some hidey-hole out there.

As we start out, Lance says, 'Say, beauty, what's your name?'

Rayo turns to him, walking backward. 'Cleo.'

'I doubt that, but it's a good name. And your last name should be… Shade. Cleo Shade. Nice, huh?'

She laughs and pirouettes back around and follows us out.

We scoot downstairs and out to the porch, where Judson is snorting and gagging, snot and drool webbing from his chin, the veins standing out on his forehead. We shouldn't have left him ball-gagged for so long. I remove the gag and fling it away and wipe my fingers on his shirt. He's gasping like he's just been pulled up from underwater, then throws up on himself, and we realize how close he'd come to drowning in the way I'd warned him about. I tell him Lance will be down in a minute to remove the cuffs, but he doesn't look up at us, doesn't say anything, just sits there gasping like there's not enough air in the world. One of those hard guys who's never before been so badly scared, never before faced a moment when he was certain he was about to die. I'd say his bodyguard days are done.

* * *

Lance called our travel time almost exactly right and his directions to the Ramhorn building are faultless. With only a few brief stops for gas and a last stop to wash up and change into fresh shirts – though Frank and I forwent the shaves we could use – we enter LA's river of morning traffic with the sun blazing in our mirrors. When I find a spot in a parking lot almost directly across from Ramhorn, we've got more than fifteen minutes to spare, and Frank tells Rayo she's not going in. If she did, we'd have to explain her – who she is, why she's with us, and so on – which would only enlarge the pretense we'd have to hold together and increase the odds of a slip-up. I agree. The smaller the lie, the easier to support it.

She's irked but knows this isn't a time to argue. We get out and put on the windbreakers but leave our weapons in the vehicle. There's a café next to the parking lot, and I tell Rayo she can watch the front door from there.

'Watch for what?' she says.

'For anybody who looks like a porn producer ready to jump at the chance to sign a sizzling prospect like Cleo Shade. Leave us a note if you decide to run off to a new career.'

She smiles flatly and gives me the finger.

* * *

We present ourselves to the lobby receptionist and she phones someone to report that the 'Texas people' have arrived. An attractive blonde appears and introduces herself as Miss Nelson, Mr Dolan's assistant. She gives us a brisk appraising look and says she hopes our long drive wasn't too tiring, then escorts us into the elevator. We exit at the top floor and follow her to a door near the end of the hall. She raps it twice and conducts us into a spacious office of paneled wood walls and black leather furniture. 'Your nine o'clock, Mr Dolan,' she says.

'Gentlemen,' he says, coming around from behind a massive desk positioned catty-corner to large, abutting windows that offer a grand view of the city. He's tall and lanky, dressed in brown tweed, and has the ruddy complexion of a sportsman. Lance had said he was in his early seventies but looked vigorous for his age, and despite the white hair and baggy eyes I have to agree.

He dismisses Miss Nelson and extends his hand to us. 'Nolan Dolan. Pleasure to meet you boys.' His voice has the deep resonance of the late John Huston's, and it occurs to me that he looks a good deal like the famous moviemaker and even emulates his tight ironic smiles and narrow-eyed looks of cagey assessment. We shake his hand, Frank first, introducing himself as Thomas Hudson and me as his partner, Alex McPope, of the Texas Starlight Group.

'Yes, of course. Shall we sit?' Dolan nods at a conference table on which are set a large pot of coffee, cups and saucers, creamers and spoons, napkins in ornate holders. He sits across from us and says to help ourselves to the coffee. We both decline. Frank tells him we're still fairly wired on all the coffee we drank on the drive from Tucson and apologizes for our casual dress and somewhat bleary aspects. 'When we got to Tucson yesterday evening, we had no idea we'd be driving all night to meet with you this morning.'

'No apology necessary,' Dolan says. 'I admire both your zeal and your stamina. I suggest, however, we not waste any time. Ben Steiner tells me you're interested in an actress under contract to me.'

'Yes, sir,' Frank says. 'Kitty Belle. According to Mr Steiner she's contractually obligated to do one more picture for you but it hasn't yet begun production.'

'That is correct on both counts.'

'Well, sir, we chose to drive here straightaway rather than wait for your return from South America precisely because of our zeal – as you so aptly termed it – to gain her participation in one of our upcoming cable films. We'd hate for her to begin work on another project before we can at least present ours to her.'

'Why Kitty? There are any number of actresses with much more experience. She's only made three pictures.'

'And we've seen only one. But it was enough to convince us she has exactly the right blend of sexiness and audacity we want in the character she'd play. It's the lead role and we think she's ideal for it. If we could meet with her to discuss the project, and should she wish to be part of it, we're sure we could all – she, we, and you – arrive at some satisfactory contractual arrangement.'

'I see.' He smiles his tight smile. 'Well, I'll tell you what

I'm sure of. *I'm* sure you're lying through your teeth. During my phone talk with Steiner I had him stand by on a pretext while I inquired about your company. I know people who know *everything* about such matters, you see, and it didn't take five minutes for me to know that the Texas Starlight Group is a total fiction. It's not in any of the registries, and none of the cable outfits has heard of it, never mind contracted with it for a production. What say you cut the horseshit and tell me who you really are and why you're looking for Kitty.'

'What about your flight?' Frank asks.

'What flight?' Dolan says with a smile.

'I see,' Frank says. He turns to me and raises his brow. I hold his look for a three-second count, then nod. It's a ploy we sometimes use to give a questioner the impression we've agreed between ourselves to be forthcoming with him.

'We should've known a man of your experience could easily find us out,' Frank says. 'The truth is we're private investigators from Dallas under contract to locate the girl.'

'So why the artifice?'

'It's our experience that people in the adult entertainment field are usually disinclined to answer questions about the business, especially from investigators.'

'That's generally true, yes,' Dolan says. 'Dallas, you say. Is that where she's from?'

'It's where her family lives.'

'Who hired you? Her father, husband, fiancé? Her pimp? There's always some man trying to track down some girl who ran away to join the porn circus.'

'We've been retained by a legal firm that's handling a substantial estate she and her brother recently acquired in consequence of their father's death,' Frank says. 'The mother passed away some years ago, and Kitty and her brother are the family's sole survivors. The brother has been notified of the inheritance, but in accordance with the terms of the will it can't be claimed by either sibling except in equal division with the other, or unless the other signs a verified quitclaim to his or her share, or unless it can be proved the other is dead. The firm somehow learned she'd been in *The Love Tutors*, under the name Kitty Quick, and we took it from there. Our charge is simply to find her and inform her of the circumstance so that she can respond to it as she chooses.'

Lance was dead right about Frank's gift for extemporaneous invention. Actually, just about everyone in the family can lie with expert facility. It's in our bones. But only Frank and Catalina also possess the equally valuable talent to know a lie when they hear one.

'I see,' Dolan says. 'And her real name is... ?'

'I'm sorry, sir, we're not at liberty to say. Nor to divulge any details beyond those I've already given. Legal restrictions.'

'Well, she's not the first rich girl who's ever ventured into the wide, wide world of fuck films,' Dolan says. 'The richies all tend to do it for much the same reason. The outlaw adventure of it, I suppose we could call it. The thrill of wagging their ass at the world they grew up in. I can usually spot them at a glance, but Kitty's never showed any sign of privileged upbringing. If she comes from money, it's not old money.'

'I wouldn't know anything about that, sir,' Frank says. 'Where can we find her?'

He looks at me. 'Do you ever speak, Mr... McPope?'

'When occasion necessitates.'

He chuckles and nods. 'All right then, fellas. Now *I'll* come clean with *you*. When I learned your company was a phony, I pegged you for hired trackers of some kind or other, and I thought we might be able to work a deal. I'll tell you where I think she is *if*, should you find her, you'll bring her to me before you take her to Texas or cut her loose. There's something I need to discuss with her, and a short meet is all that's required. After that, she can return to Dallas or whatever else she might choose. I'll pay you off-the-books. Name your price.'

'What if she doesn't want to see you?'

'I would expect you to bring her to me anyway. Which is why you can name your price.'

Frank gives me the raised brow again as if asking if we should agree to the offer. I nod. He takes a little notebook from his pocket and writes in it, tears out the sheet, puts it facedown on the table, and pushes it across to Dolan. 'That's our off-the-books fee for the sort of service you're requesting,' he says. 'It's payable in cash when we turn her over to you at this office and it buys you exactly half an hour with her. Alex and I will wait in the hallway and time you.'

Dolan picks up the paper, considers it, and puts it in his coat pocket. 'Agreed.'

He tells us she's in Mexico. She went there with a man he describes as 'a top executive of a Mexican business organization heavily invested in Ramhorn.' She met him at a party Dolan hosted for him four weeks ago at his Hidden Hills home. Every three months he throws a party for this man and around a dozen or so of his associates, and to ensure there are plenty of girls to go around, he also invites more than a dozen Ramhorn actresses. In addition to a fairly lavish buffet, Dolan tells us, his parties always include an open bar, a dance floor, and a live band. The party in question was the first one since Kitty had come to work for him, and he invited her to attend as his personal guest and seated her next to him at the head table, a detail I'm sure piques Frank's curiosity as much as it does mine. In the course of that evening, the Mexican executive and his translator – the man doesn't speak English and Dolan knows no Spanish – came over to Dolan's table and introduced himself to Kitty and asked if he might have the honor of a dance. When she answered in Spanish, the man grinned and said something more to her, at which she laughed and in turn said something that made him laugh. Dolan hadn't had any idea Kitty could speak Spanish and was impressed by her obvious fluency. She and the executive went off to have their dance, then had several more in succession. Then the next time Dolan looked, they were no longer on the floor or anywhere else in the room. The executive's translator was dancing at that moment, so Dolan went to the executive's table with a Ramhorn actress proficient in Spanish and asked the man's friends if they knew where the couple had gone. The men all grinned, and one of them said they'd gone to have a drink. Dolan asked where, and the man said Mexico and winked at the actress, and the men all laughed.

'I haven't received a word from her since that night,' Dolan says. 'Her landlord says he hasn't, either. Nor have any of her friends, not that she had many. Her phone doesn't answer.' He looks off for a moment, then back at us. 'I really *must* speak with her. I'm depending on you boys to make that possible.'

'Where in Mexico are they?' Frank says.

'I'm not sure. I asked his pals at the party, but they all shrugged and yukked it up some more. But the fella himself once told me he has a seaside place in Ensenada. Invited me to visit him there sometime and we'd go marlin fishing on his boat. I have a hunch it's not his only residence, but as it's the only one I know of, I'd say it's the place to start your search.'

'I suppose so,' Frank says. 'But now I'm curious about something, Mr Dolan. I've never been in Baja, but I've looked at a few maps, and if memory serves, Ensenada's what... only sixty or seventy miles below the border? A couple of hundred miles from where we're sitting? So I have to wonder why you haven't hired somebody to go check out the guy's place down there, see if she's with him. LA's got loads of top-flight private investigation companies and it's hardly more than a one-day job. Of course, no legit company is going to kidnap her and risk the legal shit storm that could bring on them, but they could probably find out easily enough if she's there. If she is, you could whiz on down and have your talk with her.'

Dolan nods. 'As a matter of fact, I've spoken to a number of local agencies, all deemed among the best in town. But, you see, I don't know the fella's Ensenada address, and in order to find the residence, the investigators would need the name of its owner. Being the sort of close-to-the-vest fella he is, I wouldn't be surprised if he bought it under an alias, but what choice did I have but to give them his real name in the hope it's on the deed so they could find the house? However, as soon as they heard the name, well, that was it. They got their hats. All of them.'

'Really? What's his name?'

'Jaime Montón.'

Frank leans toward him over the table. '*The* Jaime Montón? Better known to the news media as El Chubasco?'

'The very same. But you boys don't strike me as the sort to be as easily intimidated as the people I've tried to engage. I wouldn't expect *you* to bow out of our agreement simply because –'

'We *are* bowing out,' Frank says, and stands up. I do, too. 'Neither our Dallas contract nor our deal with you obligates us to risk our asses by possibly antagonizing the likes of Chubasco. We're going back to Dallas to report our findings, Mr Dolan. For what it's worth, we'll leave your name out of it. Could be her family's lawyers will want to hire a Mexican investigation team to look for her in Ensenada, who knows? That's their business. But *we* are withdrawing from the matter altogether.'

'Now hold on, fellas. Let's talk about this. If it's a matter of more money –'

'Good day, sir,' Frank says, and heads for the door.

If I didn't know him better he'd have *me* convinced we

were quitting the hunt. But I know he's just grabbing the opportunity to break us clear of Dolan. We're halfway across the room when Frank stops and looks back at him, saying, 'Almost forgot to mention. We have a certified birth certificate. She's very much underage. What you California fellas refer to as San Quentin quail. Maybe you already knew that about her, maybe you didn't, but if the law should somehow get wind of the kind of work she's done with you, there's no way you'll dodge a child-porn conviction. I strongly advise that you destroy her contract and every video and movie you've made with her. Hell, if I were in your shoes, I'd clear my records of *all* traces of her. Every photo, every form she's ever signed under any name. Any document that makes mention of her in any way. Just a suggestion.'

Dolan nods dolefully.

At the door, I cut a look back at him. He's staring down at his folded hands on the table, his face showing every day of his age.

* * *

As the elevator doors begin to close, I ask Frank how much of a fee he'd presented to Dolan on the notepaper.

'Fifty grand. Expected him to laugh and haggle it down, but he didn't bat an eye.'

'I know why he didn't.'

'Me, too. He's in love with the kid.'

'Exactly. That important talk he wants to have with her? Bet you the ranch he wants to ask her to marry him. Or maybe just "come live with me and be my love and I will give you plenty".'

'Poor old bastard.'

'Got that right. To be in love with somebody more than fifty years younger than you is about as poor old bastard as a man can get. But the hell with him. How *about* this kid?

This no-big-deal assignment, bro, is no big deal no longer.'

'Said a mouthful. *Chubasco*, for Christ's sake.'

'You know, Frankie, we *could* tell the Cat we couldn't find her. "We're truly sorry, señora. We traced her as far as LA and hit a dead end. Makes us ashamed because we pride ourselves on our expertise, but even more because you were counting on us and we let you down. But still, she's vanished… We *could* tell her that. I mean, hell, man, it's almost the truth. Be done with this fool's errand.'

'*Or*,' Frank says, 'we could call Mateo and see what the Jaguaros can give us on Chubasco's whereabouts. *And* if we get a lead on that, try to find out if she's still with him. *And* if she is, try to figure out how to detach her from him.'

'Or we could do that, yeah.'

III

THE CROSSINGS

RUDY

Frank wheels us back the way we came into the city but this time turns south when we hit I-5. Rayo's in the back seat, leaning forward between our buckets as I tell her about the Dolan meet.

'She's in Mexico with *Chubasco*?' she says.

'That's how Dolan tells it. Says she speaks pretty good Spanish. Add that to her looks, and I have to think the kid might be at least part Mex.'

'And fearless us,' Rayo says, 'we're going down there and fetch her ass.'

'Fetching is an apt inflection to describe it,' I say.

'I have to wonder how much you guys would enjoy this job if she had an ass like a bus.'

'Speaking of buses,' Frank says, 'if you want out, we can drop you at the next station.'

'Up yours, Jack. I wouldn't drop out of this for love or money. I mean, *woo*, this girl hunt has crossed over to a whole other thing.'

'Listen to her,' I say. 'She grooves on this. The riskier, the better.'

Frank eyes her in the rearview. 'Lives for danger, our gyno-American associate. Ain't no buncha Sinas can spook *her*.'

'Gyno-Mexican,' she says, 'and read between the lines.' She holds up her hand, the back of it toward us, the thumb and pinkie folded into her palm so that we can see only the three middle fingers, an old schoolyard affront that prompts all of us to laughter for no reason except our shared rush in a job whose jeopardy factor has taken a sizable jump.

* * *

She'd had coffee while she waited in the café but held off on breakfast, thinking we'd probably be hungry after the meeting and would want to grab a bite somewhere. She thought right. An hour down the road we pull off into Santa Ana and the parking lot of the first restaurant we spot. Frank tells us what he wants for breakfast, and Rayo and I go inside to wait for him while he calls Mateo.

It's not long before he joins us in our corner booth, and the waitress ambles over with a coffeepot to fill his cup and refill ours and says our food will be ready in a minute. He holds off on the particulars of the call until our plates arrive and the waitress again withdraws.

Because of our pledge of confidence to Aunt Catalina, he had to fudge the facts a little with Mateo, though he didn't like doing it. He told him we'd been engaged by an old friend of Harry Mack's, a Houston oilman named McCabe, to find his eighteen-year-old daughter, Kitty Anne. The girl ran away from home a couple of years ago, leaving a note saying not to bother looking for her, and hadn't been in touch with her family ever since. Then the day before yesterday McCabe received a call from a young woman in Los Angeles who said she was Kitty's roommate and best friend and frankly confessed they had both been working in porn films for the past year. She told McCabe that about a month ago she and Kitty had gone to a film production party in Tijuana, and Kitty took a shine to a man she met there, but it wasn't until after she and the man left the party together that somebody informed the roommate he was none other than El Chubasco. Neither she nor any of Kitty's other acquaintances has heard from her since. They all supposed she'd stayed in Mexico with him, but then they began to worry he might be keeping her there against her will. Kitty had confided to the roommate about her wealthy father and his many political connections in Texas, and the girl finally decided to phone him in the hope he might somehow be able to find out if Kitty was all right and help her if she wasn't. McCabe then hired us to try to find her and get her home to Houston, irrespective of her wishes.

Mateo agreed with Frank that it didn't look like a kidnapping or daddy would certainly have received a ransom demand by now. But he said we must owe McCabe a hell of a favor to get involved in something that could put us crosswise with the Sinas. He told Frank that just last week a Durango chief whose gang was suspected of trying to steal a Sina drug shipment had found a sackful of his men's heads at his front gate. However, Mateo said, since all we wanted to steal from Chubasco was a girl, we might not be risking the loss of anything but our dicks. Then he'd laughed and asked how he could be of help. Got a quirky sense of humor, Mateo, especially about death. That happens with some guys who have come as close to dying as he has. A couple of years ago in Mexico City he was seriously wounded, and if Rayo hadn't been on the spot and tended to him as capably as she did, he wouldn't be around today.

Frank told him we'd been informed that Chubasco has a residence in Ensenada but it's a good bet that like most cartel chiefs he has several other homes, too. Where are they? Does he have known routines? Favorite hangouts? We want everything Mateo can come up with that might help us find him so we can do a little close-up reconnaissance and see if the girl's still with him. Mateo said he was sure he could uncover that information and thought most of it might already be in the Jaguaro files. He said he'd get back to us at eight o'clock on the dot, our time.

* * *

In San Diego we buy swimsuits at a shopping plaza and then check into a beachside hotel – a room for me and Frank, another for Rayo. The place has a laundry service, and the maid says she'll have our clothes cleaned and back in the rooms in two hours. The sun's still fairly high and the sea breeze light when we carry folding lounge chairs and a cooler of pale ale out to the beach, Rayo's high-cut one-piece displaying most of her glorious butt and attracting lots of attention even in the swarm of pretty women in skimpy swimwear. The waves are large and breaking loudly, two or three dozen surfers having a grand time. We open up the chairs and uncap some bottles and fully relax for the first time since leaving Texas.

I nod off before I finish my ale, and when I open my eyes again Frank's dozing in his chair, an empty bottle next to it. I hear Rayo's laughter from out on the water and have to scan hard before I spot her. She's on her stomach on a surfboard at the fore of a growing wave and paddling hard with her hands, several surfers flanking her to either side and doing the same. When the guys flex up onto their feet, knees bent and arms out, she does, too – and lets out a gleeful yowl as the wave swells higher under her and gains speed. She told me once that she'd always wanted to try surfing but had never been to a beach with adequate waves. Now the one she's riding begins to crest, and she maneuvers the board left and right with shifts of her weight and rides down the wave's face with as much panache as if she's been doing this all her life. The wave breaks and she rides the foamy rush all the way into the shallows, nimbly hops off into knee-high water, and grabs up the board.

'*Wa-hoo*, Pixie!' one of the surfers yells at her. 'Third try's the winner, babe! You *rock*!'

She tucks the board under one arm, raises a fist, and shouts, 'You guys are great teachers!'

'One more!' another of them calls to her, but she laughs and waves so long. She slogs out of the water and goes over to a tall, bearded guy off to our right who's been standing there watching her. She hands him the board, saying, 'Thanks for the loan!' They bump fists and he goes off with his board. She comes over to me and I hand her a towel.

'*Pixie?*' I say.

'The surfer name they gave me,' she says, grinning wide with the excitement of the ride. 'Because of the haircut, I guess. Little embarrassing, the wipeouts the first two times, but I *knew* I could do it on the next one.'

'I missed the wipeouts,' I tell her, 'but I woke in time to see that ride just now. Damned impressive for a rookie.'

'Hear, hear,' says Frank, who's awake and smiling. He opens an ale for each of us and we toast her triumph. The breeze has picked up, and she wraps the towel around herself from armpits to thighs. We sit on the lounge chairs and sip our ales and watch the surfers begin to thin out, carrying their boards over to a nearby parking lot.

'I don't know about you guys,' Rayo says, 'but I'm so hungry I could eat this chair if I had a little salt to put on it.'

We rinse the sand off us under the hotel's beach showers and repair to the rooms to get dressed, then amble down the street a few short blocks to a seafood diner the desk clerk recommended. We pick a window table overlooking the ocean and begin with a pitcher of beer, platters of raw oysters on the half shell, and bowls of peel-it-ourselves boiled shrimp. For main courses we order steamed crab claws, fried scallops, and grilled swordfish and share the dishes with each other. It's a nice place, small, not at all loud, and we linger over the last of the beer before heading back to the hotel.

The street traffic is thick with tricked-out wheels of all kinds but heavy on low-riders and jacked-up pickups, most of them packed with high school or college kids, their speakers blasting a hodgepodge of pop-music styles. A lifted Chevy truck with a front-fender flame job slows down as it comes alongside us. A Latino kid sticks his head out the passenger window and calls out, 'Hey-hey, *yo*, mamacita! You are *sooo hot*!' He looks about seventeen and is wearing a baseball cap backward. Rayo smiles without looking his way. I step around her to the curb side of the sidewalk and stare at him. He grins, points at me with both index fingers, and shouts, 'You *lucky fuck*!' And the truck guns away.

She gives me one of her sly smiles. 'I'd say that young man has your circumstance pegged perfectly.'

* * *

The sun has set when we take the lounge chairs out on the beach again and sit ourselves facing the fading pink streak along the ocean horizon. The dusky shoreline is now deserted except for us and a few couples strolling by hand in hand. It's exactly eight o'clock when Frank's phone hums. He checks the screen, nods at us, looks around to see if anyone else is in earshot, and says into his phone, 'Hey, cuz, what's the story?'

He listens, then tells us to get out our phones for a group call. Mateo wants us all to hear his report together, the better to avoid mix-ups. My phone buzzes faintly and my screen shows his number and the alias under which he's in my contacts roster. 'I'm on,' I tell him. A few seconds pass and Rayo's phone beeps low and she answers, 'Bueno, cousin.'

Mateo says for us to hold off on questions until he's finished, then does all the talking for a while. He tells us Chubasco has four residences, two of them on the

Baja peninsula, and that we were correctly informed that one of them is near Ensenada. That one's a large seaside ranch called Vista Pacifica, a few miles south of the city and just off the coast highway. Its deed is held by the CEO of a multinational investment corporation. The ranch perimeter is lined with multiple types of alarms and a triple row of barbed-wire fencing – the middle row electrified – and is patrolled around the clock by armed crews in Jeeps. Chubasco usually takes his Sinaloa people there in a pair of private planes that land at the airstrip of an aircraft parts factory a mile south of the ranch. The other Baja place is named Finca de Plata and is in the southern part of the peninsula, deep in the state of Baja California Sur. It's an old hacienda and silver mine up in the mountains, at the end of a rugged trail that winds almost thirty miles up from the nearby gulf coast city of Loreto. It's a tough drive with no guardrail on it. Because the Finca compound is so much more difficult to access than any of Chubasco's other homes, it's also much easier to defend against attack, for which reason it's reputed to be his favorite. The place is completely enclosed by high stone walls, and its entrance gate – a huge thing of iron bars – is the only way in or out by vehicle. Chubasco used to go up there by helicopter, but those mountain winds are unpredictable, and last year his chopper nearly crashed in a rough-weather landing that broke a skid and scared living hell out of everybody on board. That was it for going to the Finca by helicopter. Now he flies to a private ranch about twenty miles north of Loreto, and from there to the Finca it's strictly by wheels. His other two domiciles are a hacienda in the foothills of the western Sierra in Sonora state and a mansion on sprawling grounds in Culiacán. All his compounds have resident girls and guards. He moves from one place to another pretty much at random except for the Baja places, both of which he always visits two weekends a month. The Vista Pacifica ranch is within easy proximity of the various headquarters of his top Sonora and Baja subchiefs – the guys in charge of his most valuable smuggling routes and who operate the outfit's biggest meth labs. Ever since last year, when an upstart Tijuana outfit called Los Fuegos began trying to cut into some of the Sinas' routes, those regional chiefs have become more important to Chubasco than ever. He likes to get together with them at Vista Pacifica on every other Friday to discuss business and do some partying. Today is one of those Fridays, and he and those cronies are there right now. Most of the subchiefs take their lieutenants with them, and Chubasco always takes along a group of women from his stable in Culiacán to supplement the girls who live at the ranch. In order to ensure a variety in women every couple of parties, he tends to take his most recently acquired girls – which is why, if Kitty McCabe is still with Chubasco and has found favor with him, there's a good possibility she's among the girls he took to the ranch this time. It's of course also possible that she won't be with the group or isn't even with Chubasco anymore. It shouldn't be hard to find out, though, because part of the Ensenada routine is that, on the Saturday morning after the party, all the girls, sometimes as many as two dozen of them, are taken to a high-end mall in town to spend freely for three hours on lines of credit arranged by Chubasco. They go there in several vehicles with Sina escort crews, who wait outside the mall while the girls do their shopping. While that's going on, another crew goes off to collect a bimonthly shipment of meth from the Sinas' regional lab, which is rumored to be somewhere east of Ensenada, way the hell out in scrub and vineyard country. The place is so well concealed that even Jaguaro scouts haven't been able to find it. In any case, the meth pickup is never made there but always at some different transfer point. The collection crew then goes back to the mall and waits with the escorts until the girls are ready to go. When the convoy gets back to the ranch, Chubasco distributes the meth load among the subchiefs charged with smuggling it into the States along the border from California to the Texas Big Bend, and those guys take off. The remainder of the group – Chubasco, the Culiacán women, a few other subchiefs – then go off to spend Saturday night at Finca de Plata. Next day they go down to Loreto and fly home from there. Mateo gives us the address of the Ensenada mall and says it opens at nine and the party girls usually get there just before the doors are unlocked. They shouldn't be hard to spot, all those great-looking women arriving together at the front steps of the place in a line of vehicles. If the Kitty girl's not among them, then that's that and we might as well go home and break the bad news to her daddy. But if she's with them, then all we have to do is spirit her away without her or any of the other girls raising a fuss and attracting the attention of the escorts, who won't hesitate to shoot us on the spot. If she's with the group but we aren't able to get her away from it, and if we're still alive after the Sinas leave town – Mateo *laughs* when he says that – he wants us to know he remains ready to help us out any way he can.

'That's it,' he says. 'Questions?'

'Yeah,' Frank says. 'How'd you get all that so fast? I mean, your intel system's always been A-number-one, man, but it's become nothing shy of stupendous. You could probably subcontract with the CIA.'

Mateo chuckles. 'They couldn't afford us, Frankie. As you know, we keep files on all the outfit chiefs. There are inside people constantly reporting about them to others who in turn report to us. As I expected, all the information I just gave you was already at hand. Inside people, man – the best of all assets in this brave new tech world.'

'Where are you?' I ask.

He's in Guaymas, on the eastern coast of the Gulf of

California, also known as the Sea of Cortéz. The town's around 400 miles from Ensenada as the crow flies and something like 130 from Loreto. He had to go there on business and will stay another few days. A small security crew is with him, and in addition to ground transportation he has a helicopter and a speedboat at his disposal. 'Just so you know the resources that are fairly close to hand, should you for any reason require any of them,' he says. He also has some resident agents in Ensenada, not many, but all highly capable. By sunrise tomorrow, two of them will be keeping a telescopic eye on Vista Pacifica's front gate from a woody hilltop a quarter mile east of the coast highway. Another Jaguaro, one familiar with Chubasco's planes, will be overseeing a sham road-repair gang working near the aircraft plant's hangars and with a clear view of the landing strip. 'Any of them see anything to report, they'll give me the word and I'll relay it to you.'

'I gotta say, man,' Frank tells him, 'you're going a lot of extra miles for us on this one.'

'Hey, you noticed. Well, truth be told, Frankie, this assignment of yours greatly appeals to me. How could a search for a beautiful girl *not* appeal to me?'

'Did I say she's beautiful?'

'You said she's eighteen and been working in porn, so what are the odds she's a mug? Whole new breed of women in skin flickery, my man. Almost nothing but superfine lookers. But I digress. The point is, don't hesitate to get in touch if you need anything more – transportation, money, whatever. And I mean *do not* hesitate. Meantime, you guys tread lightly and stay quick.'

* * *

As we head over to Rayo's room where she has all the maps, she says she's heard of the Tijuana bunch Mateo mentioned.

Los Fuegos. 'They're big on using incendiary ammo, right? It's why they call themselves the Fires?'

'That's them,' says Frank. 'According to Charlie they've come up with a custom rifle grenade that's smaller than most others on the market but has an equal penetration force and blast radius. Explodes about a millisecond after entering what it hits – vehicle, wall, whatever. A hell of a blast of steel frags and a flaming paste that'll stick to everything in splatter range.'

'How lovely,' she mutters.

In her room we open the most detailed of the Baja maps, lay out our route to Ensenada, calculate our drive time, and decide on our hour of departure. Then Frank and I split for our room and we all hit the hay early.

* * *

We're up and ready at sunrise. As we get into the Cherokee, Rayo says she was watching a TV weather report and heard that this was likely to be the hottest summer on record worldwide. Russia was having its worse heat wave in 130 years, and there were nearly a thousand wildfires burning in various parts of that gigantic country.

I ask if she happened to note what *our* weather was going to be.

'Sunny and hot,' she says. 'Duh, right? Since Baja's mostly just more desert. But they said there's a good chance of rain by this evening. Something about a weather system in the Pacific just a few miles off the lower peninsula. *Weather system.* Don't you love how those guys talk?'

* * *

We get breakfast sandwiches at the take-out window of the first fast-food place we see and eat them on the go. We've reckoned that the slowest part of the drive will be this first leg through the south end of San Diego and the congested San Ysidro Port of Entry, where we cross into Mexico and meld into the raucous jam of Tijuana traffic.

We soon arrive at a toll entrance to a federal highway that runs south along the coast. It's a winding, picturesque route of rocky shoreline, vast ocean, and pale blue sky showing almost no clouds at all. Gorgeous weather. As we cruise along the seaside road we discuss various stratagems for persuading Kitty Belle, should she be with the group at the mall, to come with us. We end up sticking with Frank's original idea – the offer of a fat contract to do an adult entertainment film – and embroider the pitch with a few more details. We know Rayo's our best chance for selling it to her, and we work out a mode of approach that includes references to our meetings with Lance and Dolan, the better to convince the kid of our bona fides.

'What if she's not interested?' Rayo says.

'Then wing it,' Frank says. 'Do what you have to. Just get her ass in this vehicle.'

* * *

We roll into Ensenada at a quarter after eight. Twenty minutes later I pay a taxi driver two hundred American bucks to let us have his curbside parking spot. It's under a tree near the top of a steep hillside street facing toward the fifteen-story mall on the far side of a four-lane north-south avenue. The building is fronted by a wide set of steps leading up from a semicircle driveway that right now is occupied solely by a pair of taxis. Our elevated vantage gives us an unobstructed view of it all, and the vehicle's dark glass prevents curious passersby from seeing Frank and me peering through binoculars back and forth between the mall driveway and the front doors, where a crowd of shoppers is awaiting admission. Rayo googled the mall as we came into town and learned that its driveway is restricted to taxis and to private vehicles showing a special permit on the windshield. Parking lots flank the other sides of the building. A short block to our right is an intersection with a traffic light and a pedestrian crosswalk. A longer block to our left is a similar intersection.

* * *

The shopping party from Vista Pacifica arrives about ten minutes before the place opens. Four dark-green SUVs – Lincoln Navigators – led by a bronze Chrysler 300 sedan and trailed by an identical one. The first three SUVs have plain glass, and through the binoculars we can see the girls inside, as well as the drivers and front-seat riders, but the glass of the fourth Navigator, like that of the two Chryslers, is too dark for us to make out the occupants. All the windshields show a driveway permit, and the convoy is waved into the curving driveway by an attendant. The only vehicle that doesn't pull in is the black-glass Navigator, which continues to the intersection on our right, then turns east and out of our view. We figure it for the crew going to collect the meth shipment. The rest of the party parks all in a row along the central portion of the driveway's curbside, which has apparently been reserved for it.

Two Sinas get out of each of the vehicles, ten escorts all told. They're all wearing sunglasses and baggy guayabera shirts. The SUV drivers open the rear doors and the girls alight – six of them from each vehicle. Some are in sundresses, some in jeans, all of them carrying tote bags. Their excitement's evident in the hand gestures, the energetic body language, as they start up the steps. Except for two men who stay with the vehicles, the Sina escorts go up with them. We work the glasses on the girls as close up as we can, but they're all facing away from us, their attention shifting about from one to another as they jabber. They're nearing the top of the steps when Frank says, '*Yes!* On the left flank! Pale green dress, only one that color. Hair's shorter than in the movie.'

I find the green sundress, its hem riding high on fine legs. Her hair's been cut in a shag similar to Rayo's and just about as short. She keeps turning to talk and laugh with a girl on her right and another a little behind her, giving me a clear look at her face.

'No question about it,' I say.

Rayo taps me on the head. 'Let *me*!'

I hand her the glasses. 'Far left side. Be quick, they're opening the doors. Haircut sorta like yours.'

She steadies the binoculars on my shoulder as the mall doors come open and the crowd surges through them. Then she laughs. 'Yep! That's her.'

'Let's hook up phones and get you going,' Frank says.

She phones Frank, then me, then curses for not having recharged her phone on our way here. I offer to swap units with her – mine's got plenty of juice and I can use hers while it's plugged into the dashboard and charging – but she says no. Her phone's smaller than either of ours and easier to hide. 'It's still got nearly fifty percent juice,' she says. 'That'll hold.'

She changes from her chambray shirt to a black tunic she had specially made for assignments like this. Like us, she's wearing her Toltec ID badge out of sight on her belt and has her Mexican carry permit in her pocket. She inserts audio buds in her ears and plugs their cord to her cellphone and slips the phone into a little pocket just below the front of the tunic's neck. The pocket's near enough to her mouth that we'll hear her clearly even when she speaks softly as long as she keeps her distance from loud noises. But because the tunic makes a holstered gun or one tucked in her pants too awkward for quick access, she takes out a small tote bag, shoves a wadded-up T-shirt into it to serve as a cushion for the gun and to disguise its shape against the bag bottom, then puts in the Glock and extra magazines. Frank and I have our pistols under our shirts. She hangs the tote on her shoulder and puts on an orange baseball cap and a pair of sunglasses. 'Okay, dudes, let's rock and roll.'

She gets out and strides down the hill to the avenue and then over to the intersection on our right and joins the waiting crowd at the crosswalk just when its light turns green. As she's crossing the avenue our phones are louder with crowd talk and the sounds of idling traffic. Then comes her clear voice – 'You read me all right?'

'Just dandy,' Frank says. 'If you hear me okay, give a wave.'

She pretends to wave at somebody down the street. Then she's across the avenue and mounting the steps.

The Sina escorts are lounging in the shade of an overhang near the mall entrance, smoking, batting the breeze, checking out the passing women, most of whom give them a wide berth and ignore their salutations. As Rayo nears the top of the steps, some of the men address her. Without slowing down as she passes, she points at one of them and says something and they both laugh. She puts a little more verve in her strut and the men applaud. Then she's in the building.

RAYO LUNA

She's taken off the cap and glasses and is murmuring to Frank and Rudy as she seeks after Kitty from floor to floor, bobbing her head rhythmically as though singing along softly to some tune issuing from the earbuds. The search is slow going. She consults the directory stand at each escalator landing, then makes a circuit of the floor to check out every jewelry shop, shoe store, and boutique on it, scanning the crowd closely as she moves through it. Given their loveliness and self-possession, most of the party girls are easy enough to spot as she makes her way up the floors.

'The flock has scattered all over the place,' she says. 'Mostly in twos and threes.'

When she'd studied Kitty through the binoculars, she had also focused on the girls nearest to her, the ones she'd seemed most vivacious with. If those were Kitty's close friends, then wherever in the mall she sees any of them, there's a chance Kitty will be nearby. By the time she arrives on the thirteenth floor – whispering, 'No fear of unlucky thirteen in *this* place' – it's after eleven and she's begun to fret that she's missed her, has simply failed to spot her on a lower level.

She checks a shoe store and two jewelry shops, then enters a dress boutique that's not very crowded and immediately spies a couple of girls she'd made special note of through the binoculars. They'd been babbling with Kitty in the animated way of good pals as they went up the front steps, and they're unmistakable, one with a black buzz-cut and wearing a flower-print sundress, the other with a short brown ponytail and in jeans and an LA Dodgers T-shirt. Taking a casual look around, Rayo doesn't see Kitty.

The two girls are browsing the cocktail dresses on revolving racks near the center of the store, the buzz-cut one with a tote bag on each shoulder, the other girl with only one bag. Ambling up to a neighboring blouse rack, Rayo whispers the situation to Frank and Rudy and tells them she's removing the earbuds to try to eavesdrop on the girls. She's affecting to look through the blouses when the buzz-cut girl holds a short yellow dress against her body and, addressing the other one as Rosa, asks her how it looks.

Ay, Lupita, that's so perfect, Rosa says. You *have* to try that on!

Lupita grins and hands the two totes to Rosa and heads off toward the left side of the row of dressing rooms against the far wall, apparently headed for the next-to-last room in the row, the only one whose door is open. Then the door of the last room opens and Kitty Belle comes out holding a black cocktail dress on a hanger, and Lupita stops to admire it.

'*Whoa!* She's here!' Rayo hisses into the phone. 'She was trying on a dress!'

Lupita holds up the yellow dress, and Kitty smiles and nods and says something, and Lupita grins and goes into the room and shuts the door. Now Rosa has seen Kitty and goes to join her at the register, where a clerk enters the sale and Rosa hands Kitty a tote to put the dress in. Kitty checks her watch and says something, and Rosa nods and they both give a little wave and Kitty departs. Rayo exits behind her, the buds in her ears again as she tells Frank and Rudy she's on Kitty's heels.

'I *know*, man, I've got a watch,' she says in response to Frank's reminder that the girls are due back at the vehicles in less than forty minutes.

* * *

She follows her down to a food court on the ground floor and stops to observe from a short distance as Kitty goes to the serving window of a concession. Her order – a clear-wrapped sandwich and a can of soda pop – is served on a small plastic tray, and she pays for it out of a wallet she takes from the tote, then carries the tray to an unoccupied table near the far end of the court.

Rayo tells Frank and Rudy she's removing the buds again so she can talk to the girl. She puts them into her phone pocket, then buys a cup of strawberry yogurt from the nearest stand and begins eating it with a plastic spoon as she casually ambles in Kitty's direction. She's almost abreast of her table when she stops and stares at her with feigned surprised. My God, she says. It's *you*!

Kitty looks up from her sandwich and says in her distinctive rasp, What's *your* problem?

Oh, God… I'm sorry, Rayo says. She casts a quick look around as if making sure there's no one near enough to overhear them, then steps closer to the table and says softly in English, 'You're *Kitty*, right?… Kitty Quick? Or Kitty Belle, last we heard.'

Kitty's expression becomes quizzical. 'You in the business? We ever work together or what? I think I'd remember.'

'No, no, we haven't. Jeez, I can't *believe* this. We got here yesterday and been looking all over town for you – theatrical agencies, photo studios, TV and radio stations. We've tried everywhere in town we could think of where you might've had some professional dealings, but we came up with nothing. We finally gave up this morning and were just about to leave, but my partners had to convert some money at a bank down the street and I came in here to get a snack and… *damn*, here you are! It's mind-blowing!'

'Who the fuck's *we*? And what do you want?'

Rayo takes another look around and says, 'May I sit, Miss Belle? I think you might be interested in what I have to tell you.'

'Oh, yeah? Like what?'

'Like a movie offer. One that will pay you very well.'

Kitty stares at her for a moment, then nods at a chair. Rayo pitches the rest of the yogurt into a trash can and moves the chair to within low-voice range of the girl.

She tells her that *we* is herself, Rayo San Luna, and her two partners, and that the three of them work as talent agents for an adult entertainment company in Texas. They're always on the lookout for new actors, and it so happened that just as the company was working out a deal to produce a sex-sword-and-sorcery flick called *Throne of Eros* for a satellite TV group, she and her partners saw *The Love Tutors* and were totally convinced that Kitty would be ideal for the lead part in the throne flick. They showed the producer the *Love Tutors* DVD and got a quick okay to look her up and see if she's interested.

'The producer said he wants me?'

'*She* wants you. Stella Lupino. Not many women honchos in this business, but she's better than most men. Great eye for casting. We knew she'd jump at you. And here's the best part… the job pays twenty thousand.'

'*Twenty thousand?* For a little skin flick? They make most of them in about a week.'

'This movie's several levels above most, and the company doesn't pinch pennies when it comes to getting what it wants. And Miss Lupino wants *you*. As it stands, the shooting schedule's around three weeks, maybe four. The thing is, shooting starts next Friday and the cast has to be in Dallas no later than Tuesday, just three days from now. Naturally all the contracts have to be signed and verified no later than Monday. Miss Lupino's already optioned a backup actress to play the lead if we couldn't find you, or, if we did, you weren't interested. But if you want the job it's yours, as long as we get you to the company office in Dallas by day after tomorrow, and we can do that.'

'How'd you know I was in Ensenada?'

'We didn't know, but it was the only lead we had. We went to Tucson to see if you were still with Mount of Venus, but Lance Furman said you'd gone to LA.'

'*Lance*,' Kitty says with a chuckle, and shakes her head.

'I *know*.' Rayo grins. 'You believe he wanted to put me in a movie?'

'Oh, God, yeah, I believe it!' Kitty says, and they burst out laughing. 'He's always on the watch for sexy girls. His eyes musta got *this* big when he saw you! He say he could make you a star?'

'He did, yes!'

They laugh all the more.

Rayo tells her that Lance put them in touch with Ben Steiner, who sent them to Nolan Dolan, who said he'd heard she'd gone to Ensenada with some Mexican big shot a few weeks ago. But that was all he knew. 'All that matters now is, do you want the job?'

'Yeah, I want it,' Kitty says. 'But I have to tell you, that one movie's all I'll do. Sometimes they want you to sign a contract, says you're gonna do two or three or however many, but I'm only gonna do this one and that's that. That's all I'll agree to.'

'Okay. If that's what you want, no problem.'

'Hey, look, I won't bullshit you. I always liked sex, right from my very first time when I was fifteen. And when I did my first sex movie, the one with Lance, I really loved it. To get paid so good for doing it in a movie with nice, good-looking guys seemed like the best job in the world. I mean, yeah, Lance can make you roll your eyes with some of the stuff he says – *you* know that – but he always made the job fun. And most of the other actors were new to the business, too, and were great to work with. We joked around and laughed a lot between takes and felt sorta close in a way that's hard to describe, but still it's true. One of the girls even admitted she'd once had to do a little hooking for a while and said making sex movies was a thousand times safer and could never ever be as lonely as hooking. Anyhow, right after that movie for Lance, I went to LA where I knew the pay was better, and I made a couple of movies for Nolan Dolan. But it wasn't the same. The pay was better, yeah, but nobody joked much and everything was all the time strictly business. I still liked it in some ways, but in some ways it pretty soon started feeling different even though I couldn't say why. Then one day when I was making the second movie for Dolan, I was watching them film a scene where this girl was doing three guys at once. I'd done two at a time but never three, and I'm watching her real close and she suddenly gets this *look* on her face that… ah, man, it made me feel awful bad for her. Like I was seeing something about her that was way more, I don't know, *personal*, more… *private* than even her pussy could ever be. I knew the final cut of the movie wasn't gonna include that look, and I couldn't help wondering if I was gonna get it, too, or maybe sometimes already did and didn't even know. All I knew was that whatever she was feeling just then was something I didn't *ever* want to feel. She wasn't but a coupla years older than me. Ah hell, I wish I could explain it better.'

'I think I understand,' Rayo says.

'Anyway, that's when I started to hate sex movies. But see, as much as I hate them, I'll damn sure make one for twenty thousand dollars, because with that much money I can take care of myself awhile and maybe even –'

She suddenly focuses her attention on something behind Rayo and flaps her hand at it in shoo-away fashion. Rayo turns and sees Lupita and Rosa staring at them from the entrance to the food court, Rosa scowling at Kitty and tapping a finger on her wristwatch. When Kitty gives them a more vigorous hand flap of dismissal, Rosa responds with a hand sign of 'Up yours,' then tugs Lupita away by the arm, and they stalk off into the crowd.

'Sorry about that,' Kitty says. 'Friends of mine, but they can be a real pain in the ass.'

'I totally understand, Miss Belle. I have a pair of friends exactly like that. Anyhow, you set to go?'

'You can call me Kitty. Down here they call me Gatita. And yeah, I'm set to go but, ah, did Dolan tell you the name of the fella I came down here with?'

'Yeah, honey, he did. I didn't want to bring it up if you didn't.'

'Chuy was awful sweet when we met. He asked me to come stay with him as his guest for as long as I cared to and said he'd pay for everything and I'd have nothing to worry about. I knew it meant having sex with him whenever he wanted, but I figured that was better than staying in sex movies, so I said okay. It didn't really surprise me when I saw he had a lot of other girls living with him, too. To tell you the absolute truth, I was glad I wasn't the only one. And I gotta admit he's real generous. Lets us buy clothes at some real nice stores in Culiacán and like today at this place. What I'm saying is, it was all pretty okay for a while. Then one night we got in an argument about something, and in the middle of it he told me to suck his dick and I told him to suck it himself, and he grabbed me by the neck and said if I ever talked to him like that again he'd let every one of his men fuck me and then, if I made him mad enough, he'd give me to a guy he knows who makes snuff films. You know what that is, a snuff film?'

'Yes.'

'The awfullest thing, see, is that once you been so scared that way by somebody, you can't really feel about him no other way after that, not even when he's being nice. Ever since that night, I'm all the time scared of him. About the only time I have fun and don't feel really nervous is when I go shopping with the other girls or there's a party and I can dance. I *love* to dance. The bad part about a party, though, is I gotta have sex with any guy who wants it. I guess that's a funny thing to complain about, huh? Seeing as I've been in those sex movies.'

'That's all done. You're coming with us.'

'Well, hey, I really want to but there's a problem. Some of Chuy's fellas are waiting out in front for me and the other girls, and they're not about to let me go off with somebody else, especially not some strangers.'

'Don't worry, sweetie,' Rayo says, and pats her hand. 'I've gotten to know this place. We'll leave by a side exit and give them the slip.'

'Think we can? Oh, man, if they catch me trying to –'

'They won't. I'll give my guys a call and we're on our way.' She glances at her watch and takes out her phone and is irritated by the screen warning that the battery power is now nearly drained. She puts in the earbuds, telling Kitty it's so she can hear better in all the food court noise, then pretends to tap a few numbers and says, 'Come on, man, answer.' Rudy's voice says, 'Well done,' and she tells him to pick them up at the building's north door, which is nearest to the food court.

'All right, amiga,' Rayo says, putting the phone and buds back in the tunic pocket, 'let's hit the trail.'

As they head for the food court exit Rayo asks her how old she is.

'Seventeen as of two months ago. How about you?'

'Twenty-seven.'

'*Really?* I *never* woulda guessed you're that old. You sure don't look it.'

'Thank you so very much.'

'And hey? I been wanting to tell you. I like your haircut.'

Rayo laughs. 'Yeah? That's cool, kid, because I like yours, too.'

RUDY

The sun's past its meridian but we're in good shade, and a breeze has kicked up and we've lowered the front windows about halfway to let it flow through. We've taken turns getting out to stretch our legs and take a piss in the restroom of the coffee shop down the street, but the wait's making us a little antsy. As we've listened to Rayo's talk with Kitty, we've been keeping close watch on the mall entrance. Most of the girls, a dozen so far, have returned to the vehicles and been divvied into the two Navigators parked just ahead of the rear Chrysler. Behind that Chrysler is the black-glass Navigator, which ten minutes ago got back from wherever it went to make the meth pickup. It pulled in at the tail end of the line of vehicles, and four guys got out and traded fist bumps with some of their fellows. All the escorts are now loitering down near the vehicles except for two guys still up by the front doors and waiting for the last of the girls.

Three more party girls come out the front doors, and the escorts up there – one wearing a New York Yankees cap, the other a white narrow-brim Panama – gesture for them to hurry on down to the vehicles, where they're directed into the Navigator directly behind the lead Chrysler. Two minutes afterward another two girls emerge, one of them with a buzz-cut who had been impossible not to notice when the girls first arrived and we were glassing them in search of Kitty. The Yankee-cap guy gives them a palms-up shrug as if he's asking something, and the buzz-cut's ponytailed pal answers him, looking pissed off and pointing back at the front doors as she speaks. Whatever she says clearly irks the Yankee-cap guy, too. He says something to the Panama hat guy and then heads into the mall as the Panama hat conducts the two girls down to the forefront Navigator.

'What's all that, you think?' I say.

'What else? It's time to go and they're still a girl short, so the guy's gone to fetch her. Christ. We can't give Rayo a headsup, she's not wearing the buds. We better quick –'

He's cut off by Rayo telling the girl she's going to give us a call and then pretending to and urging us to answer. I tell her she's done well, and she says to pick them up at the north doors and I say we're on the way.

'Let's get over there,' Frank says – but as he reaches for the ignition, there's a sudden and sustained blaring of vehicle horns from the intersection on our right, where we'll have to make the turn to get to the mall parking lot and the building's north doors. The avenue light is green, but a pair of black Yukon SUVs side by side at the head of the southbound double lanes aren't moving. Because horn blowing is something of a national pastime among Mexicans, who rarely step on the brakes ahead of leaning on the horn, the hubbub is drawing scant notice from avenue pedestrians or the Sinas at the driveway.

Now the green light's flashing to signify it's about to turn yellow, but still the Yukons don't budge and the squall of horns gets louder.

'The hell're those Yukes doing?' I say.

We put the binoculars on them and see they've got black glass. The light changes to yellow and the Yukons start across the intersection in no hurry at all. And now we see two silver Yukons directly behind them. They've got black glass, too, and start creeping toward the intersection, then abruptly stop, the drivers behind them braking hard and laying on their horns even more furiously. Then the light goes red and the silver Yukes leap forward, leaving the traffic behind them stuck at the stoplight as they speed across the intersection just ahead of the coming cross traffic, which also gives them a lot of angry horn blares.

'Kids getting kicks?' I say.

Frank shrugs.

The black Yukons slowly roll by the mall driveway, the one in the outside lane moving over behind the one in the inside. When they come abreast of the driveway exit, they halt, blocking it off. At the same time the silver Yukons come to a stop about ten feet shy of the driveway entrance, the Yukon in the outside lane almost a full length ahead of the one closer to the curb. It takes me a moment to recognize it as a common attack alignment that affords both a wider barrier of defense and a better field of fire to anyone shooting from this side of the vehicles, and it blocks both of the traffic lanes behind them. Frank's picked up on it, too, and says, 'It's a hit!' in the same moment that some of the Sinas point at the Yukes and start yelling in alarm.

Then everything happens fast.

All the Yukon doors facing our side of the avenue fly open and men spring out, nine or ten, including the drivers, all of them armed with AK-47 rifles, some of which have a grenade launcher attached under the barrel. '*Fuegos!*' Frank says as the Sinas scramble for cover behind the vehicles and grab for their guns under their guayaberas. But before any of them can get off a shot, a Fuego fires a grenade through the back window of the black-glass Navigator carrying the meth load and God knows how much gasoline – and a bright orange blast bucks the vehicle off the ground, blowing off its doors and making spray of its glass. The Navigator crashes on its side in a raging fireball, and the Chrysler in front of it is also hit with an incendiary and explodes into flames, and then the two Navigators ahead of the Chrysler – each one holding six girls – blow up almost simultaneously. Through the dense black smoke and roiling flames we see at least half the Sinas sprawled on the sidewalk, on the steps, their clothes smoldering, their hair. There's a swelling chorus of terrified shrieking from all along the avenue. Traffic's at a standstill at both the right and the left intersections, vehicles being abandoned in the street, people fleeing in all directions away from the mall driveway. The Fuegos are now cutting loose with automatic fire, and the Sinas who are still able are fighting back with handguns, both factions ducking and sidestepping, trying to get clear shots at each other from around the burning vehicles while maintaining cover behind them. A Fuego with a ready grenade launcher peers over the hood of a Yukon and starts to take aim, but his head snaps back and he drops in a slack half-turn. The Chrysler at the head of the Sina convoy pulls away from the curb and zooms toward the exit and the foremost of the black Yukons blocking it. A trio of Fuegos sprint away from the Yuke as others drill the Chrysler with automatic bursts just before it rams the Yukon aside and then swerves across the empty northbound lanes to this side of the avenue, crashes into a sidewalk tree, and bursts ablaze.

The only Navigator still intact and not on fire contains the last five girls to exit the mall. It's now at the forefront of the burning row of vehicles and the nearest to the driveway exit, but the Fuegos either can't see it for the flames and smoke or are out of incendiary rounds. Sidling toward it are the five or six Sinas still on their feet, a couple of them being assisted by comrades, all of them crouching low and out of the Fuegos' line of sight.

'The entrance!' Frank says, his binoculars on it.

I take a look and there's the Yankee-cap guy. He's got a pistol in his left hand and is holding a girl close to him on his other side, but we can't see her face until they start running toward the far end of the steps and a thick, bordering row of palm trees that slopes down a knoll all the way to the sidewalk. 'Kitty!' Frank says at the same time I recognize her. I cut the glasses back to the mall doors to look for Rayo, but there's nobody else there. It wouldn't surprise me if she'd risk coming out into the war zone, but I'm hoping like hell she doesn't. I grab up my phone and yell, '*Rayo!* You hear me? *Rayo!*' Nothing.

We both scan our glasses along the full length of the front of the building but see no sign of her. Police sirens are closing in from every direction.

The Yankee-cap guy and Kitty are barely detectable in the shadowy palms as they scuttle their way down through them and then we lose them altogether behind a hedge at the bottom of the steps. But in a moment the guy's head pokes around the end of the hedge as the other Sinas are piling into the remaining Navigator. Tugging Kitty along, he runs out to the vehicle, his mouth working, shouting. The door starts to close and then swings open again and the Yankee-cap guy shoves Kitty inside and dives in after her and the door shuts and the Navigator wheels into the gap between the exit and the black Yukon with the bashed-up front end. It hits and dislodges the Yuke's front bumper and speeds toward the south intersection and the stalled traffic facing this way as volleys of AK fire form pale starbursts on its bulletproof back window. A Fuego runs over to the guy sprawled in blood beside the AK with the ready grenade. He grabs up the weapon and takes hasty aim and fires at the escaping Navigator as it makes a hard right turn at the traffic light and the grenade misses and detonates against a garbage truck across the intersection. The blast jolts adjacent vehicles and sets some of them afire.

The Navigator's gone, the sirens getting louder.

Frank turns to say something – then his eyes cut past me and he grins big.

The rear door jerks open and Rayo slides in and slams

it shut, shrugging the tote off her shoulder and taking her phone out of the tunic pocket even as she's saying, 'My stupid no-good fucking battery died and I couldn't tell you I lost her! I told her stay there, stay right there, don't move, I'll be *right back*, and I go off and come back and she's gone who the hell knows where. I wanted –'

'She's okay but they got her back,' I say. 'One of them went in after her and came out with her. They took off in a vehicle with some other Sinas and got clear. Only ones who did, them and a few other girls.'

She flops back in her seat with her hands over her face and lets out a long breath. Then sits up and passes me her phone and asks me to plug it into the charger.

The sirens are piercing. Cop cars are picking their way through the jam of traffic both north and south along the avenue, ambulances behind them, TV news vans. Flashing lights everywhere.

Frank cranks up the Cherokee, saying we better clear out before they cordon off the area. He wheels a U-turn and then whisks us up to the crest of the hill and onto a connecting street that winds down past an industrial zone. A trio of cop cars goes wailing by us toward the mall. At the bottom of the hill we turn onto an avenue with an arrow sign advising that the bayside business district is nine kilometers ahead.

Rayo tells us she and Kitty were almost to the mall's north exit when they heard a lot of horn honking and her first thought was it might be a traffic jam that would keep us from getting to the parking lot. They went out and saw the lines of traffic backed up along the north side of the intersection, but they hadn't gone another ten feet before there was an explosion somewhere in front of the building and everybody around them started freaking. Then there were more blasts and gunfire, and people were screaming and running everywhere. She hauled Kitty back into the building, and they huddled against a wall not far from the doors, in case they had to exit fast. She tried to phone us and see where we were, but her battery was dead and Kitty didn't have a phone. The Sinas don't let the girls have them and punish anybody caught with one. So she told Kitty she was going to check things out and would be right back and made her promise not to move from where she was and she swore she wouldn't. Rayo then hurried out and ran along the wall to the front corner of the building, gripping the Glock in the tote and hoping like hell she wouldn't have to pull it. She peeked out and could hardly believe the carnage in front of the mall but was relieved to see the Cherokee still on the hillside. She figured she and Kitty could go a little way up the north side of the intersection, cut across the avenue through the stalled traffic, then make their way over to us. But when she went back the kid was gone. She tried looking for her but the ground floor was so packed with panicked people it was hopeless to think she might find her in that mob. Besides, what if Kitty took off *out* of the building? Who knew in what direction she'd gone? And what if Frank and I made it over to the north exit while she was out looking for the girl? All she could think to do was run back out to the avenue and work her way across it, hoping we wouldn't move from our hillside spot before she got to us. And here we still were.

'We *had* her,' she says. 'You guys heard. She was coming with us. What a dumbfuck I was to leave her alone for even a minute.'

'Not your fault the guy found her,' I say. 'You didn't want to risk her getting shot out there. The girls who saw her with you told the escort and he went in after her. Those guys probably know every foot of that mall. When he didn't see her in the food court or around the front doors, he knew the north exit was the next nearest. He went there, spotted her, and grabbed her. If you'd been with her, he wouldn't have hesitated to put you down.'

'That right? Well, *I* wouldn't have hesitated to put *him*

down. Listen, a couple of her pals saw her with me. One with black buzz-cut hair, one in a Dodger shirt. *They* come out?'

'They did,' I say. 'Went off in the same vehicle with her.'

'Ah, hell... They'll tell those guys she was talking to me.'

'So what?' Frank says. 'She'll tell them what you told her. You're a gringa in the porn biz who's seen her in a movie and was happy to run into her by chance and offered her a job. Nothing suspect about that. Chubasco knows she's been in skin flicks, probably seen her in some. Hell, he met her at Dolan's. She'll say when the explosions broke out and people started screaming and running around, the two of you got separated and she didn't know what to do but she sure didn't want to go out into the street. That's why she was where the escort guy found her. She's clever enough to come up with something that solid and simple, don't you think?'

'Yeah. Actually she is,' Rayo says, and stares out the window.

* * *

Along a bayfront street we spot a bar and grill that looks inviting – overlooking the water, outer deck with umbrella-covered tables and not a soul sitting at any of them, the parking lot half empty. We even find a shade tree to park under.

Inside, the place is dim and cool and full of talk about the violence at the mall. The counter stools are occupied by patrons enrapt by the large TV above the back bar. The volume's turned down but closed captions run across the bottom of a screen full of burning vehicles in front of the mall, ambulance crews collecting the dead and wounded off the street, some of the bodies charred, some still smoking, reporters babbling excitedly into the cameras. We order a pitcher of beer and take it out to the deck, which we have to ourselves, and sit at a table in a seaside corner. I pour three glassfuls and we all take deep pulls off them. Beer never tastes better – *nothing* ever does – than right after an extremely vivid reminder of just how suddenly things can take a mortal turn.

Frank's phone hums.

'Mateo,' I say. 'Heard the news about the skirmish and wants to see if we're among the quick.'

He checks the screen, nods at me, and says into the phone, 'I was about to call you... Yeah, we were. Practically had a front-row seat... Nah, we're fine... No bullshit, man, not a scratch among us. We're at a joint by the bay having a brew... Yeah, actually, we *did*. But they got her back while the fight was going on. Got her back without even knowing *we'd* had her... Naw, she was fine. Last time we saw her, anyway. She and a few other girls were in a vehicle that got clear.'

He then listens for at least a minute without looking our way or injecting a word other than 'yeah' or 'right.' Then says, 'Hold on. I'll run it by them.'

He tells us Chubasco must've been notified of the attack even while it was happening. The hilltop Jaguaros staking out Vista Pacifica saw him and some of his people – men and women both, some of the guys carrying automatic weapons – come out of the house and get into three white Chevy Tahoes. They stayed put, though, until a green Navigator with shot-up rear glass came wheeling up to the front gate and was waved through by the guards. It parked out of sight behind the house, and then a small bunch of men and women came running around to the Tahoes and got in, and off they all went down the road toward the aircraft plant. Shortly afterward Mateo's man working with the road crew reported that both of Chubasco's planes had taken off. Mateo then called a contact in Civil Aeronautics who was able to learn quickly that the two planes had filed plans for Loreto.

'Ten to one they're headed for the Finca,' Frank says. 'If

we want to try getting her back, Mateo thinks he can work out some kind of gun-delivery ploy to get us into the Finca tonight without any problem, but getting out of there with the kid or even without her could be a different matter. So… What do we want to do?'

'He really thinks he can get us in there?' I say.

'That's what he said. What do we do?'

'Get her back,' Rayo says.

Frank stares at her a moment, then turns to me.

'Ah, hell,' I say. 'Can't be any riskier than telling Catalina we failed. Let's get her.'

'It's a go,' Frank says into the phone. He listens, then says, 'Yeah, sure, no problem. We'll do it right away… No, what?' He looks around at the sky and says, 'Well, up here it's just another day in paradise. But what the hell, about the worst it can mean is we might get a little wet, right?… Okay, cuz, we'll be waiting.'

He puts away the phone and says, 'Could take him a few hours to set it up. When he calls again, he wants us to be someplace close to the airport.'

'What's he got in mind?' I ask.

'Didn't say.' He scans the sky again, then says to Rayo, 'By the way, you were right about us getting some rain tonight. That weather system in the Pacific you mentioned is now a tropical storm. It's clocking winds of fifty-plus and heading for Baja's south end. Mateo said they expect it to blow through the peninsula and into the Gulf. Then either it'll keep pushing east into the mainland and beat itself out or it'll cut north and come our way and probably get stronger as it does. The weather people aren't giving odds yet.'

'Just what we need,' Rayo says. 'One more thing to liven up our visit to Chubasco's place.'

'Not *our* visit,' Frank says. 'You're not going.'

'*What?* What're you – ? The hell I'm not going! How'd you come up with *that*?'

'Use your head,' Frank says. 'Even if the Kitty girl's cool enough to hide her recognition of you, as soon as either of those pals of hers saw you, that's it, we'd be had. As it is, none of the girls know me and Rudy, but Kitty knows you've got two male partners. That's our approach to her.'

'Look, Frankie,' she says, 'it's not a problem. I can wear a disguise, a wig. I can –'

'Don't talk like a dope, it doesn't suit you. Besides, you can't disguise that you're a woman. And when was the last time you saw a gun delivery team with one? And what if Chubasco wants a roll with you? You okay with that? What if he decides to share you with his troops? You willing to pull a train? Like hell. We'd have to fight and they'd kill me and Rudy right off and then gangbang you two or three at a time before snuffing you, too. Given those very real possibilities, cousin, you ain't going. End of story.'

She turns to me.

'He's right and you know it,' I say.

She gives me an exasperated look, then throws up her hands and says, 'Yeah, I know, I *know*. So what am I supposed to do while you guys are up there?'

'We'll see,' Frank says.

'I meant to tell you, Stella Lupino was a nice touch,' I say, trying to soothe her a little.

'Just popped into my head,' she says. 'I figured a woman boss might make the kid more agreeable to the whole thing. Not that she needed much coaxing, as you heard.'

'We also found it interesting that you've got a couple of pals who can be real pains in the ass just like her two buddies,' Frank says. 'We were trying to guess who you might've had in mind.'

'Oh, yeah? I guess I should've given a fuller description and said a couple of *dimwit* pains in the ass.'

* * *

As we pass by the bar on our way out, we pause to view TV footage of the smoking ruins of some street-front business. The captions identify the place as a Tijuana restaurant destroyed by a rocket attack a half hour ago. Among the known dead are a dozen members of the crime gang Los Fuegos, including its head man.

They shouldna fucked with the Sinas, the bartender says to the TV.

* * *

We've finished a leisurely meal at a restaurant three blocks from the airport and the sun's almost down to the sea when Mateo calls back. He directs us to hook up in a four-way connection and, as before, withhold all questions until he's finished his report.

He'd called a Jaguaro subchief in Los Mochis – about 150 miles east of Loreto, almost directly across the Gulf from it – to whom he'd sent a load of brand-new submachine guns the day before yesterday, and was happy to hear the subchief hadn't distributed them yet or even opened the crates. Mateo ordered him to ship the load via private charter and without delay to the Loreto airport, where it would be signed for by a Toltec Seguridad agent who would ensure its transfer to a certain vehicle in the terminal parking lot.

He had then phoned El Puño, Chubasco's number two man, and claimed to be Diego Soto, chief of the Sangreros gang in Juárez. The deception was necessary, Mateo tells us, because even if we don't succeed in getting the McCabe girl away from them, the Sinas are going to be infuriated by the attempt and almost certainly figure it for the work of whoever sent us to deliver the guns – and the last thing the Jaguaros need is hostilities with the Sinas. The Diego Soto pretense ensures that if the Sinas go after anybody, it'll be the Sangreros, which is nothing less than those

Juárez fuckheads deserve for playing out of their league.

He told Puño he'd gotten his phone number from Miguel Soto, his closest cousin, who had been the Sangreros chieftain until he and his brother were shot dead in their home last week by unknown assassins. Puño recalled meeting Miguel Soto at a Sina party in Ensenada not long ago. He and Chubasco had been introduced to him by Tico Ruíz, a subchief from Hermosillo who had since then also been murdered, his throat cut by a cunt who was quickly found and her remains fed to the crabs at a remote estuary. Mateo said he and Miguel had known Tico Ruíz for years and it was good to know his killer had been properly punished. And he was glad Puño remembered Miguel because, according to Miguel, Chubasco had been pleased to learn the Sangreros dealt in guns and said he was always in the market for submachine guns. He had told Miguel that whenever he had some for sale he should contact his segundo before offering them to anybody else, then told Puño to give Miguel his phone number. Puño said he remembered it all very well, and Mateo said good, because if Chubasco was still interested in submachine guns, he might like to know that the Sangreros had just come into possession of two crates of nine-millimeter Heckler & Koch MP5s with folding stocks, plus one crate of ammunition and one of forty-round magazines. They had acquired the shipment from a German connection working out of Central America and got it at such a bargain rate that they could in turn give the Sinas an excellent price and still make a profit. Puño asked how much for the load and Mateo told him and Puño said they had a deal. Mateo said good, but he wouldn't accept payment for the guns until Chubasco himself had examined them and was fully satisfied. Puño said that wasn't necessary because he had the chief's full authority to make weapon purchases for the organization. Mateo said he understood, but he was determined to establish the Sangreros as the Sinas' most dependable supplier of arms, and the only way he would ever sell guns to them was on the condition that their chief inspect them personally and even testfire as many of them as he wished before any money changed hands. Puño laughed and said all right, what the hell. If the chief didn't feel like test-firing, he wouldn't. He asked where the guns were right now. Mateo said in Baja Sur, in Loreto, because for reasons of his own, the German dealer had always found it most expedient to make the deliveries there for any Mexican buyer west and north of Durango City. However, the Sangreros were willing to relay the shipment from Loreto to wherever Chubasco might prefer to receive them. Puño said there was no need for that, Loreto was perfect. The chief was having a party tonight at a place not too far from there, and to get a load of machine guns at the fiesta would only add to his pleasure in the evening. He asked Mateo if *he* was in Loreto, too, and Mateo said no, he was in Juárez, and because he had been looking forward to meeting Chubasco, he was sorry to say that for reasons of other pressing business he would not be able to deliver the guns himself. But his two best men, Franco Gómez and Rudy Muñez – who at the moment were in Ensenada – could arrive in Loreto this evening sometime around seven, go pick up the guns, then meet with Puño and accompany him and the load to Chubasco. Puño said all right, and the meeting was arranged for eight o'clock at the south end of the Loreto marina parking lot. Mateo told him we'd be driving a black Ford Expedition with a white plastic baseball dangling from the inside rearview. Puño said he'd be in an orange two-door Silverado pickup with Maya Ingeniería and a La Paz address printed on both doors. The mention of La Paz shifted their subject to the tropical storm, which – if we hadn't heard (and we hadn't) – had given La Paz a beating and flooded most of its streets as it tore through town and then turned north on reentering the sea. It's holding to a northerly course almost directly along the centerline of the gulf, Mateo informs us, its winds gusting to more than sixty. If it holds to its present speed and heading, it should reach Loreto sometime around midnight. The weather guys say there's no way to know if it'll speed up or slow down, get stronger or slacken, turn left or right into a coast, hit Loreto directly or just pass by. When Mateo told Puño that even if the storm just brushes the town, it'll still give it a hard time, Puño said he didn't give a damn because by the time the thing reaches Loreto he and the Sangrero gunrunners will be up in the mountains, enjoying the chief's party.

As soon as he got off the phone with Puño, Mateo fixed us up with a flight to Loreto via Aerolíneas Vientos, a small charter airline owned by the Mexican Wolfes through front companies. He also arranged for one of his men to collect our Cherokee from the Ensenada airport and return it to Félix García in El Paso. We're to leave its keys with the attendant at the parking lot gate. Our plane is a small turbojet that can normally make the flight from Ensenada to Loreto in about an hour and forty minutes, but given the headwinds we're going to meet as we close in on Loreto, the trip will probably take close to two hours, maybe a bit more. Which is still soon enough to make the meeting with Puño. A man named Gallo with a black patch on his left eye will meet us at the Aerolíneas Vientos gate and take us to the Expedition. The shipment for Chubasco will be in it. Gallo will then guide us to the Loreto marina and point out where Puño's waiting.

'So,' Mateo says, 'there's your way *in*. Then all you have to do is find the girl and get out of there with her, maybe with the Sinas on your tail. God alone knows how you might do that, but I look forward to hearing about it.'

'I appreciate your confidence,' Frank says.

'Confidence, hell. Big-ass hope is more like it.' He tells us that if we somehow make it back to Loreto with the girl, we not only won't be able to fly out because of the storm – which is certain to shut down all air traffic – but won't even be able to make a getaway by road. There are only a few routes out of town, all of them simple to cover, and the main highway can easily be roadblocked at intervals north and south by state cops on the Sina payroll. The only possible escape will be by way of the Gulf, which is why a black thirty-eight-foot speedboat named *Espanta* and its two-man crew, Disco and Raul, will be waiting for us at the marina – Gallo will show us where. It's equipped with a self-bailing system and radar with a fifteen-mile range. The cockpit's big enough to carry four men, but we can jam Rayo and the girl in there, too. The trip across to our landing point is about 120 miles, but even though *Espanta*'s top speed on a calm surface happens to be 120 miles-per-hour, it sure as hell can't go even half that fast in a tropical storm, much less a hurricane. Disco's a top pilot, however, and Raul's a navigation whiz, and even in a storm they should get us across in about two hours. We'll be met by a helicopter and ground transport both. If the storm isn't a real monster by then, the chopper should be able to fly us to an inland ranch with an airstrip and a waiting plane that'll take us all the way to Matamoros. If it's too rough for the chopper, we'll be driven to the ranch.

'So,' Mateo says. 'Questions?'

'Nope,' Frank says. 'You covered the ball park.'

'Ditto,' I say.

'Well, I have one,' Mateo says. 'Rayo going to the Finca?'

'No,' Frank says.

'Good,' Mateo says. He suggests she wait for us at the boat. He's already told Disco and Raul to expect her. How long the boat should wait for me and Frank to return from the Finca is for us to decide.

'Sounds like a plan,' Frank says.

'All right, then, get moving,' Mateo says. 'Your pilot's waiting at the Aerolíneas Vientos counter. Javier Reyes.

He'll be in a 49ers jersey and Giants cap, what he always wears on the job. Dude's loony for Frisco. Hell, all pilots are loony. Good luck, cousins. Hope we talk again.'

* * *

We take off a little after five. We've left our bags in the Cherokee going back to Félix. Besides the pistols under our windbreakers and extra magazines in the pockets, we're carrying only our Mexican gun permits and Toltec IDs.

Even though the turbojet is a lot more powerful than the Wolfe Associates' twin-props, it's about the same size and its interior design is similar. The cockpit's open to cabin view and we can see Javier Reyes at the controls. He's a young, goodlooking dude, and while his interest in Rayo was very clear when we met him in the terminal, he's all business in the air.

Thirty-five minutes from Loreto the plane begins jouncing and the windows are suddenly streaked with rain. Just some of the storm's advance activity, Javier says. Minor stuff. It's moving up the Gulf but still a good way from Loreto. Twenty minutes later the plane's shaking more vigorously. Javier again apologizes for the turbulence and says we're almost there. He has a few terse exchanges with the control tower, and then, pitching and rolling, we begin our descent. The windows are blurred with rain. The windshield wipers beat against it with little effect. Javier tussles with the yoke and talks to the tower. He's flying strictly by instruments and tower instructions. By the time we can vaguely see the runway lights, I estimate we're well less than a hundred feet from the ground. We touch down with a small bounce, then roll smoothly. It's 7:11 by my watch. Slightly better time than expected. A truck with yellow roof lights leads us to the apron in front of the Aerolíneas Vientos gate at the far end of the terminal. We say so long to Javier, deplane into the gusting rain, and jog to the gate.

Gallo's just inside the entrance and greets each of us with an abrazo. A matching pair of gold canine teeth enhances the piratical impression of his eye patch. Everything's ready, he says, and leads us to a door marked solo personal autorizado. It's attended by a uniformed security guard who exchanges nods with him and lets us pass without a word. As we go down a long dim hallway, Gallo tells us the authorities have announced the airport will cease operations at nine o'clock. We come to an exit door manned by another guard. There's a large cardboard box on a table next to the door, and from it Gallo takes out hooded raincoats for everybody, including himself. No need to get any wetter than you already are, he says.

A small van's waiting just outside the building. We get in and the driver wheels us away to the parking lot.

* * *

The Expedition's parked near the exit gate. Gallo tells us it's got run-flat tires. If punctured, they will retain enough air to keep us moving at up to fifty miles an hour for at least another forty miles. The airbags have been deactivated so they won't hamper us if we have a minor collision that would set them off. The glass is bullet resistant, the radiator and engine block are shielded both front and sides with steel plates, the chassis's reinforced, and the iron front bumper could probably knock down a brick wall. The vehicle has a reworked ID and is registered to a nonexistent owner of a false address in the town of Tepic. It can be abandoned anywhere.

We pull up beside it and all get out. Gallo tells the driver he'll see him later, and the van leaves. We go around to the rear of the Expedition, the wind yanking at our raincoats, rain blowing off our hoods, and Gallo opens the hatchback to expose the tarp-covered shipment. There's a flashlight in there and he hands it to Frank, then draws the tarp aside and Frank runs the light over the four crates. The content information is stenciled in German, but it's easy enough to comprehend which crates hold the guns, which the ammo, which the magazines.

He tucks the tarp back in place, and Frank turns off the flashlight and leaves it there. Gallo shuts the hatchback and goes to the driver's side and extracts a plastic baseball from under the seat. It's attached to a little chain that he hooks to the rearview mirror. He takes a key from his pocket and asks who's driving and puts it in Frank's outstretched hand, then takes out another key and gives it to me. Spare's good to have, he says. I put it into the coin pocket of my jeans. Rayo's quick to claim the shotgun seat, Gallo and I get in back, and we head out of the airport.

The marina's only a short drive away. Gallo directs Frank to a small bridge just two blocks from the Gulf. It spans what looks like a churning river gushing out to the sea but which, he tells us, is only a shallow arroyo that's bone-dry most of the year. It will be running even stronger as the storm closes in. The latest updates say it's maintaining a northward course through the Gulf and its winds are now in the high sixties. We cross the bridge and cut over to a narrow road that runs along the seawall against which waves are spraying high. Gallo says he hasn't seen so little traffic in Loreto on a Saturday night since the last tropical storm that blew through here. We pass a plaza on our left where most of the windows have been shuttered or boarded up, though at some places workers are still laboring to install protective covering. The streetlamps are rain-hazed, the trees flailing, blown papers flapping in their branches. Trash cans tumble along the streets.

There, Gallo says, nodding ahead and to our right at a

throng of swaying boat masts in the glow of the marina lights. He has Frank pull over to the curb of the marina parking lot and near the pedestrian entrance to the dock area. He points northward at a brightly lighted billboard advertising a local brewery and tells us it stands at the far end of the marina lot and El Puño is waiting alongside it. Up the street and to our right is a lane that connects to the lot. Pointing in the other direction, he tells us the *Espanta*'s in a slip right beside the marina's entry to and from the Gulf. If the power's out when you get back, he says, just remember the boat's at the south-side dock and near the exit. He tells Rayo the *Espanta* crewmen are waiting for her, then wishes us the best of luck and exits the vehicle.

Hold on, Frank says. He gets out, and he and Gallo move off a short way. Frank does all the talking and Gallo now and then nods. Frank pats him on the arm and Gallo strides off into the shadows.

'What was that about?' Rayo asks when Frank gets back behind the wheel. She's taken off her windbreaker and tossed it into the back seat and now puts her raincoat back on.

'Just wanted him to know how much we appreciate his help.' He checks his watch and tells Rayo there's no telling how long we'll be in retrieving Kitty. The way he figures it, if everything goes without a hitch, we should be back sometime around eleven, but if we're not back by eleven thirty she's to shove off without us. 'We'll make it back home some other way,' he tells her.

'Yeah, right,' she says.

'I'm not joking, girl. The reports say the brunt of the storm will hit here around midnight. By that time you should be close to halfway across the Gulf. You better –'

'You better get going, what you guys better do.' She gets out and pulls the hood over her head.

'We're not there by eleven thirty, you split,' Frank says.

'You betcha.' She heads off toward the marina.

I take her place in the front seat. 'She wouldn't go without us.'

'I know,' Frank says. 'I told Gallo to call the speedboat guys and tell them if we're not there by eleven thirty they're to ignore whatever she says and cast off. Cuff her to the rail if they have to, at least till they're out in open water. Now let's meet our guy.'

* * *

As we approach the orange Silverado next to the billboard, we put our extra ammo magazines under the seats. A large man emerges from the driver's side and we see the maya ingenieria sign on the door. He puts his hands in the pockets of his black raincoat and watches us from under a crownless long-billed visor that bares his bald scalp to the rain. We stop near him and abreast of the truck.

'He didn't come solo,' I say, nodding at the dark form of a baseball-capped man sitting in the Silverado shotgun seat.

We get out, and the big man introduces himself simply as 'Puño' but makes no offer of a handshake and neither do we.

Let's have a look, he says, taking his hands out of his pockets. They're as large as we've heard, the biggest I've ever seen. In one of them is a short pry bar.

We go to the rear of the Expedition, and Frank opens the hatchback and pulls back the tarp and shines the flashlight on the crates. With a few deft moves of the pry bar, Puño unseals the lid of the gun crate, raises it, and takes a look inside, then puts the lid back in place and flaps the tarp back over the crates. Frank cuts off the flashlight and sets it down, and Puño shuts the hatchback.

You and me go in this one, he says to Frank. Your guy follows with my guy.

Fine, Frank says. He starts for the Expedition's passenger side but Puño says, No. You drive. I'll direct.

Frank shrugs and goes around and gets behind the wheel.

You're driving the truck, Puño says to me. The guy riding with you is Osmayo. Stay close enough for me to see you and don't use your brights. And hey, Osmayo doesn't like talk on the road, so don't irritate him with any. Let's go.

Osmayo looks at me as I get in. The light from the billboard lets me see the long hair from under his cap, his wide nose, a pencil mustache. He turns to stare out the windshield. He neither looks at me nor speaks as I crank up the engine and we get moving. Because I always like to know how far I've gone from one point to another, I set the trip meter to zero. As the Expedition exits the marina lot, the plastic baseball sails out the passenger window.

* * *

I trail them westward across town to the federal highway, then south and across a larger bridge than the one we crossed earlier over the same arroyo. The rain's rattling against the truck like gravel. Traffic has thinned to a meager scattering of slow-moving vehicles. I'm keeping within two to three lengths of Frank as he turns off the highway at the San Javier Road that bears west toward the mountains. We follow its gradual curve around to the southwest for a few miles before Frank makes a right onto a rocky trail that takes us into a narrow mountain pass. I'd bet my last dollar that only Sina vehicles ever come through here. It's an uphill route that becomes increasingly serpentine as it steadily ascends, and we're soon so deep in stormy darkness that all I can see before us is the Expedition's blurry taillights and the short portion of trail illuminated by my headlights through the glitter of the rain. We've seen our share of tropical storms along the South Texas coast and I've driven in most of them, but never on terrain like this. In places, segments of the shoulder on one side or the other have eroded away. The Expedition slows almost to a stop in order to negotiate a very tight turn, and now the road becomes even steeper and narrower and ruttier. Before long we're passing by sheer mountain walls barely ten feet to our right and by cliff rims about the same distance from us on the left. The curves are following closer on each other, and the Expedition's taillights go in and out of view. Our headlight beams at times glare against a mountain wall directly ahead but beyond the next sharp bend, and at other times lance out into the empty blackness beyond a cliff before they swing into the curve and brighten the trail again.

We've been driving an hour and covered a hair over twenty-six miles when I round another tight curve and see the Expedition come to a stop with its headlights blazing on the entrance to the Finca not thirty yards ahead. It's blocked by a barred double gate about a dozen feet high, set between higher stone walls, and manned by a pair of guards in a well-lighted shack just inside the gate and off to its side, a bright pole lamp over the door. I pull up behind the Expedition. Frank hits his brights on and off three times in quick succession – at Puño's direction, no doubt – and one of the double gates rolls open sideways just enough to permit a guard in a flapping slicker and tied-down cowboy hat to come out, a flashlight in one hand. He goes to the driver's window and shines the light into it, then waves at the other guard, and the gate opens wider to let us enter.

The guard in the shack is on a line phone as he watches us go by.

I follow the Expedition into the compound through the blowing rain and across an expansive courtyard – blurrily lit by tall lampposts and centered with a large stone fountain – toward the largest building in sight. It shows light in every window of both floors. In dimmer view are smaller buildings occupying farther reaches of the compound, but except for us and the gate guards there's nobody else in sight.

The big building is fronted by a circular driveway with a

porte cochere. About fifty feet beyond the drive are several rows of roofed parking stalls, most of them occupied and mostly with SUVs and pickups. We turn onto the driveway and park under the porte cochere, next to a set of low steps in front of a tall double-door entrance, one of the doors closed against the wind, the other open and projecting a broad shaft of yellow light. We all get out and Puño tells Osmayo to fetch some guys to carry the shipment inside, and Osmayo bounds up the steps and into the building. Through the drumming of the rain there's an audible resonance of rock music coming from the open door.

We'll join that party in a little while, says Puño. Right now I need to know if you guys are armed.

Yes, Frank says.

I'll hold them till you leave.

Your place, your rules, Frank says, and we hand him our pistols.

Good weapon, Puño says, looking the Berettas over. They seem much smaller in his hands, and I can't help thinking that the trigger guard would be such a tight fit for his finger he'd run the risk of an accidental discharge if he tried to stick it in there. He puts the guns into his raincoat pockets, and, as if he'd heard my thoughts, he draws his pistol from under his arm and holds it in the light for us to see. It's a Sig Sauer 226 with an extra-large trigger guard and an oversized butt that, in addition to accommodating Puño's hand, looks like it can take a doublestack magazine of at least forty rounds.

Nice custom work, Frank says.

Guy in Mazatlán did it, Puño says. Best gunsmith on the coast.

He returns the Sig to its holster and tells Frank to take off his raincoat and put his arms out and spread his legs. Frank stares at him a moment, then does it, and Puño gives him a quick, efficient frisk.

Trust but verify, eh? Frank says.

Puño shrugs and says, You know how it is. He turns to me and we repeat the process.

Osmayo comes back with eight men who make quick work of unloading the shipment, two men to a crate, then he drives off in the Expedition. As we go up the steps with Puño, the shipment carriers behind us, I note the general area of the parking stalls where Osmayo's parking the vehicle. So does Frank. Always know where your weapons and your wheels are. Basic rule.

We cross a spacious foyer, passing by a wide stairway to the second floor and by the open doors of a large room where all the good-time racket is coming from. I catch a glimpse of a busy dance floor in there before we turn off into a hallway, the first of a half dozen corridors we pass through until we come to one that ends at a closed door.

Puño opens it and we follow him into an anteroom of sorts. There's another door directly ahead, padded benches and hat stands along the walls, a table in the center where a red-haired guy wearing a sleeveless black T-shirt is sitting with a magazine. He hops to his feet, grinning broadly at Puño, and says, About goddamn time! We thought the storm mighta blown you away.

Never, Puño says as they clasp forearms in a Roman handshake. He opens the other door and tells the carriers to take the crates in and set them on table number one. He removes his raincoat and hangs it on a hat stand and indicates for us to do the same, then introduces the redhead to us as Rojo Romero, the resident chief of Finca de Plata when Chubasco and Puño aren't here. Romero gives us a nod and says he's glad to know us. Then we all go into the next room.

It's a very much larger one, comprising a shooting range of four parallel firing lanes about a hundred feet from a target wall at the other end of the room. The shipment crates, their lids removed, are on a sturdy waist-high table of unpainted wood against the wall to our left. An adjoining table holds a variety of gun-cleaning tools, solvents, and cloths; a metal tray full of individual pairs of earplugs in little ziplock bags; a cardboard box full of shooter earmuffs; and one containing chest-strap magazine pouches.

Puño dismisses the carriers and goes to a wall phone at the far end of the maintenance table. While he speaks into it in a muted voice and Romero busies himself loading one of the curved forty-round magazines, Frank and I take in the room. Unlike most ranges I've seen, this one has no individual shooting stalls along the firing line, just waist-high stands topped by small tables on which to lay a firearm. At the end of each lane, a white torso-silhouette target with a red heart about the size of an actual human heart in the center is attached to a frame connected to an electrically operated ceiling rail. By way of a button on the table stand, the shooter can retrieve the target or adjust its distance from the firing line. As at many indoor ranges, the walls and ceiling are padded to absorb the concussive blasts of gunfire and reduce the risk of hearing damage. On this side of the room are a few tables with chairs. Along the right-side wall is a small, untended bar lined with unoccupied stools.

Puño ends his call and begins helping Romero at loading magazines and putting them into ammo pouches. A minute later, the outer room door opens and El Chubasco walks in.

There's no mistaking him. Not after seeing his face in so many newspaper and TV pictures. He's said to be in his late thirties or early forties. Looks in good shape. Short and thickshouldered, pale-complexioned, bushy mustache, thick black hair. He's wearing running shoes, jeans, a blue-and-white baseball T-shirt with three-quarter sleeves, and a pistol in a harness shoulder holster. With him is a thin, sharp-faced man in a black tracksuit and black baseball cap. He, too, carries a pistol in a shoulder rig, plus a small brown bag slung on a strap.

Chubasco raises a hand in greeting to Puño and Romero; comes over to me and Frank, taking us in with a quick, intense once-over; and smiles wide. Welcome to Finca de Plata, my friends, he says as we shake hands. I am Jaime Montón. You can call me Chuy. Most of my friends do. As you know, we're having a little party tonight, and as soon as we finish our business here, we'll join it. Also, you will of course stay here tonight as my guests. The storm is terrible and may get worse. No need to go back to town until tomorrow.

We introduce ourselves, say it's an honor to meet him, and thank him for his hospitality. I now see his pistol's a ninemillimeter Browning Hi-Power. Good gun. The man in the tracksuit has closed the door of the outer room and positioned himself beside it. His weapon, too, is a Browning.

I was sorry to hear of the killing of Miguel Soto, Chubasco says. I met him only once, but I liked him. As you may know, Puño has spoken on the phone with Miguel's cousin Diego. He tells me he seems a capable replacement as the Sangrero chief.

He is, Frank says. Miguel and Diego grew up together and were close. Both good men, good leaders.

Glad to hear it. And glad Miguel told Diego of my interest in automatic weapons. Also, I must say that his refusal to accept payment until I have personally examined the guns is an unusual courtesy.

That's how he is, Frank says. Won't accept a penny until he knows the chief is happy with the shipment.

Chubasco goes to the crate of MP5s and extracts one. With evident familiarity he flicks open the stock and then locks back the charging handle. Puño hands him a loaded magazine and he snaps it into the gun, then takes a set of earmuffs from the box and gestures for Frank and me to do likewise and to come with him.

We go to the nearest firing lane and put on the muffs. He

sets the selective-fire switch on semiautomatic, slap-releases the locking handle to insert a round in the chamber, puts the stock to his shoulder, and with five fast trigger pulls delivers five rounds into the target. He presses a button on the shooting table and the retrieval rail brings the target to us. It has five small holes in the heart.

I give him a thumbs-up and Frank nods in agreement. Chubasco smiles and takes the target off the frame and replaces it with a fresh one from a stack next to the table stand. He presses the rail button and the target hums off to the end of the lane. He thumbs the selector switch and this time triggers a sequence of four three-round bursts through the target heart without a miss. He then sets the switch on full automatic and, in a single long burst, fires the twenty-three remaining rounds into the target. He brings it back to the firing line and there are no holes outside the ragged red-edged cavity where the heart had been.

We all remove our earmuffs and he says, Beautiful weapon. One of my favorites.

You handle it well, I say.

He looks at our empty holsters. Puño take your guns?

He did, Frank says.

Doing his job, Chubasco says. Come on.

We go over to the shipment table and he tells Puño to give back our pistols. Puño goes out to the anteroom, makes a quick return, and holds the guns out to us, not knowing which belongs to whom. I know mine by a scratch behind the front sight. Frank and I check the chambers for a seated round and then eject the magazines and hand-test their weight to be sure they hold a full load, then reinsert them and holster the guns.

Very wise, Chubasco says. Never trust a loaded gun that's been out of your sight to still be loaded the next time you pick it up.

He tells Puño and Romero to go ahead to the party and

we'll join them in a minute. Then calls to the skeletal man, Hueso!

He comes over, and Chubasco says, Give it to them and go.

The man takes the bag off his shoulder and holds it in front of him for either of us to accept. Frank takes it and the man departs. Frank unzips it, has a look inside, then zips it closed and hangs it across his chest.

Don't you want to count it? Chubasco says.

Would you cheat us and lose a reliable source of machine guns?

More wisdom, Chubasco says with a laugh. Assure Diego Soto that I'm always in the market for automatic weapons and I never cheat a seller.

We'll tell him.

All right, then, party time. And, oh yes… I should tell you that probably every man at the party will be armed. I have always permitted weapons at parties because you never know when another gang or the police or the military, *some* fucking enemy, might attempt to raid us, and we would not want to be unarmed if that happened. But at a party last year a couple of the boys got into a drunken argument at the bar and shot each other several times before they both dropped dead. A miracle nobody else was hurt. So I gave an order that nobody was ever again to pull out a gun at a party for any reason except defense against raiders. If anybody did, I myself would shoot him. I am pleased to say that, ever since then, only once has that order been violated.

Did you shoot the violator? I ask.

Of course. What good is an order that is not enforced? Now let's go have some fun.

* * *

We pass the stairway to the second floor and enter the party room and the reverberant blast of music issuing from large floor speakers at either end of a dais holding a DJ table. The dance floor takes up most of the center of the room and is packed with couples rocking out. Some of the partiers are at tables flanking the perimeter of the floor, drinking, laughing, conversing in shouts; some are at the bar along the back wall. Everyone's dressed as casually as Chubasco – guys and girls both. He tells us the girls usually prefer to wear their sexiest dresses, but they live in a dormitory at the far end of the courtyard and didn't want to get their party clothes wet in the storm.

The high windows brighten with a quivering pale glare of lightning. The thunder that follows is audible through the party noise.

Getting mean out there, Frank says.

No problem, Chubasco says. We have generators as big as trucks all over the place. Their fuel's piped from storage tanks way outside the compound. There's no way in hell a tanker truck can get up here, of course, so every now and then we send a bunch of SUVs to Loreto to fill up with gas and then transfer most of it to the storage tanks when they get back.

He exchanges quips with partiers as we cut around the dance floor and over to the bar. He orders a shot of gold tequila, so we do the same. To friendship! he says. We clink glasses and down the shots, then switch to bottles of beer. I spy Romero out on the dance floor, then follow Chubasco's gaze toward the far end of the room, where Puño and another guy at a table are waving him over.

Scout around, Chubasco says to us. Check out the girls. Do some dancing, have some fun. If you want to get laid, take one upstairs. The second floor is just for that. Nothing but bedrooms and a crew of maids to keep them clean and tidy all through the party. Now I have to go see about a few things.

He goes off to join Puño at the far table.

* * *

We stand with our backs to the bar, sipping our beer and casually scanning the dance floor and tables in search of Kitty – and work up a rough-draft escape plan, trying to keep to the basic rule that simple is best. We'll have to move soon and fast, while the storm can still give us cover but before it's too strong to drive through. Because hot-wiring a vehicle in the dark can be a bitch, Frank praises Gallo for having given me a spare key to the Expedition. What we need to know are the locations of all the building's outer doors and we're hoping the girl can tell us. If we try to leave by way of the lobby and front door – unaccompanied by Chubasco and with Kitty in tow – there are sure to be people who will want to know where we're going, and the jig, as they say, will be up.

Maybe she's not here, I say, low-voiced and sticking to Spanish because the sound of English might attract the curiosity of others nearby. Could be he didn't bring her and she's still in Ensenada.

Why would he leave her in Ensenada?

I don't know. But that doesn't mean he didn't.

We scan some more. No sight of her.

And then there she is. Not twenty feet off to our right. Among a bunch of dancers near the periphery of the floor. In running shoes and snug faded jeans and a purple T-shirt, slinging her hips and pumping her arms to the thumping beat, bopping with a long-haired Indian-looking dude she doesn't even glance at. She could be dancing by herself. The guy doesn't take his eyes off her.

When the number ends the Indian says something to her and jerks his head toward the bar. She says something in turn and does that little bounce-in-place move some girls do when they're entreating. He gives her an irked look and summons her with a hand flick.

He wants a drink, she wants to dance some more, I say, pushing off the bar.

Move, Frank says, deferring to me because I'm the better dancer of the two of us.

As I work my way through the tables flanking the floor, the Indian beckons her more forcefully, clearly angry now, and the DJ puts on a slow-dance tune. She makes a face and flaps her arms in resignation and starts toward him, but I intercept her as she comes off the floor.

Pardon me, miss. May I have this dance?

She stares at me blankly for a second, then returns my smile and says, Yeah, sure. She takes my hand with both of hers and draws me onto the floor.

Hey, you!

I turn and set myself as the Indian starts toward me. Then Rojo Romero steps between us, stopping him short.

She's with *me*, the Indian says to him. We were about to have a drink when this prick –

Enough, Vicente, Romero tells him. You know the rules. She can dance or drink with anybody she wants to, she can go upstairs with anybody she wants to. You don't like it, too bad. Go cool off.

The Indian gives me a 'Fuck you' hand sign and stalks away. The couples dancing nearest to us are grinning at the diversion.

Enjoy yourself, Romero says to me, and returns to his dance partner.

I cut a look at Chubasco's table. If he noticed the wrangle, he's already lost interest and is conversing with Puño. I take Kitty in my arms, and as we start dancing I tell her my name's Rudy and she smiles back and says she's Gatita. The slow dance is a timely break. It's softer music and we don't have to yell to hear each other.

Listen and don't stop smiling, I say to her. I'm one of Rayo San Luna's partners.

Her eyes go wide. *Rayo!* she says. My God! Is she all right? I was *so* worried she –

Easy, girl. *Smile.* And keep your voice down. Rayo's fine. She talked to the movie people and they're very excited you want the job. We're gonna take you to them.

You mean the job that pays twenty thousand dollars?

That's the one. But Rayo said Chubasco probably won't let you go, so we're not gonna ask him. I'm here with our partner Franco. Rayo's waiting for us in Loreto and we're taking you to her tonight.

Tonight?

Yes. *Smile* and don't ask questions, just answer. Do you know this building pretty good?

Yeah, I guess. Yeah.

What other exits are there besides the front door?

She says there's a side door at both of the far ends of the building and two other doors in the back, a wide one for big stuff like furniture and the kitchen's rear door.

Keep that smile going, I say. Besides the main staircase, are there other stairs between the two floors?

Yeah, there's a couple of little stairwells at either end of the second floor that connect to the side doors downstairs, she says. Some of us sometimes use them to leave a party and get back to the dormitory when it's real late and you don't want to go down the main staircase again, because you don't want to run into even one more guy who wants to take you upstairs. There's a little lavatory next to each of the stairwells, you see, and when you finish with the guy you're with, you tell him you have to pee real bad and you'll see him downstairs. You go to the lavatory door and look back to make sure he's gone, then you quick go down the stairwell and out the exit and hurry over to the dorm.

Is there a doctor in the compound?

Doctor González. Him and his nurse live in the clinic at

the corner of the courtyard, right next to our dormitory. Why? What's he – ?

Are the parking stalls on the same side of the building as your dormitory?

Yeah. On *that* side. She tips her head in the direction she means.

Perfect, I say. Now we need a girl for Franco so we can all four go upstairs at the same time. Some friend of yours. All you tell her is you're going up with a special guest of Chuy's you just met and that a friend of mine has been admiring her and would like to take her upstairs.

She looks around, then smiles wide and waves. That's Lupita, she says, and points her out.

It's the buzz-cut girl we saw at the mall. She's at a table with some people and waves back at Kitty and includes me in her smile. She's in jeans and a black buccaneer blouse with a thin red scarf around the collar.

The number ends. I tell her to get Lupita and meet us at the bar. Then I hustle back to Frank and fill him in fast.

The girls soon appear and Kitty introduces Lupita and I introduce Frank, and he and Lupita exchange grins. As we head for the door, our arms around the girls, Frank and I take a gander at the far table where Chubasco and Puño are looking our way. Frank pumps his fist high in a gesture of good-time camaraderie, and when the girls look over to see who he's looking at, I tell them to blow Chubasco a kiss. They do. Chubasco smiles and raises a fist in response.

Then we're out of the party room and ascending the big staircase, and I quickly tell Kitty what we're going to do.

* * *

The second-floor landing is at the center of a softly lighted hallway, the clamor of the party somewhat muffled up here by the rain's overhead pounding. At the ends of the hallway are the doorless thresholds to the stairwells. We're greeted by a woman Kitty addresses as Griselda and whose duty is to direct arriving couples to a room or line them up on the landing in ready turns as rooms become available. There's only one room ready at the moment, she says, and because Kitty and I preceded Frank and Lupita onto the landing, we get it. Number seven, she tells Kitty, who says, Thanks. As she starts to lead me to it, I grab my stomach and hunch over with a loud moan. She puts her arms around me, asking, What is it, sweetheart, *what*? Frank and Lupita come up and help her hold me up. Griselda rushes over and asks what's wrong.

Rudy just all of a sudden feels sick, Kitty says. I better get him to the lavatory before he throws up.

God, yes! Griselda says. Don't let him do it out here. Come, come!

She leads us to the lavatory at the end of the hall, but before we reach the door I slump against Frank and moan louder. *Jeeesus!* My *gut*!

He doesn't need to throw up, he needs a doctor, Kitty says. We better quick get him to González.

Griselda agrees, and Kitty says they can get me out of the building a lot easier by way of the stairwell than having to go through the crowd in the lobby. Yes, yes, Griselda says, and flaps a hand at us to hurry.

We go into the dimly lit landing and out of hallway view, then scurry down the stairs to the exit, Kitty behind me, then Frank, holding Lupita by an arm. *Hey*, Lupita says, he's not sick! What going on? Frank tells her to shut up. At the bottom of the stairwell he sits her down on a step and tears her scarf into two strips. He uses one to tie her hands behind her and around a baluster, then gags her with the other, placing it between her tongue and top teeth. She's wide-eyed and weeping. He kisses her on the nose and tells her not to worry, somebody will be along very soon and set her free.

* * *

We rush out into a darker night and stronger storm than when we arrived. No thunder and lightning now, just a ferocious wind and whipping rain that stings my face. In seconds we're soaked. The vehicle stalls are scarcely discernible as we advance on them, shielding our eyes with our hands, our heads bent into the storm. Kitty totters and falls to one knee and I snatch her upright by the back of her jeans. She clings tight to my arm as we stagger toward the section of stalls where we saw the Expedition get parked.

It doesn't take long to find it. Frank says he'll drive and I give him the key. When the door opens the interior roof light comes on and I break it with my pistol barrel. Then I go around to the rear of the vehicle and shatter the taillights as well. I tell Kitty to get on the floor behind our seats and curl up into a ball as tight as she can, then cover her with Rayo's windbreaker.

Franks backs us out of the stall, turns on the wipers but leaves our lights off, then slowly advances through the storm.

We go around the far side of the courtyard fountain, guided by the hazy light of the lampposts. There's no sign of anyone else out here. When we see that the big building's front doors under the porte cochere have been shut against the wind, Frank switches on the headlights and turns us toward the murky light of the front gate's guard shack.

As we approach the gate we can see the two guys at the shack window, watching us. Frank flicks the brights on and off three times. We're hoping the let-us-in signal also works for an exit. He pulls up a few feet from the gate and in the glow of the light above the shack door, the Expedition rocking in the pummeling wind. The gates don't open. Through the window we see one of the guards put on a raincoat and pull the hood over his head.

'Stay low and small, girl, and don't move,' I say.

The raincoat guy comes out, a hand in his pocket, Frank lowers the window a little, admitting a hard spray of rain, and says, What the hell's the holdup?

Need to give me your pass! the guard says shouting to be heard in the shrilling wind.

Pass? Frank says. Chuy didn't say anything about a pass when we said so long! Hey, we're the guys who just brought your chief a load of guns! Open the fucking gate if you want to keep your job!

We know who you are! the guard says. But nobody goes through without a pass! That's the order!

I lean over in front of Frank so the guard can see me better and to keep his attention from drifting rearward and possibly spotting Kitty. Hey, man, I say, we know you're just doing your job! That's fine! Let me call Puño on your line phone and he'll clear us!

Before he can say anything more I scramble out my door and start around the front of the Expedition, leaning into the wind, a forearm at my brow against the rain. I intend to disarm them as soon as we're in the shack and I'm sure Frank knows it. But the guard raises a hand at me and says, *I'll* make the call! Get back in the vehicle!

I halt and shrug and say, Yeah, yeah, all right! and take a step back, and the second he turns to the door I rush up and grab him in a bear hug from behind, pinning his arms to his sides, and start tugging him backward toward the gate. He writhes and bucks and tries to hit me with the back of his head, yelling, You're fucked, man! You're *so fucked*! At the gate I sling him around hard and ram him headfirst into the bars. He hits them with an audible crack and goes limp and I let him drop – then flinch at the sound of a gunshot and pull the Beretta as I spin around and see Frank standing outside the Expedition with his pistol pointed at the shack window. He darts to the door and ducks down as he opens it. Then stands up and goes in and I follow.

The guard's on the floor, faceup, eyes open, a neat little red-black hole just above his brow, his head in a spreading pool of blood. There's a big patch of blood on the wall opposite the window. The phone receiver's lying beside him, and even through the din of the storm we can hear an unintelligible tinny voice shouting from the earpiece. Frank reaches down and yanks the line out of the wall. 'As soon as you grabbed the other guy this one was on the horn,' he says. 'Had time enough to give an alert before I could pop him. Be a war party here in a minute.'

Another phone on a table across the room begins ringing in short bursts.

'Move the other one out of the way,' Frank says. 'No need to run over him.'

I scoot out as he goes to the gate operation panel.

The gates draw apart as I drag the guard clear of them. He issues no sound, makes no movement. The phrase *dead weight* comes to mind, and I resist the inclination to check for a pulse. Frank hastens out and slides behind the wheel. I hop into the other side and he guns us through the gate. Kitty's sitting up now and hugging herself, her eyes huge. The rear window is a watery glare against the shack lights. Then we're into a wide curve and there's nothing behind us but darkness. Frank takes off the money bag and hands it to me. 'Bothers my driving,' he says. I hang it across my chest.

'Who *are* you guys?' Kitty says. 'You're not like any movie people *I* ever met.'

'Like I said, we're friends of Rayo,' I say. 'That makes us friends of yours. Everything's cool, kid. We're on our way to her.'

'Don't call me kid!'

'Forgive me. I meant to say everything's cool, my lady.'

She laughs along with us. Good sign.

My watch reads 11:16.

EL CHUBASCO

The dance floor is still thronged and the traffic of couples to and from the second floor continues. Romero joins Chubasco's table and says the storm is now officially a category one hurricane with winds of seventy-six miles an hour and expected to intensify.

Who cares? Puño says. This party's stormproof.

Now the supervisor of the Finca's telephone switchboard crew pushes through the crowd around the chief's table. He leans down close to Chubasco and tells him of a call an operator received from one of the gate guards a few minutes ago to report that the two Sangrero gunrunners had driven up to the gate and demanded to be let out, and when a guard refused because they didn't have a pass, one of them began to assault him. The operator then heard a gunshot and the guard on the phone went silent. The operator kept asking what was happening, but the guard made no reply and then the connection was broken. The operator tried a backup connection to another phone in the shack and it rang and rang, but there was no answer. He then told the supervisor about the call and the supervisor sent a runner to the gate. The runner called from the shack's backup phone to report the gate was wide open and both guards dead.

Fucking whoresons! Chubasco howls, lunging to his feet. He tells Puño to dispatch replacement guards to the front gate and have pursuit crews with satellite phones ready to go *right now*. He directs Romero to the range room to fetch a pair of MP5s, two strap bags of extra magazines, and a set of earplugs. He tells someone else to bring him a waterproof jacket. Within minutes a pursuit party of three big-cab pickup trucks – three men in each cab, rack lights on each roof – roars out the front gate and past the replacement guards. The dead guards will be kept in the kitchen's meat locker until the weather permits their burial in the graveyard behind the compound.

* * *

Cuervo – a crow-voiced little man and the Sinas' best driver – is at the wheel of the lead vehicle and increasing its distance ahead of the other two trucks. He knows every foot of this trail, every bend and rise and rut and shoulder from one end to the other, and he guides the Ford F-150 through the curves like it's on rails. Chubasco sits beside him, an MP5 propped against his leg, an ammo bag strapped across his chest. Puño's in the rear, armed and equipped the same way.

Via sat phone, Chubasco has contacted the Sina subchief in Loreto and told him to post a crew of gunmen at a point a little north of the Finca trail's junction with the San Javier Road. The first vehicle to emerge on that trail will be their target, and because there's nothing to the south except wilderness, it is almost certain to turn north on the road to town. If it should turn south, the ambushers are to notify him and go after it. In either case, they're to disable it any way they can without killing the two men in it. If they abandon the vehicle and try to escape on foot, shoot them in the legs but don't let them bleed out.

I don't understand why they had to try to sneak away, Chubasco says to Puño. Why not just tell me they wanted to go back to town? Thanks for the offer of a bed but we gotta get back because blah-blah whatever. I have you call the gate and out they go. But no, they gotta sneak off like thieves. Were they stealing something? Afraid they might get searched and caught?

Puño shrugs. Stealing what? he says. They had no access to cash, to jewelry. There aren't any drugs there. What could they steal that's worth killing two of our guys and the punishment they'll get for that?

Chubasco sighs. So why'd they run?

The phone trills. Puño answers, Yeah? He listens, then says, All right. Let me know if she turns up.

He cuts off the call and says, That was Romero. Said Griselda told him they left the Lupita girl tied up in a stairwell. The other girl who went upstairs with them, Gatita, she can't be found. She's not at the party, not at the dorm, not anywhere on the compound. Looks like they took her.

Gatita? Why take *her*?

A hostage to get past the guards? Open the gate or we'll kill her.

No, Chubasco says. Open the gate or we'll kill *you* is what they'd tell the guards. Hell, it's what they *did*. Christ, who *are* these guys? I hope to hell the fools don't kill themselves on this road before we catch them.

They go through a sharp curve that ends in a long, slowwinding series of descending curves and Cuervo cries, *There!*

Far ahead and through the glitter of the rain, the dark form of the Sangrero vehicle is visible against the forward cast of its headlights.

Busted their taillights like it was gonna make them invisible, the dumb shits, Cuervo says.

The Sangreros disappear into a sharper curve.

RUDY

With the windshield wipers working at full speed, Frank's zipping us down the snaky little mountain trail like some hillbilly who grew up running moonshine on roads like this. He's always been a masterful driver, quick to learn a particular road's character and adapt to it. The drive to the Finca was all he needed to get to know this one. Although we never touched thirty miles an hour on the way up there, we haven't dipped below it driving down, in spite of the wicked wind that's corkscrewing through the passes and walloping us from all sides. Despite my faith in his skill, I can't help pressing back into my seat and bracing an arm against the dashboard every time we swing out toward a cliff or a rock wall. Kitty sometimes lets out a small squeak on those turns, but all in all she's being a trouper. The way Frank looks at her in the mirror, I can see he's impressed, too.

We have to assume there are chasers after us even though none has come in sight. And then on a fairly straight stretch that, as Frank recalls, will become a sharp bend leading into the exit pass, he looks in the rearview and says, 'Here they are.'

I turn and see the headlights and roof-rack lights appearing out of and disappearing into the curves behind us. They're between two hundred and three hundred winding yards back. Kitty's looking back at them, too. 'Fuck you bastards,' she says.

'That wheelman's very good,' Frank says, his eyes cutting between the mirror and the trail ahead.

We go into the bend and out of their sight. And there, directly ahead, is the pass opening. '*Yes!*' Frank hisses.

We plunge into its greater darkness, our headlights reflecting off the flanking walls as we follow the tightly winding trail downward. The chaser's not going to gain on us in here, but the next span of minutes seems endless. At last our lights show the gap at the end of the pass just ahead.

We exit into the open, still going downhill, and are nearly blown off the trail by a wind that hits us broadside from the south. If it's not hurricane force it's damn close to it. The scrub is leaning almost flat against the ground and quivering like it's trying to tear free. Frank fights the wheel all the way down the trail to its junction with the San Javier Road, which doesn't show vehicle lights in either direction. He hangs a left onto it and speeds up. I look back and see the reflected glow of the chaser's lights approaching the mouth of the pass, then the hazed and shuddering brightness of headlights and roof lights emerges and begins nosing down toward the road.

I look ahead again just as a set of headlights comes on about seventy yards away, glaring from the shoulder on our right.

'What's *that*?' Kitty says.

In the same instant that I think, *Shooters*, Frank apparently has the same thought and cuts off our headlights just as automatic gunfire begins flaring from both sides of the ambush vehicle. The rounds ring against the plates protecting the engine, then our front end sags a little when the tires are hit. But they're obviously not called run-flats for nothing, and despite their slight sag we're going over fifty as we close on the ambushers, still pouring a barrage of fire into our shielded motor.

'They're trying for disablement or they'd shoot the

windshield till they drilled through and nailed us!' I say.

'Their mistake,' Frank says. 'Hold on!' He swerves to the right and off the road, and we go jarring and jouncing over the rocky ground a short way before he cuts back hard to the left and hits the headlight switch – only the right light now working, set on bright – and accelerates toward the shooters' SUV. The blaze of our headlight is stark on the five or six of them in their flapping raincoats as they scatter, and Kitty yelps just before we ram the rear door of the SUV with a hellacious crash that sends the vehicle spinning onto the road, knocking down two of the shooters and running over them. We skid off the road on its other side, and Frank wheels us around and back onto the pavement and we speed away on the spongy tires, the engine holding fine, the sole headlight casting a long beam.

'Sweet Mother Mary! Gallo wasn't bullshitting about the bumper and run-flats!' Frank says.

'*Wow!*' Kitty says in a tone a kid might use after her first roller-coaster ride. Frank cuts a look at her in the rearview and grins. I turn to look at her in the glow of the dashboard and see the bright excitement in her eyes. She rubs her forehead and I ask if she's hurt, and she says no, she just took a knock on the door pillar, then asks, 'Who were *they*?'

'Non-friends of ours,' I say.

Through the rain-smeared back window I see the lights of the chaser slowly approaching the smashed-up SUV blocking the road, then stopping short of it. Farther behind, two other vehicles with roof-rack lights – more chasers – have come out of the pass and are creeping down the trail to the road.

By the time the lead chaser slowly eases off the road and around the wreckage, it's only a speck of light to us. We have a lead on it of nearly two miles when we curve out of its view on a long bend of the San Javier Road heading to Loreto.

It's 11:44.

Frank catches the glance at my watch. 'We'll make sure she's gone,' he says, 'then hijack whatever boat looks strong enough to get us across and that's got a full tank. Reimburse the owner later if we're still kicking.'

'Sounds like a plan. And you sound like Mateo. *If* we're still kicking.'

'Make sure she's gone?' Kitty says. 'She *who*? You mean *Rayo*?'

'Don't fret, dear lady, everything's cool as can be,' Frank says, wrestling the wheel against the sidelong buffeting of the storm. I don't know if I could keep us on this road like he's doing. Some driver, Frank. Some guy.

* * *

The San Javier Road transitions into the crosstown avenue at the south end of Loreto. The city's taking a beating and is in neartotal darkness, its electric power knocked out. Only a scattering of windows show light, undoubtedly generator produced. The streets are all but deserted, the few vehicles on them moving slowly, discernible solely by their misty lights wobbling in the wind.

'Here come headlights,' Frank says, peering at the rearview.

I take a look. They're about two-thirds of a mile back, the only lights behind us and very slowly gaining. 'If it's them, they're not using the roof rack and they've made us by our broken taillights,' I say, 'but they don't look in any hurry to catch up.'

'They're not dopes,' Frank says. 'They figure we've seen them and if they come up fast we'll turn off the avenue and cut our lights and lose them. Sneak away on side streets. Maybe lay for them. They'd rather keep us in view as long as they can and then close in fast when we stop.'

Because we don't know if the Sinas have lookout posts

along the route that Puño showed Frank for getting out of town, we don't turn off at the federal highway intersection but opt for the route Gallo showed us to the marina. We follow the avenue past the closed airport and toward the arroyo bridge near the seawall. But now there's a yellow light there, flashing intermittently.

'Oh, man, don't tell me the bridge is out,' I say.

* * *

The light proves to be the roof flasher of a power company truck. Frank pulls up alongside it and asks a workman if it's safe to go across. He has to yell to make himself heard through the wind. The guy says yeah, they just finished securing a transformer connection and now have to see about a downed power line near the seawall plaza, and so we better go ahead if we don't want to get stuck behind them. We ease around the truck and cross over the bridge, the surging water now risen to within a foot of it, and it seems like we're driving across on its surface. Then we're on the seawall road, and the truck crosses over behind us.

Waves are exploding against the seawall. The trees thrashing as if berserk.

EL CHUBASCO

Cuervo speeds them out of the long San Javier Road bend and onto the city's south crosstown avenue, the truck rocking in the wind, its roof lights off, the better to keep the Sangreros from spotting them. In the back seat with Puño now are two Sina gunmen who narrowly evaded injury when the Expedition rammed the SUV – Nico and Moisés, armed with M4s.

Chubasco has again been in sat phone contact with his Loreto subchief and this time gave him descriptions of the Expedition, of the two Sangreros, and of the girl who may or may not be with them. He ordered him to post lookouts at the federal highway's north and south exits from the city and at the north and south ends of the city's coast road. He had then phoned the two chase crews behind him and instructed one of them to help the lookouts on the highway, the other to assist the coastal route guys.

So where's their way out? he'd said to Puño after the calls. There's no air traffic. We got the exit roads covered. What're they gonna do? Take a boat? In *this* storm?

If it's their only choice, said Puño.

There! Cuervo yells, and points straight ahead. No taillights. And look at their headlight glow. It's brighter to the right of them because the left light's busted! It's them!

Chubasco has Cuervo close in on them slowly. No need

to risk spooking them into the backstreets and losing them.

Now they see the whirling yellow light at the avenue's far end. The Sangreros drive up to it and stop. Chubasco makes Cuervo lower their speed even more. There are no other vehicles on the avenue at the moment. As the Sinas draw closer and see it's a utility truck light, the Sangreros go around it and over the bridge, and then the truck crosses over behind them.

They're heading for the marina and a boat, Puño says. Where else by *that* route, and what else *can* they do? Hide till the storm blows over, then drive out or fly out? Bullshit. They'd never get by us and they know it. A boat's their only bet and damn the risk. Hell, maybe they already arranged for one.

That seawall road's too narrow for us to go around the truck! Chubasco says.

That road's the shortest way to the marina from here, Cuervo says, you know that, chief. But it catches the most litter in a storm. Tree branches, driftwood, all kinds of crap that's gonna slow them down. The highway route's longer but it never gets as much obstruction in a windstorm. We can make better time on it and get to the marina almost as fast as they do.

Go! Chubasco says.

Cuervo switches on all their lights and executes a fast Uturn. As they start back to the federal highway bridge, the truck joggling in the wind, Chubasco makes a sat call to the coastal ranch north of town where, in addition to berthing his helicopter, he keeps his powerboat racer – *La Ninfa* – in a boathouse within the estate's private inlet. It's a fifty-footer with oversized fuel tanks that are always kept full, a pair of huge quad-cam engines that can propel it at almost 160 miles per hour on calm water, and a radar system with a thirty-mile reach. The boat's two-man crew lives in a cottage on the grounds. One of the crewmen answers the call and Chubasco tells him to bring the boat to the mouth of the Loreto marina at once.

On the way, chief, the crewman says.

But even though *La Ninfa*'s crewmen are superior boatmen, the estate is twenty miles away and the boat will be coming directly into the wind and waves. Chubasco knows it could take as long as half an hour to arrive.

RUDY

We don't spot the marina until we almost drive past it. Frank slowly wheels into the lot and parks next to the pedestrian entrance. If there are other vehicles here, we can't see them in this darkness. We step out into the slashing rain and hold on to the Expedition to keep from being blown off our feet, then interlock arms with each other and stagger to the entrance. We go past a lightless front office and out onto the main dock and the loud clatter of dozens of hulls against their moorings on the undulant water. The only light is a pale glow from the far side of the marina, most likely from some boat. It's barely bright enough for us to see that the layout of the marina is as Gallo described, three docks branching from the main one – one on either side of the basin, one down the center – and a cross dock on the other side. There doesn't seem to be an empty slip anywhere, but no other boats show light or any sign of occupancy, their owners evidently having chosen to wait out the storm somewhere other than on board.

'That light across the way!' Frank says, yelling through the hull knockings and the hammering rain. 'Isn't it about where Gallo said the *Espanta*'s moored?'

'Ah, Christ! You think she's still *here*?'

'She damn sure *is!*' says Rayo's voice as a bright light comes on behind us and casts our shadows far down the middle dock.

We whip around and squint into the glare of her flashlight, unable to see her behind it until she turns the light upward right below her face, producing a Halloween effect, her eyes wild, her grin lunatic. She's wearing a hooded slicker and clutching a mooring line to keep her balance against the wind. She laughs and lowers the light.

'*Rayo!*' Kitty says. She rushes to her and they hug, and Rayo says to us, 'What took you guys so long?'

'Why the hell aren't you gone?' Frank says.

'Because when those guys said it was time to go, I was ready for it and got the drop on them!' Rayo says. She opens the slicker and shines the light on the Glock in her waistband. 'I told them we were waiting till you got here, then took their flashlight and told them to leave the cockpit light on and I sat on a bench over on the right-side dock there, where I could guard against them sneaking up on me and still be on the lookout for you coming through the entrance! Let me tell you, it's been –'

A bright shaft of light flashes briefly through the pedestrian entrance, and through the keening wind comes the sound of a crash.

'Could be Sinas!' Frank says.

'Come on!' Rayo says, hustling past us.

As we follow her down the center dock she flicks the flashlight off and on just once and there's a deep rumble of engines firing up. At the cross dock, the *Espanta's* tossing in its slip, moored with the bow facing out, ready to go, its two crewmen in the front seats. We hustle into the cockpit and the pilot cuts off the panel light and Rayo switches her flashlight off and we're in full darkness. The four of us hunch low and press tightly together against the back seat as the pilot eases us out of the slip and bears left, the engines growling low. I get the sense that he knows this place so well he could maneuver into or out of it with his eyes closed. Then there's a shout from the main dock and he works the throttle and we accelerate out of the marina as automatic weapons open fire, the gunmen shooting wildly toward the sound of our engines.

We exit directly into a furious head sea that starts the boat bucking like it's becrazed. There's less chance at the moment of being hit by a bullet than of being bounced overboard or of the bow plowing into the foot of a head-on wave that takes us under. The pilot turns us sharply to port – out of the Sinas' narrow field of fire and broadside to the waves – and we're suddenly hoisted so high and tipped to our left so steeply that I'm sure we're going to capsize or get smashed against the outer wall of the marina. But the pilot cuts back into the wave at an angle and begins zigzagging obliquely through the heave and roll of the broadside swells, the bow rising and dipping. It's the only way to navigate such a sea and he's an evident master of it. As he settles into this steering pattern, he turns the cockpit light back on. The other crewman pats him on the shoulder for his expert seamanship and then shouts introductions of him as Disco and himself as Raul. In case you haven't heard, he says, we're now in a hurricane! He gestures at the instrument panel, saying, Seventy-nine-point-six on the meter!

He passes out life vests from the equipment compartment and we strap them on. The money bag's a hindrance, so I take it off and give it to Raul to put in the compartment. He hands us rolls of nylon-web safety lines with D rings, clip-on connectors, and quick-release buckles. Twelve feet long! he says. Might want to hook yourselves up to each other so that if somebody goes overboard you can pull him back in! Unless he pulls you out, too! *Ha!*

Frank clips one end of his line to his vest and the other to Kitty's, and I do likewise with Rayo. Raul then provides nylon rain jackets, saying they might at least warm us a little. Try to enjoy the trip for the next two hours! he says. Like a long carnival ride that's windy and wet! And don't worry if someone comes after us! There's not another boat in that marina can catch this one!

EL CHUBASCO

Cuervo wheels them into the marina lot, their headlights sweeping past the pedestrian entrance and fixing on the black Expedition parked next to it. Ram it! Chubasco yells. Smash the fender into the wheel! Disable the fucker!

Cuervo does it with a loud crash. Chubasco tells him to stay with the truck in case the bastards try sneaking back out. The other men get out with him, leaning into the wind, weapons ready. As they get to the entrance they hear engines start up somewhere within. They rush out onto the main dock as a boat rumbles on the other side of the marina. Puño shouts that it's heading for the exit – and the boat roars and the Sinas fire flaring bursts into the gloom in that direction.

Enough! Chubasco says. They made the turn out and we're shooting blind, wasting ammo! Did you hear those engines? They're no match for our boat's! We'll catch them!

* * *

Roughly twenty minutes later *La Ninfa* arrives and the two crewmen – the pilot Tuco and the mate Javier – toss bow and stern lines to Sinas who lash the big boat to mooring posts just outside the marina entrance. The crewmen swiftly top off the fuel tanks with jerry cans of gasoline as the boat bobbles on the incoming waves, thumping against the pilings, its engines growling like enormous carnivores. They fling the empty gas cans up onto the dock, and then Chubasco, Puño, Moisés, and Nico carefully lower themselves aboard. Left behind to take the truck back to the Finca, Cuervo frees the mooring lines and tosses them into the boat.

La Ninfa makes a quick turn to port and begins running parallel to the waves, weaving through them as the *Espanta* did. Chubasco is seated between the two crewmen and watching the Sangrero boat's blip on the radar screen. It's twenty-five miles ahead of them and moving at an erratic fifty miles an hour – which, all things considered, Chubasco reflects, is an impressive speed. They've evidently got an excellent pilot. But of course Tuco's an excellent pilot, too, and has the more powerful boat. Under his expert hand *La Ninfa* crisscrosses the grueling waves at a steady sixty.

We're gonna catch those bastards! Chubasco says.

RUDY

We rise and fall, tilt this way and that, veer into and out of wave after high-cresting wave. Time and again there's a moment of near certainty that we're about to overturn as another hard wave bursts against our starboard side. But each time we stay upright and only get wetter, and I thank the gods for the self-bailing system as water sloshes around our shins. The boat at times goes airborne and then smacks down into the trough with such force that one or another of us is nearly bounced from the cockpit, and we clutch to each other more tightly. It's amazing that Disco can hold our present speed in such a sea. Raul is monitoring the radar screen, which shows nothing within its fifteen-mile range of us in any direction.

It's like we're the only people in the whole world! Kitty says, looking about at the encompassing blackness of heaving sea and raging wind, Rayo hugging her close.

How deep is it out here? Rayo asks.

That depends! Raul says. The Gulf isn't so very wide but it has many deep basins! We're going to cross over one that goes down a mile and a half!

Is that the truth?

That's what all the charts say! And you wouldn't believe the size of some of the things that live down there! There are fishermen who swear they've seen whales in this sea bigger than submarines! *I've* seen sharks the length of this boat and half its width!

Damn good thing it's so deep! Rayo says. Or it could get pretty crowded down there!

* * *

An hour and a half out of Loreto, we're seventy-five miles into the Gulf, well more than halfway to our landing point. The wind's at eighty even, and the waves are raising us higher and tilting us more steeply.

Somebody coming up from behind! Raul says.

We all lean in to look at the screen. There's a blip near the bottom of it, a bit less than fifteen miles away and perceptibly gaining.

Who the hell's *that*? Disco asks. The dudes Mateo told us you might piss off?

Who else? Frank says. I doubt it's the Coast Guard coming to help!

That's some boat! Raul says. Moving that fast through these waves! I thought *we* were zooming! We have to speed up!

Any faster on this sea, Disco says, we'll be risking a rollover! Whatever kind of boat that is, it's bigger than this one and better built for running in a storm!

They'll catch up before we make land! Rayo says.

They get close enough we'll get out the M16s and start shooting! says Disco.

They'll start shooting, too! Frank says. Not that anybody in either boat would hit anything except by wild chance, bouncing around like this!

* * *

Forty-five minutes later we're holding as tightly to the boat as to each other. The wind's notched down to seventy-eight, but the waves don't seem any smaller. Disco's cursing as he grapples with the wheel. We're less than seven miles from our landing point, and the pursuit boat has closed to within two miles of us.

Oh, dear mother of God! Raul says, staring at the radar screen.

What? says Disco.

Raul looks off to the darkness on our right and says, A wave's coming! Then looks back at the screen.

Been nothing *but* waves coming! says Frank. Waves and that bastard chaser behind us! What's the big deal?

I mean a *big* bitch of a wave! Coming fast! And *long*! Coupla miles at least!

Frank and I regard the screen. It's a big one, all right. A rogue wave rising out of a collision of currents God knows how deep. It's advancing very swiftly and growing taller as it closes on our starboard side. And now the boat starts rising precipitously. Raul orders us all closer to the port side and yells that if we start to capsize we shouldn't jump away from the boat but just drop out of it as it starts to roll over, so it'll be more likely to fall ahead of us rather than on top of us. Frank pulls Kitty up against him, and Rayo draws closer to me and we get a grip on each other's life vest.

We're rising higher and higher, slowly tipping to port, then suddenly go up on beam-ends – the deck perpendicular to the sky for a trembling moment – and we all tumble out as the boat is carried forward on the crest of the wave that crashes over us.

And then I'm in wild underwater blackness, whirling in all directions, not knowing up from down. My eyes and nose and throat are burning and I've never before felt such panic. I'm certain I'm about to drown. And then suddenly I'm moving sideways and my held breath gives out just as my head breaches the surface and I suck a gasping mouthful of seawater and have a hacking fit so harsh it feels like my Adam's apple might rip loose and my eyes pop from their sockets. My vest keeps me afloat. And now I realize I'm being tugged by the safety line clipped to it.

'I got you, baby! I got you!'

Rayo. The champion swimmer, pulling me to her. She gets her arms around me and holds me close and my coughing eases.

* * *

Dark hours pass and the storm begins to abate. The wind slackens to sporadic gusts of reduced force. The rain quits. The waves lessen. Bobbing like corks, we take turns hollering for the others as loud as we can. The more we call without response, the greater our fear we may be the only ones left. I'm hoarse by the time we hear faint cries of 'Over here! Over *here*!'

Frank! It's hard to get a fix on the direction of his voice as we twirl this way and that, rising and falling on the swells, calling to him, though our cries are so weakened it's doubtful he can hear us.

Then we don't hear him anymore.

* * *

Small gray breaks are showing in the black cloud cover and there's no telling how much time has passed when we make out the sound of an approaching helicopter. We laugh and Rayo hugs my neck. Then she quits laughing and says, 'Wait! Whose *is* it, you think?'

'I don't know!'

'Could be the guys chasing us!'

Now a searchlight is playing over the water, and at times we see the dark form of the aircraft as it passes below some gray portion of sky. It's flying a meandering pattern, the light sweeping in all directions.

The helicopter suddenly veers out of its pattern and circles around and descends to about fifty feet above the water and holds that altitude in a wavering hover. It's maybe fifty lateral yards from us, its light fixed on something or somebody that's blocked from our view by the swells. A moment later we make out the vague form of someone on a rescue line being lowered from the chopper through the searchlight beam and swaying in the wind until he's out of sight behind the waves. A minute passes and we see two forms clutching each other being raised to the aircraft. The procedure then repeats and another person is hauled up to the chopper. Then a third.

'If they're not our guys they wouldn't be picking us up, would they?' Rayo says.

'Unless they want to interrogate us! Give us a ration of pain!'

The chopper moves off to our right and for a moment I think it might be leaving. But then it pauses and hovers again. And once again the guy goes down on the safety line and retrieves somebody. Whoever's chopper it is, if it's picked up only our people it's picked up everybody but Rayo and me.

The helicopter starts coming our way, now flying in tight circles and working the searchlight with wide sweeps. Whoever they are, we have to chance them. Out here on our own we're dead for sure. We wave our arms and yell as if it were even remotely possible to be heard above the engine and the wailing of the wind. The light is flashing everywhere except on us as the chopper passes overhead.

'God damn it!' I say.

'*Stupid blind asshole dipshit motherfuckers!*' Rayo bellows – and the beam swings back and flicks past us and then whips back again and holds on us.

We bust out laughing. 'Oh, man,' she says, 'is *that* what it takes? Give the bastards a good cussing?'

The chopper comes around to hover directly above us, pinning us in the glaring shaft of light, its downdraft agitating the water all the more. And now here comes the guy on the rescue line. As I help hook Rayo to him and work the rescue harness under her arms, I ask him who they are and he says, The best friends you got in the world right now! He waves up at the chopper and the line hoists them away.

The chopper keeps its light on me and moves along with my drift. Then down comes the guy on the line again. He hooks me to him and I put on the harness. He waves up at somebody, and the line reels us up.

At the cabin door another crewman pulls us in and yells, *That's it!* The chopper swings around and off we go.

The cabin has no seats. Frank's sitting with his back against the wall, Kitty and Rayo are on one side of him, Raul and Disco on the other. *Everybody's* grinning at everybody else, including Mateo, who's hunkered near the cockpit.

'As I've informed the others,' he says to me, 'I would never have put you guys on a boat that wasn't equipped with a location sender.'

EL CHUBASCO

When the radar spots the rogue wave coming at their starboard side, Chubasco asks Tuco if *La Ninfa* can go up and over it. Tuco's sure she can. Chubasco laughs and punches him on the arm. *Do it!* he says.

Tuco steers the boat toward the coming wave and revs the engines. Just before they meet it head-on, he veers to port and speeds up even more, and they climb the wave at an angle. As *La Ninfa* steadily ascends the wave, every man of them cheers. But then just shy of the crest, the boat slows and falters, and the bow begins rising like a rearing horse. Realizing they're going to overturn, Puño grabs Chubasco from behind and lunges with him out of the cockpit just before *La Ninfa* topples backward and falls free of the wave. The boat hits the water topside down, crushing both crewmen and the two gunmen. The prow narrowly misses Chubasco, but it clouts Puño's shoulder and shatters both it and his collarbone.

Puño howls and struggles with one arm to stay afloat. He calls to Chubasco for help. Chubasco starts toward him, then spies one of the cockpit's white flotation pads and strokes over to it and hugs it to his chest, gasping with relief.

Help me, chief! Puño yells, trying to keep his head above water. He goes under for a long moment before he resurfaces, coughing and gagging. *Chieeeef!* he cries. Then goes under again. And comes up no more.

* * *

The storm passes.

The waves diminish to easy rolls.

The wind gentles to fitful gusts, and the remnant clouds come apart in gray tatters.

The flotation pad under his torso bears him easily. Its side straps are a comfortable fit over his shoulders and they afford his arms ample freedom to stroke through the water toward the pale beach he estimates to be less than two miles away.

Despite his exhaustion he maintains a steady rhythm of stroking and kicking, fueling his strength with his hatred, with thoughts of the retribution he will take on the Sangrero sons of whores – *all* of them, not just the two deliverymen they sent with the guns, but, yes, those two in particular, who killed two of his men and stole one of his women. He grins as he envisions the reckoning to come, the bastards chained to a wall or bound in chairs in one of the special rooms designed specifically for the purpose of introducing certain enemies to varieties of pain greater than any they've ever imagined. They'll beg for mercy. They'll plead for death.

He'll laugh at them.

Just above the mountains, the lower sky has slowly transformed into a long bright band of interwoven reds and pinks. He pauses to admire the lovely sunrise and smiles at its assurance of yet another day. He rests for a moment, then strokes even harder toward shore.

He's within a half mile of the beach when he hears a peculiar sound behind him. He pauses and turns, holding tight to the pad, and stares in icy terror at the huge black dorsal fin hissing through the water toward him.

His scream is shrill and short.

RUDY

A crewman passes out beers to all of us. Mateo sits against the cabin wall with us, watching Rayo and Kitty, huddled under a blanket to their chins, sipping their beers and gabbing about who knows what. He excuses himself and goes to them, says something that makes them laugh, then goes over to talk with Disco and Raul.

Frank tells me in a low voice that he introduced Kitty to Mateo by her first name only and was relieved when Mateo didn't address her as Miss McCabe and initiate confusion. Then says he supposes the bag of money went down with the boat.

'All the way down would be a sound supposition,' I say. 'I shoulda kept it on me.'

'Or I shoulda kept it on me. Mateo's shipment, his money. I told him we lost it and he shrugged it off. Said the loss of cash now and again is a hazard of the trade and for us to forget it. Some guy.'

'Got that right,' I say. 'And I don't think we should worry about it, either. I think we just send him the money as soon as we get home.'

'Sounds like a plan.'

The sun's high over the mountains when the chopper lands at the Sonoran ranch airfield. There's a twin-engine business jet out on the runway. Mateo asks if we'd like to wash up and change clothes, have something to eat, and rest a bit before taking off for Matamoros, and we all say yes.

* * *

The afternoon is sunny when we go out to the plane, the girls laughing at the ill-fitting jeans and baggy men's shirts they're wearing, the floppy sneakers on their feet. Mateo tells me and Frank we'll land at a ranch airstrip just outside Matamoros, then be driven over into Brownsville. From there we can make our own arrangements to take the girl to her father in Houston.

At the steps up to the plane, he hugs each of us goodbye, giving the first hug to Kitty, then watching her go up the steps. 'I *knew* she was a beauty,' he says. We exchange abrazos with him and go aboard.

Within minutes of takeoff I fall asleep, Frank in the seat beside me, Rayo and Kitty across the aisle. When I wake, my watch tells me we're more than midway through the flight. Frank and Rayo aren't in their seats, and Kitty's curled up asleep in the seats she and Rayo occupied. I look aft and see them in the rearmost row, conversing across the aisle. I go back there to join them. They've been discussing how we should tell Kitty we're not taking her to Dallas to sign a Starlight contract. We work up a story.

* * *

We're forty minutes from Matamoros when Kitty awakens and sits up, rubbing the sleep from her eyes, blinking at the three of us now sitting in the aisle seats nearest her. 'We almost there?' she says.

'Almost,' Rayo says.

'I never in the world thought I'd go to Dallas,' she says. 'I hear it's really big.'

'Actually, sugar, we're not going to Dallas after all,' Rayo says. 'We just spoke to the Starlight people on the cockpit radio and found out the financial deal for *Throne of Eros* fell apart. Starlight tried its best to save the project, but nothing doing. That deal's dead as stone. We're going to Brownsville.'

Kitty's mouth tightens. 'God *damn* it! I knew it was too good to be true. That money was… ah, *damn*.'

'Well now, easy there, girl, because here's the good news,' Rayo says. 'Even though Starlight had to pull the plug on the movie, it's honoring its promise to you about the money. You'll get the twenty grand.'

'I *will*? You kiddin' me?'

'Nope,' Frank says. 'Starlight's good about honoring its pledges.'

'I can't believe it,' Kitty says.

'That doesn't make it any less true,' Rayo says.

The money is of course coming from the three of us, but why tell the kid and have to explain more than we'd care to? Frank and I will each pony up $6,666.66. Rayo's share is two cents more because it was her idea we go ahead and pay her. 'You should've seen her face when I told her she was getting twenty for the movie,' she'd told us. 'She saw it as her ticket out. Ticket to what, I don't know, but what's it matter? *That's* why she came with us. No matter what Aunt Cat decides about her, I think we ought to give the kid the money.'

Frank and I said okay.

'You say we're going where… Brownsville?' Kitty says. 'How come we're going there? Is it farther than Dallas?'

'No, it's a lot closer and we'll be there shortly,' Rayo says. 'It's where we live. We figure you can rest there awhile, think things over till you decide what you'd like to do, now you'll have some money to work with. Plus, we'd like you to meet our cousin Jessie and our Aunt Catalina. We'll be seeing them tonight.'

'Cool.'

Rayo grins back at her. 'So happens we think *you're* pretty cool. We'd like to know more about you.'

'Really? What do you wanna know?'

'Oh, where you're from, about your family, how you came to meet Lance Furman. If you don't mind telling.'

'I don't mind. Not really a whole lot to tell, though.'

* * *

Her name, she tells us, is Alejandra Katrina Harris. Everybody at school called her Allie. She was an only child, born and raised in Salinas, California, the only place she ever lived until she was sixteen. Her mother was Tina Mendoza – she was born in California, too, and grew up all over the San Joaquin Valley – and her daddy was Jimmy Jack Harris, a car mechanic from Louisiana. Allie was six when he deserted them. Her mother burned all his pictures and hardly ever spoke about him again and never nicely. After he left, her mother always had to work at two jobs to support them in their little rented house at the edge of town. She mostly cashiered at grocery stores and fast-food places, and it helped that she could speak Spanish. She had learned it from *her* mom, and she taught Allie to speak it, too. It came in handy for making friends with the Mexican kids in the neighborhood and at school. Allie sometimes asked about her mother's family, but Tina didn't like to talk about it and never did. What she liked was to have a good time with men. One night she and some fella were coming back from a good time in Watsonville and he ran off the road at pretty high speed and hit a tree and they were both killed. Allie was sixteen and there was only seventy-odd dollars in her mother's bank account, so for the rest of that school year she lived at the homes of different friends. Some of the other kids started calling her Gypsy because of it and she came to like the name and sometimes used it. She'd lost her virginity the year before and now started fooling around so much she pretty soon got herself a reputation but didn't care. Her best friend was Connie Amado, who did a lot of fooling around, too. One day she told Connie about this Los Angeles movie agent she'd read about online. His specialty was in getting pretty girls good-paying acting jobs in sex movies, and from there some of them went on to being in real movies like you can see in mall theaters and on HBO. She thought they ought to go to LA and see if that agent could get them started, too, and Connie said okay. But the day before they were going to leave, Connie backed out, saying she just couldn't do it. So Allie went to Los Angeles by herself and found the agent and told him she was Katie Moore from Fresno and wanted to be in the movies. He explained about having to start out in porn, and she said that was all right with her. He sent her to a doctor to get a full exam, then had a photographer take a bunch of pictures of her, some dressed, some bare-assed, and next thing she knew, she was in Arizona, making *The Love Tutors* with Lance Furman, and was calling herself Kitty Quick.

'I guess you pretty much know the rest,' she says.

'Speaking of Kitty,' Rayo says. 'What name you want to go by with us? Kitty? Alejandra? Allie? Gypsy? Something else?'

'You know, I really do like Kitty. It's why I chose it when I could be somebody new. You think it's maybe too slutty on account of I used it in sex movies?'

Rayo chuckles. 'No, baby, I don't. You want to be Kitty, Kitty it is.'

'I like it myself,' I say. Frank nods. Kitty beams.

* * *

We land at the Matamoros ranch airstrip in the rising darkness of early evening. There's a car waiting for us, and we have the driver take us across the river and out to the Landing, where the girls get in Rayo's truck and head off to the beach house to clean up and change clothes and round up Jessie. We all know Catalina would never forgive us if we wait until tomorrow to tell her we've got Kitty. She's going to want to see her tonight.

When I come out of the shower, Frank tells me he's given Catalina the news and asked when she'd like to see the girl, and she said right now would be satisfactory. 'Not a hooray or a thank-you or is everyone all right,' Frank says. 'Just, "Right now would be satisfactory, Francis".'

Frank told her the girls were getting ready and we'd be there in about an hour, then called Rayo. He could hear Jessie and Kitty talking and laughing in the background like they were college roommates.

* * *

Catalina's porch is cast in the amber glow of the overhead light. A note taped to the front door informs us the maids have been given the night off to visit relatives in Matamoros and won't return until tomorrow. It invites us to enter, make ourselves at home, feel free to dance, and help ourselves to the beer.

The furniture has been pushed to the walls to provide a small dance floor. On a table in a corner of the living room is a big plastic tub of beer and soda pop on ice, and next to it is Catalina's old phonograph – at the moment playing Artie Shaw's rendition of 'Stardust' at low volume. Like Frank and me and Charlie, she loves the music of the jazz age and big band era, which she'd come to relish at the height of its popularity in the twenties, thirties, and forties.

'Stardust' ends and 'Temptation' starts playing. Frank beckons Jessie for a dance, and I dance with both Rayo and Kitty at the same time, an arm around each of them, all three of us laughing in our efforts not to step on each other's feet. Not until the number ends and we hear her applauding do we become aware of Catalina watching us all from the hallway entry, wearing a white half-sleeved dress that very much becomes her.

'I see we have a special guest,' she says, smiling at Kitty, whose own smile at that moment is the shyest of hers I've seen.

Frank steers her to Catalina and introduces them to each other as 'our dear friend Kitty Harris' and 'our dear Aunt Catalina.' Aunt Cat says she's delighted to make her acquaintance. They hug closely and I see Catalina whispering in her ear. Kitty looks up at her and nods. Catalina tells us they're going to have a private conversation in another room and will return shortly. In the meantime, we're to help ourselves to the beer, keep the music playing, and dance, dance, dance.

As soon as she and Kitty disappear down the hall, Frank turns to me and Rayo and Jessie and asks what we think. We all shrug.

'Yeah,' Frank says. 'Me, too.'

* * *

We've gone through maybe a dozen numbers, Frank and I trading off on Rayo and Jessie as partners on every other one, all of us now and then pausing to have a pull or two off a bottle of beer, and we've just put on a Glenn Miller record when Cat and Kitty return. Catalina gestures at the player, and I go over and take the tone arm off the record and turn off the phonograph.

'My dear people,' she says, 'this young lady and I have had a very interesting conversation whose purpose is no secret to any of you. I had told you that if I could see her in person, hear her voice directly, and ask a few questions of her, I would know – know in my bones, the surest means of knowing of which I am capable – if she is or is not a descendant of my sister, Sandra. And I now know beyond all doubt that she is not.'

We all cut looks at each other.

'However,' she says, 'having heard her life story to date and her account of a harrowing adventure she shared with you in Mexico, I believe that, although not of my birth family's blood, she is certainly of our Wolfe family's character. Its essence. Its *bone*, if you will. I have asked if she would like to become a member of our family and she has said yes. Now I ask that you welcome her into it, this young woman who wishes to assume the name Kitty Alejandra Wolfe. And so shall it become officially.'

Catalina's smile is small and pleased, Kitty's smile wide in spite of the tears she wipes from her cheeks. The rest of us grin like lunatics.

And just like that it's done. We hug and kiss Kitty, laughing with her, she and Jessie and Rayo crying and laughing at the same time.

Frank starts the Glenn Miller record and 'Moonlight Serenade' fills the room. Catalina says Miller has always been her favorite dance musician, and Frank says that's why he put him on the player. He gives her a gentlemanly bow and asks if he may have the pleasure. She responds with a half curtsy and says it would no less be her pleasure. Then Frank and the oldest person in the world are dancing. And though in deference to her years he keeps their footwork to a minimum and they mostly sway in place, she is no less graceful for that or, as evidenced in her radiant smile, any less exhilarated. As Rayo and I foxtrot around the floor, Jessie bows to Kitty and asks her for a dance, and Kitty laughs and says of course, and then they're at it, too. When that number draws to a close, the marvelous opening notes of 'In the Mood' come welling from the speaker, and Frank and Jessie and Rayo and I really start swinging. Kitty watches us avidly and asks Catalina what kind of dance we're doing. Rayo steps away from me and gestures for the kid to assume her place. I teach her the basic swing steps, and by the end of the number she's an ace. Then 'String of Pearls' is playing, and I'm taking a careful turn with Catalina, and Frank's dancing with Jessie, and Rayo and Kitty are spinning each other around with some fancy improvisational moves of their own.

And so does it go, the laughter and the chatter and the beer and the music and the dancing, dancing, dancing, deep into the night.